Victim of Love

Barbara Woster

Cover by Ashley Creatives

DEDICATION

For my family, without whose love and support,
I could never have written this book. I love you all, very much.

Other titles by this author can be viewed at:
www.LiteraryAdventures.weebly.com

DISCLAIMERS:

This book is a work of fiction. Any similarities to individuals, real or implied, is unintentional. This book is not accurately representative of the Arapaho nation and makes no claim at being an expert on the lives of Native Americans, their customs. It is with the highest regard that I choose to use them as characters in my novels.

CHAPTER 1

"What do you think you are doing?"

The voice that rose above the din was distinctly feminine and unquestionably irate. Although not screeching, the tone was shrill enough to silence every movement within audible range, including the man wielding the whip.

Cara Martini pushed through the crowd and stopped nose-to-nose with the castigator. More precisely, nose-to-chest, but in her current state of agitation, she was as foreboding as he—despite her diminutive stature. The stench arising from his sweating body was repugnant, but she remained firmly planted, for the nearness prohibited her from viewing the bloodied individual tied to the whipping post behind him.

Although she wanted nothing more than to aid the person strapped, hanging slumped and nearly lifeless; eyeing the tortured soul wasn't a mandatory part of that help as far as she was concerned. So, she stood with her nose only inches away from Rankle's dirt-covered, sweaty chest, lifted her gaze and speared him with a look meant to bore a hole in his brain.

She'd watched from her bedroom window as Rankle hauled the protesting person across the main street, and cringed. She couldn't make out the person meant for the beating, as Rankle's large frame overshadowed the petite form of the person he intended to assail; but to her it didn't matter, for she knew that Rankle was not a man known for his restraint with a whip. Too many times, she had seen justice meted and then watched as the man continued to raise and lower his whip as if deriving some perverse pleasure from the infliction of pain. She'd seen it too many times and had had enough. If she couldn't help them all, perhaps she could assist one from a lengthy stay at the doctor's quarters, or a fitting for a coffin from the undertaker.

Common sense told her to remain safely ensconced in her room, but she was not much for listening to sense, common or otherwise.

"Good day to you, Miss Martini," Harold Rankle murmured, taking a polite step back before tipping his hat. He pulled a dirty handkerchief from his equally filthy jeans pocket and wiped the sweat dripping down his face. "What is it that I can do for you on this fine day?" He returned the brim of his hat to shade his eyes and tucked his handkerchief back into his pocket, waiting patiently for her response.

Cara knew that his polite demeanor was a ruse. Just as he, no doubt, could see the angry disgust in her own gaze, she saw the angry irritation in his. He only treated her with regard because of who she was and because she was a lady. That didn't mean that he was pleased at having his task interrupted. He was having the time of his life and it riled him that someone would dare interrupt his pleasure—especially a tiny whiff of a girl. Were this a man, he'd have just punched him immediately. His jaw clenched and re-clenched as he waited for her to speak, but within a minute, the clenched jaw loosened and a grin formed as his brain envisioned this nosy, interrupting female strapped alongside the other one. He'd derive a great deal of pleasure from beating her too. His gaze said as much.

"I'm not certain why you find the beating of a helpless person so amusing, sir, but I am quite certain he's suffered enough." Cara whispered, appalled at the smile forming on Rankle's too-big mouth.

"Beg pardon, miss, but that simply isn't your call to make."

"Well, I'm forming a formal, and quite public, complaint. There is no way that anyone will agree with you that this person deserves further assault."

"The person is a criminal, Miss Martini, and crime must be punished. Are you saying that crime shouldn't be punished?"

"Short of murder, there is no reason for you to be thrashing a person to within an inch of his life. Did this person in point of fact, sir, take another's life?"

"No."

"Then the penalty and torment is certainly sufficient for the crime committed, or do you truly think that removing the entirety of flesh from a person's back proper punishment for a crime?"

"Your father left those decisions to me, Miss Martini, not to you."

"Yes, well, I'll take up your misplaced fanaticism with my father presently. Something tells me that he is unaware of your constant abuse of these so-called offenders, especially to the Natives of this land."

"Those Natives, Miss Martini, wouldn't think twice about removing that lovely blond hair from your head to take as a trophy, and leave you for dead, all for a loaf of bread."

"In this instance, sir, I cannot see how you are much better than they are then. Still, I am not here to debate the rightness or wrongness of their actions, merely to defend the unjust punishment of the one hanging behind you. Now, will you cease the excessive execution of this so-called justice, or do I find someone capable of stopping you?"

"As daughter of our esteemed governor, I will bow to your bidding," Rankle said amiably. Too amiably, Cara estimated. There was a catch. There had to be. Just as Rankle's reputation for meting punishment too severe for the crime was known far and wide; so was his reputation for not backing down from a confrontation. She waited for the hammer to fall, and was stunned when it finally did. "If you wish for the punishment to cease, I will do so, providing you take the place of the criminal."

"Surely my hearing deceives me," she gasped, along with several of the spectators that had gathered to view the on-going confrontation. A confrontation they found amusing until that ultimatum was issued.

"You heard me well enough, Miss Martini. You are interfering with the discharge of my duties, but because you are a woman of some importance, I will bow to your request, providing you are willing to take your place on the whipping post and complete the punishment that I started. I can hardly have spoken any plainer. So, what say you? Is this prisoner truly worth your own hide?"

"Certainly not!"

"I thought as much. Go back to your needlework, Miss Martini, and leave the justice of Martins Landing to me. Good day." Rankle turned back to face the criminal, leaving Cara standing there in stunned silence. She glanced up as Rankle lifted the whip, the sight of which snapped her out of her bemusement.

Raising her skirts, she dashed around Rankle's side, placing herself between him and the barely conscious Indian. The crowd gasped loudly in disbelief.

"No! I can't let you do this. No more! Enough is enough!" She stomped her foot against the dirt, the effect of which was laughable as the slippered sole made not a sound.

"If you don't move, I'll issue the punishment to you, strapped to the post or not, and then when you've been dealt with, I'll finish up with the heathen. Is that what you want?" Rankle was done catering to the whims of a bureaucrat's spoiled daughter.

"You wouldn't dare!"

"As I've already said, you are interfering with the duties of my office. If you continue to do so, then I will be well within my right to stop you."

"My father will see you hanging on this post if you lay so much as a finger on me, and well you know it. You will strike no one else this day, sir!" She straightened her shoulders and crossed her arms over her chest, but her confidence began to wane when he started clenching the handle of the whip.

She suddenly doubted that her standing in the community would stop his carrying out his threat. She glanced about her and decided to elicit help from those gawking nearby.

"Surely, whatever this person's crime is doesn't warrant this amount of abuse!" She said loudly. "Isn't there any person here that is willing to stand against this injustice besides myself? Or, would you wait to do something when it's your neighbor strapped behind me? What crime, precisely, was committed here?" She asked, addressing Rankle again.

"Theft."

"Of what? A prized mare?"

"Bread."

"Bread! You dare stand there and tell me that the severity of this punishment is because of hunger?"

"Hungry or not, a crime is a crime," Rankle said, shrugging his shoulders.

"Maybe she's right, Rankle," a voice interjected from beside her and Cara sighed inwardly in relief. "Heathen or not, the poor child has suffered enough for the crime committed, surely."

"Thank you, Reverend Tomlinson," Cara said with a sigh.

"I'd suggest you not get involved, Reverend," Rankle snapped. "I don't tell you how to preach your sermons, do I?"

"That is hardly the same..." Reverend Tomlinson began, but Rankle interrupted.

"When you beat at peoples' souls and I sit and watch them cringe, do I jump up and shout for you to stop your duty, cease performing that which you swore an oath to do? Well, consider this my small part of saving souls. One beating from my whip and the poor soul thinks twice about committing the same crime."

The Reverend backed away with a shrug and Cara wanted to scream, "Surely you aren't buying this rubbish?"

"He's right, Miss Cara," the Reverend sighed. "If crime isn't punished, then it won't be long before the criminals take over. As much as it pains me to watch the suffering of another, it's not my place to interfere."

"Poppycock. Justice was served several whip strikes ago. Now he's merely continuing for the pleasure he derives. Can't you see that?"

"You've had your moment of protest, Miss Martini, and no one here is willing to stand with you. Now move!"

"I can't do that." Cara looked at the people milling about, now with lowered gazes of shame. If she couldn't move them to action, she feared the person hanging behind her would die. "What if someone other than this Indian had committed this crime," she tried once more, her gaze challenging every gaze it encountered; however briefly. "Carlton," she snapped at the local baker, "what if this was your son? What if he thought it would be amusing to snatch a pie from a window sill? Would you stand by and allow the beating to go on and on and on? Or what about your daughter, Sarah..."

"Coddle criminals?" Rankle interrupted quickly, suddenly fearful that Cara's pleas would not continue to fall on deaf ears. He kept his job because he kept crime away; so just as she wanted to appeal to their sense of justice, he needed to feed their fear of sin run amok. "Is that what you're suggesting, Miss Martini? Are you saying that we should just let people behave however they wish without fear of repercussion? No, don't answer that. I'm tired of your interference. Now move or I'll move you, and deal with your father's protestations at a later date."

"No!"

"So be it." Harold cracked the whip at his side, the threat apparent. Cara remained steadfast, her heart racing, her pulse pounding. She wanted to glimpse at the crowd to see if there was anyone willing to stop him; but feared that he'd strike if she glanced away; and then he made his move.

Rankle raised his arm with such speed that the whoosh of air from the whip brushed Cara's cheek. She cringed involuntarily. She closed her eyes, awaiting the sting of the thin leather that she knew would lash at her at any moment. When nothing happened, she peered from beneath her lashes, and then her eyes flew open in utter amazement.

"You weren't actually planning on striking my fiancé, were you, Rankle?" The question was asked with a quiet authority that Cara knew most men would not dare defy, but she also knew that Rankle wasn't most men. Added to the fact that he was incensed, she could well comprehend his bold insolence, idiotic though it was.

She watched in awed silence the barely perceptible struggle that was occurring. Rankle's biceps bulged as he attempted to pull free of the iron grip of her fiancé. Casey Scott was equally determined not to let him go until he was confident that Rankle wouldn't do anything irrational. Both men were tall, brawny, formidable—and livid.

"You need to keep a tighter rein on her then, Scott," Harold snapped, tugging on his arm once more, hoping to extricate it from the ever-tightening grip. "And tell her to stop interfering with my business."

Victim of Love Barbara Woster

Casey glared at the man in front of him and drew in a deep breath. He was tempted to let loose his anger; to snatch Rankle's whip and slash away at the chief magistrate until he apologized for threatening his fiancé. A shudder passed through him as he thought of what might have happened had he not returned to town when he did.

He'd been amused at first, as he rode down the main street and his gaze fell on his fiancé causing a ruckus. She was very passionate about things, which was one of the qualities that initially drew him to her; however, when she moved between Rankle and the intended whipping victim, his breath caught in his throat and his heartbeat accelerated. She was a brave soul, he would credit her with that much, but sometimes he wondered whether God forgot to add the screws needed to mount her head properly to her shoulders. Didn't she know that Harold Rankle was a treacherous man?

Apparently, her anger prevented her registration of the peril, but it was clear enough to him. He spurred his horse into a gallop, his worry over whether he'd make it in time increasing with his horse's stride.

He heard the whoosh of the whip as Rankle's arm leapt upward just as he leapt from his horse. Another shudder ran down his spine when he thought of what might have happened had his stallion been slow to obey his command. His beloved Cara...

"You best learn how to control that temper of yours, Rankle," Casey said, "or you're going to cross paths with someone, one day, that will make you live to regret the day you lose it."

"Are you threatening an officer of the law, Scott?"

"You take it the way you want, Rankle, but you better take it to heart. If you persist in threatening my fiancé, you may find yourself strapped to that post and your own hide flayed. That's a promise."

"I could have you thrown in jail for that."

"And I could have your job, Rankle. Think about *that* the next time you threaten innocent women!"

"Innocent! Have you got blinders on, man? That woman is hardly innocent. She's a bloody nuisance is what she is."

"Yes, well, she's *my* bloody nuisance. Threaten her again and you'll pay dearly."

Casey shoved at the magistrate's arm, sending him stumbling backward, and then turned toward Cara, who hadn't moved an inch or said a word. Her eyes were round as saucers and he wondered shortly if she'd gone into a state of shock—until she dove into his arms.

"Oh, Casey! You're home!"

Casey closed his arms around her, "Did you ever doubt that I'd be back?"

"No. It's just your timing always seems to be impeccable," Cara grinned.

"Well if you'd stay out of mischief, I wouldn't have to have impeccable timing."

Cara moved from Casey's embrace and turned to look at the Indian hanging from the post for the first time. Her gloved hand flew to her mouth and she gagged slightly. "Please, Casey," she pleaded, turning back to her fiancé, "cut the poor man down. He can't be more than a boy. No one deserves this."

Casey looked at the shredded, bleeding bronzed back and felt close to retching himself. Instead, his anger at Rankle returned, and he sent the man a deadly look. He reached into his pant pocket and pulled out his pocketknife, but a hand shot out to grip his arm and prevent its use.

For the second time in a short span, both men locked grips in a barely perceptible tug-of-war.

"You don't have the authority to release my prisoner, Scott," Rankle growled, his face flushed with renewed rage.

"Enough is enough, Harold," Casey whispered. "Now let go of my arm before I force-feed you this blade."

Rankle shoved Casey's arm away, "You'll pay for this, Scott. You've interfered one too many times for me to let it pass."

"I think that you'll be the one to pay, Rankle," Cara snapped. "Once I've spoken with my father, you'll be searching for employment elsewhere, so you may as well start packing..."

"What the devil?"

Cara turned at her fiancé's exclamation, "What's wrong, Casey?" She started, and then stopped as she followed his gaze. Her shock quickly overshadowed her repulsion, as she caught sight of the bloodied person lying in her fiancé's arms.

"Oh, dear Lord above!"

CHAPTER 2

"Are you completely out of your mind?" Cara prided herself on being a lady, which, for her, meant not raising her voice above conversational. Yet, twice today, within the span of half-hour, Rankle had so incensed her that she found herself screeching like an agitated Raven.

"As I said, a criminal's a criminal, Miss Martini," Rankle said, shrugging his shoulder.

"A criminal is...?" Cara sputtered. "You, sir, are a barbarian!"

"No, Miss Martini, *she* is the barbarian, and a thief."

"She's but a girl, and no amount of thievery vindicates what was done here today. Now, I demand an explanation, sir!"

"You have done enough demanding for one day, Miss Martini," Rankle said, his ire rising again. "And since you and your interfering fiancé have deprived me of completing my duties, I will take my leave of you."

"You...you..."

"Cara," Casey whispered, "leave him go. I need you to help this poor girl. Can you manage, love, or should I go fetch Doc Parson?"

"Take her to Doc Parson," Cara whispered. "I'll offer whatever assistance I can, but...oh, dear Lord above, Casey, it's a wonder the poor child is still breathing."

Casey carefully shifted the Indian maiden closer to his chest, mindful of her shredded back. He started down the main street, ignoring the gawking citizens lining the way. He cast a glance down at the pallor beneath the tan and sighed, "If she's still breathing come morning, I'll be surprised," he said sadly, taking a moment to address his fiancé's concerns.

"If she dies, I'll see Rankle brought up on murder charges," Cara declared passionately.

"Sweetheart," Casey sighed, "you and I both know that the worst that Harold will suffer is a slap on the wrist."

"That's all this poor girl should have suffered."

"True enough, but since she received more than that, it's now up to you and the doc to see she recovers. Stay focused on that, okay? I'll focus my efforts on seeking retribution against Harold. He's long overdue. I'll go to speak to your father. Try to get Rankle relieved of his duties. That's the most we can hope for, in any case. I hate to think what the men of her tribe are going to do about this," Casey said, taking the stairs to the doctor's second-floor office, two at a time. Cara lifted her skirts, trotting up after him as quickly as she could manage. When she reached his side, she pushed open the door, not bothering to knock. She wished she hadn't.

"Oh, heavens!" She exclaimed, stumbling back into Casey and slamming the door shut behind her.

"What? What's wrong, Cara?" Casey exclaimed, trying to regain his balance. "You nearly sent me tumbling down the stairs."

"I'm sorry darling, but I just...Casey, promise me when I'm old and my sight is going, that you won't offer to purchase me eyeglasses."

"Why ever not?"

"Because I never want to see that good again."

"What are you going on about, Cara? We need to see the doctor."

"I *did* see the doctor and he is occupied at the moment," Cara started to explain, when the door opened suddenly and Doc Parson stumbled out, fastening his drawers. He careened into Cara, his face reddening to a deeper scarlet.

"Oh, dear me," he exclaimed, "I'm terribly sorry, my dear. I simply wasn't expecting...that is to say, I never thought...well, I most certainly wouldn't have been otherwise engaged had I known that someone would stop by—without knocking first," he finished lamely.

"This is a doctor's office, *Doctor*," Casey said, his irritation rising. "Dropping by is to be ..."

Casey stopped talking when the notorious madam of the whorehouse in the neighboring town sauntered out, fastening her bodice. "Next time you feel like entertaining me," she purred close to the doc's ear, "lock the door, will you? I don't believe in that sort of free advertising." She cast a glance at the girl lying in Casey's arms, and then back to the doctor. "Looks like you have more pressing business to attend to at the moment anyhow, so I'll escort myself home."

Casey pulled the girl up, closer to his chest, so that everyone could fit on the upper landing; which revealed the lash marks lining the girl's back. The madam barely cringed as she scooted past and headed down the stairs.

"Uh, Penelope ..."

"I'll see you next week, Arty. How else can I repay you for the invaluable service you perform for me and my girls?"

"How else indeed," Cara heard him mutter under his breath. "Well you two, don't just stand there, bring her inside. I don't require a medical degree to know what happened to her. What did she do to get on Rankle's bad side?" He asked, leading Casey through the main office to the back room.

"Stole a loaf of bread," Cara said, trying to regain her calm. "At least that's what Rankle accused her of doing."

"A loaf of bread, huh? Well, I hope she got to eat it at least. Otherwise, this wasn't really worth it, now was it?" The doctor leaned over the girl and immediately set to removing pieces of fabric from the seeping slash marks crisscrossing the bronze skin. "They ought to make a law that the shirt be removed before lashing," the doctor muttered to himself, picking at the larger pieces of cloth, "at least then, if the person survives, my job of healing will be far simpler."

Cara's eyes widened in disbelief at the callous observation. She was about the snap a rebuke when Casey placed a calming hand on her shoulder and shook his head.

"Not now, Cara, he whispered. "I'll be back later," Casey called out to the doctor and then placed a light kiss on Cara's cheek. "Do your best for her."

"Did you think I wouldn't, Mr. Scott?"

"Not in the least, doc."

"Very good. Be on your way so that I can get started saving this poor girl's life. You going to help me, Miss Martini?"

"That's my intention, yes," Cara said, less than enthusiastically.

"Yes, well if so, then the main thing is for you to stay lucid and erect. If you can manage that much, hand me those tweezers on that tray yonder."

"Tweezers?"

"Yes tweezers. Can you think of a better way to remove the smaller pieces of cloth from this girl's back, or did you think perhaps I was going to take the time to pluck my eyebrows!"

"Sorry," Cara muttered, passing the tweezers over.

"Now go and boil two pots of water," the doctor started, and then snapped when it looked as if Cara was going to question his next order, "and by God, don't ask me why. I'll tell the whys when I think you need to know them."

Cara sighed, and then turned to follow his curt instruction.

"And the final thing to know if you're going to stay to assist me," he called after her, "is to do first and ask questions later."

The moment Cara returned, the doctor returned to barking orders. "Find some strips of cloth—should be some in the chest just yonder—and put them in the first pot."

"Yes, doctor."

"Good. Just keep saying 'yes, doctor', and following my instructions and we may just get through this."

"If I don't kill you first," Cara muttered, pulling strips of cloth from the chest.

CHAPTER 3

"I think it's time to find another chief magistrate, Governor Martini," Casey said without preamble, the moment he strolled into the governor's office.

"We have an extremely low case of crime here in Martin's Landing, Mr. Scott, so obviously Harold Rankle is doing his job, wouldn't you say?" The governor replied, without glancing up from his reading. Being the governor of a tiny town didn't require much in the way of exertion, but Stanley Martini always affected an air of consequence, even when reading the newspaper.

"I'd say that the man is a loose cannon that's going to fire off before long and hurt someone innocent, like today."

That caused the governor to lift his head, "What transpired this day that is different than any other day?"

"Rankle nearly beat a poor Indian girl to death because she stole a loaf of bread," Casey spat.

"Stealing *is* a crime, Mr. Scott, or is it the fact that it was a woman doing the stealing and receiving the punishment that has you so distressed? I do declare that if we allowed the female population to go unpunished, then the men may well begin enlisting them to do their dirty work. Can't have that, now can we?"

"There's not even any proof that the poor girl was guilty. He just strung her up and…"

"So now you're declaring that the native population is entitled to the same justice as we are? She probably consumed the proof anyway."

"Sir…" Casey started and then stopped. He was addressing someone who cared just as little for the native population as Rankle—as well as most everyone in Martin's Landing—so he was not likely to get the magistrate fired over the wellbeing of one. He'd just have to switch tactics. "What about your daughter, sir? Is her safety less of an issue?"

That caused the governor's head to jerk up. He slapped the newspaper onto the desk and leaned forward, "What are you talking about, Casey? Last I recall, we were speaking about an Indian maiden, not my daughter."

"Well, your daughter determined that the punishment didn't fit the crime, to which I readily agree, so she tried to stop Rankle from continuing his assault ..."

"What's happened to my daughter, Casey?" Martini yelled; his face red in agitation.

"Nothing," Casey sighed, shaking his head. "Fortunately, I arrived in time to stop Rankle from lowering his whip in retaliation against her."

Martini let loose a loud whoosh and then settled back in his chair, "And for that I owe you a debt of gratitude, but since Rankle didn't actually ..."

"Fire him and send him packing," Casey inserted assertively. "He isn't fit for the post."

"I love my daughter as much as you, Casey, but please do not presume to tell me what I need to do. Besides, you stated that Rankle did not harm Cara; or am I missing something?"

"I beg pardon, Governor," Casey sighed. "It was merely a suggestion. Still, the fact that your daughter was unharmed was simply due to my timely arrival. I assure you, sir, that he fully intended bodily harm. Next time, I may not arrive in the nick of time."

"Admittedly, you state a good point, which I must consider. If Rankle strikes at innocents, then he does not deserve the post," the governor sighed. "Regrettably, we have no one to stand in until a replacement can be found. Without a magistrate, Martin's Landing would be subject to victimization on a large scale. These are perilous times, Casey, as well you know. Unless ..." the governor stopped speaking, a thoughtful look on his face.

"Unless what, Governor?"

"Well, I've always thought you to be a decent fellow; otherwise I would never have consented to giving you my daughter's hand."

Casey smiled, "Yes well, I'm forever in your debt, Governor, for that favor, and will be even more appreciative when you permit the actual wedding to take place, but I'm not certain what that has to do with our present conversation."

"Well, this town needs a decent fellow to uphold the law, see?"

Victim of Love Barbara Woster

"Yes, I see," Casey sighed. "You want me to take the oath of office and run Harold out of town."

"I'm glad you agree. I'll swear you in right now, and we'll hold a formal ceremony as soon as you've dealt with Rankle. Now raise your right hand. Oh, and Casey," the governor said, momentarily stalling the oath taking, "as soon as we're done here, do have a talk with your fiancé. She gets more and more disruptive as she advances in years."

CHAPTER 4

"Disruptive, am I?" Cara exclaimed an hour later, when Casey dropped by to pick her up from the doctor's office.

"Well, you definitely disrupt my mental state whenever you're around me," Casey grinned, drawing her into his embrace.

"I'm not quite certain if that's a good or bad thing from your tone," Cara objected, pushing at his chest.

"Both, if you must know," Casey laughed when her jaw dropped. He took advantage of her momentary state of shock to pull her tightly against him. "You don't see me complaining awfully much, do you?" He whispered against her ear, and then sent a trail of kisses along her neck.

"Casey," she protested, half-heartedly, "we're on a public thoroughfare."

Casey lifted his head, and looked up and down the empty alleyway, and then down into his fiancé's bemused face. He laughed briefly and bent his head back to his task. "It isn't exactly a main thoroughfare, my dear; still, if anyone happens down this way, I'll simply shove you into the shadows before continuing my attack upon your person."

"Hmm, sounds delightful," Cara muttered, leaning her head against the brick edifice.

Casey laughed again, then lifted his head to lay claim to her mouth, willingly offered. She responded with the same passion with which she addressed everything in her life and he felt himself respond with an ardor that had him wishing their wedding day was sooner rather than whenever her father decided.

Moments later, and with reluctance, he drew away. He grinned when he heard her mutter a protest, "Before *we* can proceed, my dear, you need to convince your father to allow our wedding to proceed."

Cara's eyes flew open and she blushed, and then sighed, "I don't know why he refuses to allow us to set a date. He's already approved of you for my mate and consented to see us wed. Still, ever since we lost Mother, he's been reluctant to let me go."

"Well, you can't remain subservient to his needs forever, you know."

"Oh, without a doubt, you'd rather me wait on your needs."

"Oh, without a doubt; and those needs mount every time I'm alone with you."

"Well, there's one way to prevent such frustrations from mounting, you know," Cara grinned.

"Don't even say it," Casey snapped. "I'll not do it."

"Well, it would help alleviate ..."

"I said, don't say it."

"Well, it's not as if I'm asking you to make love to me out of wedlock, you know," Cara laughed.

"No, you're just teasing me mercilessly," Casey growled. "You know that I can't stay away from you for prolonged periods of time, for the sake of alleviating frustrations or no. Are you saying you can part company with me until we wed?"

"Of course not," Cara smiled, wrapping her arms around his waist. "It's hard enough on me when you leave to tend to your business, and those times I know you're only going to be gone a day or two."

"Well, your father has seen to it that I won't be going away for a good long while, so I'll have to rely on self-restraint, as well as Murphy, even more."

"I won't be complaining, but do you think your business partner will?"

"Murph? No. He's just as capable as I in handling our affairs."

"Well for once, I can say a genuine thanks to my father for one of his decisions."

"Well, I will be happy to give genuine thanks if you could talk him into letting us wed sooner than never."

"I'll work on him tonight at dinner, but before then, I do believe, Magistrate Scott, that you have a duty to tend to."

"Pleasing my fiancé isn't a duty?"

"I'd rather hope that's more of a pleasure."

"Oh, I'd say it's definitely more than pleasurable, however dealing with the Arapaho is going to be much less than pleasurable."

"How do you think they are going to react when the girl is able to finally go home?"

"Violently."

"Well you can always point them in Rankle's direction, once you run him out of town, that is?"

"Might have to, if only to keep the townsfolk safe," he replied thoughtfully, genuine concern lacing his tone.

"Well, it's nice to know that we're on friendly terms with them, at least," Cara reassured naïvely.

"No Cara. We're only on friendly terms with some of them, and that friendliness is not set on a firm foundation; and unfortunately, we aren't on friendly terms at all with the younger generation, who are more deadly in a fight."

"Well, we can't exactly blame them. It's not as if they've been fairly dealt with."

"Shhh," Casey placed his fingertips on her lips to silence her outburst. "Don't let your words reach too many ears, my dear. Someone listening might take you for an Indian sympathizer and string you up for sedition."

"You wouldn't let them."

"I'm not going to be here. I'm going to be escorting that Indian maiden home in a few days, which means I won't be around to protect you from yourself."

Cara crinkled her nose at his comment and chose to overlook it, "So, you really think she'll be able to travel in a few days?"

"Yes," Casey sighed. "Fortunately for her, you arrived at the opportune moment; preventing Rankle from doing too much serious damage."

"It certainly looked serious."

"It usually does and is," Casey said, pulling back a little. "In her case, the serious was superficial. She'll bear scars, but she'll live. So, my darling, when are you going to settle down and stop interfering in perilous affairs?"

"Never," Cara stated stubbornly, raising her chin defiantly.

Casey shook his head, and then leaned down to kiss her softly. "I worry about you. I shouldn't have to worry about you," he whispered against her lips. Cara pulled back.

"Perhaps I should stop caring about others, then," Cara replied, a deep sadness in her tone. "If I don't worry about others, I have no need to care about their problems. If I don't care about their problems, I don't get in trouble trying to help, and then you don't have to rescue me."

Casey laughed softly. "I get your point. Would you at least do me the courtesy of waiting until I'm around before placing yourself in harm's way? That way, I can step in quickly."

"But it's so romantic the way you gallop in at the last minute ..."

"Cara, I'm not joking right now," Casey stated firmly.

"Very well—I will endeavor to do so, sir," Cara grinned, planting a light kiss on her fiancé's chin.

"Much obliged," Casey smiled. "Now, you head on home. I'm going in search of our former magistrate.

CHAPTER 5

"You'll be sorry?" Cara laughed. "Did he really say that?"

"Yes, and I fail to see the humor in it," Casey sighed.

"Why is it that angry people always mutter that very threat when they perceive themselves wronged? It really is absurd, considering they never do find themselves in a position to retaliate."

"Makes them feel better," Casey said, helping her climb into the carriage. "And why, pray tell, is it that whenever I tell you that you can't do something, you always manage to persuade me otherwise?"

Cara merely laughed, settling into the seat across from the young Indian girl. Her humor faded quickly however, at the pained look on the girl's face. She was still in a great deal of agony, but had refused any medication to assist in relieving that agony. That was why Cara insisted on taking the carriage instead of returning her to her people on horseback, as the men initially intended. It would be a difficult journey at times, but at least she would be more comfortable; the pain more bearable. It was Cara's hope, also, that the men of her village would see their consideration and forgo butchering them upon arrival.

"Change of heart about coming?" Casey asked, seeing his fiancé's knitted brow.

"No," Cara whispered. "She needs me with her."

"I don't think playing chaperone ..."

"I'm coming, Casey," Cara interrupted softly. "Please."

"There might be trouble," Casey tried once more. "In fact, I'd be surprised if we escape the village without gunfire—once they see the damage to their maiden."

"I'm always in trouble, remember?" Cara grinned. "Fortunately, I have you to rescue me if things turn ugly."

Casey grinned wryly, "Let's just hope I'll be up to the task if the need arises."

"You usually are, darling, but if not," Cara teased, "I'm sure that one of the other seven men accompanying us will be able to manage."

"There'll be sunshine in Hell the day I'm unable to tend to my own woman's needs. You just remember that, Cara."

"Oh, I don't think that will be something easily forgotten," Cara replied softly, her skin turning a lovely shade of pink at his blatant innuendo.

Casey laughed, and then closed the door, moving to mount his horse, "Let's ride men! The sooner we get there, the sooner we get back!"

CHAPTER 6

"I'm truly sorry for what happened to you," Cara said, finally breaking the silence after two days. "You probably don't understand a thing I'm saying, but ..."

"I understand," the Indian maiden said, turning her face from the window; startling Cara.

"Oh. Well, then, I'll reiterate, that I'm truly sorry for your suffering."

"You wish to apologize for what the man did to me?"

"I make no apologies for that overzealous fiend," Cara snapped in renewed anger, and then took a deep breath to control the memory. She didn't want to frighten the girl. "However, I do apologize that I wasn't faster in preventing him using his whip."

"It was you who I heard stand ready to fight for me?"

Cara nodded, and couldn't help the blush that crept into her cheeks at the maiden's blunt perusal of her person.

"You are not a very big person."

"No, I guess I'm not," Cara replied with a knit in her brow.

"But you have a brave heart as big as the man that whipped me." The statement startled Cara—and pleased her. She half expected the girl to call her an idiot for going up against such a huge man; instead, she called her brave. Cara smiled.

"Why did you help me?" The maiden asked softly.

"Because what Rankle was doing was wrong, that's why."

"Many people would not care," the maiden whispered, lowering her gaze.

"I've been told that I'm not most people," Cara replied with a wry grin. "What's your name?" She asked suddenly.

The girl's gaze shot up, "Why?"

"Because I like to know to whom it is that I'm speaking," Cara smiled indulgently. "And, since I now know we understand each other, I thought it would be nice if we could address each other properly."

"Oh, I did not think..."

"That I would care?" Cara finished and was happy to see a wisp of a smile form on her face. "Is the pain still unbearable?" Cara asked, when the smile vanished, replaced by a scowl.

"I will suffer the pain because I know that I will live. I am called *Adanawidvdi geladvsdi ama*."

"Did you do that on purpose, or is that truly your name?" Cara laughed, and the maiden giggled. "Can that be translated into something I can understand and actually say?"

The Indian maiden hesitated, "Hmm. This I do not know. I have learned your tongue, but I have not thought to learn my name."

"How long have you lived in town?"

"One half of your year," the maiden said.

"Six months?" Cara's brow knitted, wondering why she'd never seen the girl about town. "And what did the people call you that you worked for?" Cara asked, suddenly wondering who her employer was. She didn't think about the fact that it may have been them who turned this poor girl over to Rankle.

"Girl."

"Just 'girl'?" Cara cringed.

"Yes."

"Well if you don't mind, I'd prefer to call you something else, if we can just figure how to translate your name, that is. Have you ever played charades?" Cara asked, and then stopped. "No, I don't suppose you would have."

"What is this charades?"

"You act things out with your hands and body..."

"Signing."

"Yes, I suppose so."

"This is how my people communicate with those who do not speak our language."

"Well, I certainly fall into that category, so you act out your name, and I'll try to guess. It'll certainly make the time pass faster."

"I will try," the maiden said, knitting her brow in concentration. She placed her fingers on the palm of her hand and began jumping them slowly from wrist to fingertips.

"Hop? Jump? Skip..."

"Yes."

"Skip?" Cara clapped. "Wow, that was easier than I thought it would be, but that's not all, is it? Surely, I'm not going to call you 'Skip'?"

"No, that is not all," the maiden said, and then began acting out the next part.

"Oh, dear! This one is a lot harder," Cara sighed in frustration after fifteen minutes. "I may end up calling you just Skip after all."

The girl smiled, "If you do not wish to continue ..."

"No, no," Cara interrupted, "I'm not one to give up on something that easily."

"Yes, I see this is true about you," she replied, and Cara blushed.

"Well, let's keep at it. Eventually I'll be able to address you properly."

It took another hour and a half, but Cara was finally able to decipher the hand signals that the young girl was doing, "Skips Along The Water? That's truly your name?"

"Yes, this is what I am called."

"That's very pretty, but how in heaven's name did you get a name like that?"

Skips Along The Water grinned, "My mother said that, from a very young age, I could jump from stone to stone in the water so quick and easy, that it looked like I was walking on the water."

"Well, it's very pretty, and it's a pleasure to make your acquaintance, Skips Along The Water. My name is Cara."

"Cara," Skips Along The Water said. "I wish to thank you again for what you did for me."

"Think nothing of it," Cara said, waving a hand in dismissal, then decided to address the thing that nagged at the back at her mind. "You said you lived in town for six months, but to be honest, I don't recall seeing you before...well, you know."

"I was not permitted out of doors," Skips Along The Water said in a whisper, her head drooping.

"Weren't...you must be joking?" Cara snapped, her ire rising again. "And was it your employer who turned you in for stealing that loaf of bread?"

Skips Along The Water's head snapped up, and anger blazed in her eyes, "I did not steal anything," she declared, her chin raising a notch higher.

"Didn't steal the bread?" Cara repeated thoughtfully, now certain that Rankle had no proof; was merely abusing the girl for the pleasure he derived. She looked back to address her traveling companion, but was taken aback by the hostility that shone in the dark eyes. She pushed the unease she felt aside at seeing such hatred displayed in one so young and started to speak, but Skips Along The Water interrupted her.

"I took the bread to cut and serve," the Indian maiden snapped, crossing her arms across her chest, defying Cara to refute her claim.

"I don't understand," Cara shook her head, confused. "Why would your employer..."

"What is this word, employer?"

"A person you work for, usually for money," Cara said, and then continued when she could see Skips Along The Water trying to understand her meaning. "Usually, when a person needs help in their home, they go to someone and ask them to work for them. Then they pay them money for the job they do. Does that explain better?"

"Yes, but I was not asked to work," Skips Along The Water said, her eyes darkening again in fury. "I was taken from my people and made to work."

"You were abducted!?"

"If you mean, was I stolen from my home? Yes."

"Unbelievable!"

"You do not believe me?" Skips Along The Water asked, the rage dissipating rapidly, replaced by sadness.

"I believe you," Cara said softly, "I just find it incomprehensible that someone would do such a thing. I wish I knew who was responsible, and why none of the townsfolk knew it was happening. Do you know the name of the people who took you?"

"It was the man who dragged me from his home and beat me."

"Harold Rankle?"

"I did not know his name." Skips Along The Water shrugged.

"But if Rankle kept you for six months, why suddenly lose his temper over a loaf of bread and whip you?"

"He took me to his bed every night and I would cry. The night before he took me and whipped me, I did not cry," Skips Along The Water grinned fiendishly. "I bit his nose very hard and then I kicked him and punched him until he jumped out of bed. He was very angry, but he did not touch me. The next morning, he told me I was a thief and would be punished, but I knew he was just angry with me."

"And to think, all we did was to get him fired," Cara said, more to herself. "Well, one of these days he'll get his comeuppance."

"This is another word that I do not know."

"I just mean to say that someday, something bad will happen to Harold Rankle that will make him sorry for all of the bad things he did to you—and to others."

"Oh, yes it will," Skips Along The Water said. "My brother will make sure it does."

That one statement, said with such seething conviction, made Cara glad that she would not be the one on the receiving end of the brother's vengeance.

"What about your father? Won't he be angry as well?" Cara asked.

"I have no father, only my brother is left to me, and if Rankle had not locked me in his home, my brother would have found me long ago."

"And killed Rankle, most likely."

"Rankle will die."

"Well, without a doubt he will—one day," Cara said, "but it's not something you need dwell on. Just think about how happy your brother is going to be to see you when you get home tomorrow."

"Yes, he will," Skips Along The Water said softly, tears welling in her eyes.

Cara judged them to be tears of joy, and turned away to look out of the window, giving Skips Along The Water a moment to compose herself. When Skips Along The Water next spoke, it gave Cara pause, but when she turned to respond, Skips Along The Water had fallen asleep.

CHAPTER 7

"What's so disturbing about 'I'm sorry'?" Casey asked Cara when they stopped to make camp for the night.

"It's not the words, Casey; it's how they were said," Cara explained with a sigh, recalling the maiden's words just before she drifted off to sleep.

"And what makes you think she wasn't just apologizing for crying in front of you? The native people of this land are very closed emotionally, from what I've heard; or perhaps she was apologizing in advance for falling asleep while you two were conversing. She may have felt it was rude."

"Maybe, but...no, it was more than that. It was as if she wanted me to know she was sorry for something that was *going* to happen, not something that *had* happened," Cara emphasized. "And I can't explain any better than that. All I know is it sent shivers along my spine."

"Well, why don't you just ask her what she meant by that ominous apology?" Casey grinned.

"See, now you're just laughing at me," Cara huffed, standing and walking toward the river. "And don't you dare follow me," she shot over her shoulder, when she heard footfalls coming up behind her.

"I'm not allowed to say, 'I'm sorry'?" Casey laughed from behind her.

Cara spun on her heels and Casey had to dig in his heels to keep from colliding into her, "No, you are *not* allowed to say you are sorry, especially since I know it would not be sincere, and as for talking to me further, it might be best to wait until I do not have murder on my mind."

"Ah, now Cara," Casey cooed, stepping closer.

Cara took a step back, "I need to be alone for a while, Casey, so now would be a good time for me to go and wash up at the river."

"When you come back, will you still be angry with me?" Casey asked, feigning a ridiculously dejected look.

Cara grinned. "No, I don't suppose I will," she said, placing a quick kiss on his lips.

Casey grabbed her about the waist and pulled her close, deepening the kiss. Cara wrapped her arms around his neck and leaned closer, pressing her breasts into his chest, intentionally arousing.

"You really know how to heat a man's blood to boiling," Casey whispered when they finally came up for air. "Remind me to thank your dad for allowing you to accompany me."

Something in Cara's face made Casey pull back, "You did get your father's permission to come, didn't you, Cara?"

"I left him a note," Cara whispered, a blush staining her cheeks.

"Oh, dear Lord," Casey exclaimed, "he's going to be furious."

"Well, maybe it'll force his hand."

"Force his hand? What in blue blazes are you talking about?"

"Well," Cara said, "we've been trying to get him to set a date for the marriage, right, so maybe he'll do it now that we've spent so much time in the wilderness alone. Reputation, and all that nonsense."

"Nonsense," Casey moaned, glancing heavenward. "God, spare me from my nonsensical fiancé. Cara," he sighed, looking back into Cara's innocent eyes, overly exaggerated, "we're hardly alone."

"Well, not alone, to be sure," Cara smiled, "but certainly not appropriately chaperoned."

Casey shook in head in bemusement, "And here I thought you wanted to come along to act as chaperone to the Indian girl, when in reality you had some rather self-serving motivations."

"A girl has to look out for her interests when her dad doesn't seem to want to," Cara said, shrugging her shoulders.

"Your mischievous nature is going to come back to teach you a lesson one of these days. Still, I, for one, hope it works," Casey said, drawing her back into his embrace, "but I wouldn't put it past your old man to lock you up until you're old and gray."

Cara laughed, "I sincerely doubt he'll be *that* angry, after all, we have been engaged for nearly six months."

"True enough," Casey said, stroking her back, thoughtfully.

"Well, I'm going to head to the river and wash up, before it gets much later," Cara said, pulling from his embrace, when it appeared he had nothing further to say on the matter.

"Want company?" Casey grinned, snapping from his musings.

"If I said 'yes', you'd just laugh and head back to the fire."

"I guess you already know me too well," Casey sighed. "Kind of takes the fun out of teasing you."

"Don't worry, sweetheart," Cara smiled, turning and sashaying toward the river, "I'll let you get away with teasing me more often than not."

"I'm not the only tease, woman!" Casey laughed, watching her hips sway.

"Keeps life interesting," Cara laughed and vanished into the tree line.

"Dear Lord above," Casey laughed, turning toward camp, "thank you for sending such an interesting woman into my life."

CHAPTER 8

Cara knelt on the bank, pulled a handkerchief from her sleeve and dipped it into the cool spring. With a sigh of contentment, she dabbed the dripping cloth over every inch of her face and neck, and then sank onto her haunches. She'd insisted on making this journey, but it was far more taxing on her body than she'd assumed it would be.

She spotted a movement to her right and saw Skips Along the Water walking through the woods. *She is probably searching for privacy also*, Cara thought, dipping her handkerchief back into the water and swiping it along her arms.

Her muscles relaxed a bit as she absorbed the calm feel of her surroundings. A light breeze began to blow and she sighed, then shivered. Though it was a warm breeze, it contacted the cool water on her neck causing goosebumps to pop up on her arms. Still, the cool sensation provided a reprieve against the heat.

The word *heat* popped about in her head and her mind drifted to Casey. He'd commented on how she heated his blood, but did he know how hot her own blood ran when he held her; kissed her? She didn't much like the conversations her married friends had about their husbands though and that caused another shiver to run along her spine. Did a relationship really turn dull and ugly upon saying one's vows? Certainly, the marriage bed couldn't be as disgusting as her friends attested; especially when she'd found nothing but pleasure in the way Casey touched and kissed her. Her friends joked that they kissed a thousand toads to find their Prince Charming, only to have him revert to being a toad after marriage. She shivered again.

It was times like these, when thoughts like those entered her brain that she wished she still had a mother; but her mother had died of influenza when Cara was only twelve. At twelve, and on the verge of womanhood, her father should have seen to her womanly education by sending her to a finishing school or to live with a female relative, but he hadn't, so all she had to go by now was her own emotions and the gossip of those already married.

Unfortunately, her emotions conflicted with the gossip, leaving her feeling as if she were abnormal somehow. Surely, she thought, having feelings and desires was a normal thing, and if the feelings she had when Casey held her were enjoyable, then certainly *everything* would be enjoyable.

If only her father wasn't being stubborn about allowing her to set the date for her marriage, then she could put her unrest to sleep once and for all; learn about what really happened in the marriage bed first hand. She shuddered when a thrill of delight shot down her spine at the thought of lying in bed next to Casey. *Whew*, she thought, *I really do hope these feelings are normal.*

Her thoughts drifted of their own accord to the note she'd left for her father and hoped Casey wouldn't be too angry with her when he discovered what she'd *actually* written. Of course, she wouldn't have written it had her father shown the slightest reason in allowing the wedding to take place. After all, a six-month engagement was far too long in her opinion, and Casey's.

She sighed, dipping her handkerchief in the water again.

"Now, if I can just convince him to stop in Twin Arrows on our return trip to locate a minister. Then we can ..."

Cara screeched and struggled, but couldn't break the hold on her mouth or her waist. Whomever it was that grabbed hold of her was strong, and had little patience, she discovered, when the hand gripping her waist released and smacked her on the head to cease her struggles. Little did whomever it was realize, that smacking her was only making her angry; and she set to struggling more intensely. That was until Skips Along The Water walked around to stand in front of her. Then her struggles ceased and her gaze widened in fear, but it wasn't until the young woman spoke that the ominous feeling of the previous night hit Cara like a punch to the gut.

"I'm sorry," she said softly. "My brother will not hurt you, but you must come with us now."

"Mmm mmm mmmm," Cara muttered from behind the hand covering her mouth. She wanted to berate the girl she'd helped and befriended, but her captor wasn't allowing any leeway whatsoever. He hefted her, hand still covering her mouth, and started following Skips Along The Water. She didn't know where they intended to take her, but it was obvious they weren't escorting her back to her camp; and was equally obvious they were hauling her away from Casey.

And if they were taking her away from Casey; how would he know where she was or where she'd gone? Would he piece together clues that would let him know she'd been abducted? Certainly, he wouldn't assume she'd wandered away on her own. He said there would be sunshine in Hell before he couldn't take care of his woman. She'd known the meaning was more than intended, but he also meant that he would always be there to protect her. He always had been, even if arriving at the last moment; and generally the protection was because of her own mischievous making. Now though, she'd not been responsible and since Casey didn't know she was being abducted…. She felt tears prick her eyes, because this night there could very well be sunshine in Hell.

Fear crept deep enough into her heart and mind that she started struggling again; kicking at her captor's shins. She heard a few grunts and assumed her efforts worked, when he moved his hand from her mouth; however, that same hand smacked her upside the head and then clamped on her mouth again. It happened so quickly she failed to scream. Still, as she'd told Skips Along The Water, she wasn't a quitter; and in this case, she refused to be deterred by slight headaches, especially when she was scared beyond measure.

She began thrashing about again, kicking ineffectually, only to have him smack her on the head a third time. Her captor's speed, lighting fast, astonished her. It took two more smacks however, before she realized she wasn't going to break free, or be able to scream before he clamped down on her mouth again. He was simply faster than she. She was also starting to see persistent stars in front of her eyes, and trying to see past them was giving her an even bigger headache.

They hadn't gone too far, when they reached a pair of horses standing in a nearby glade. Skips Along The Water's brother released her long enough to reposition his hands, then hoisted her onto one of the horses. She took advantage of the situation and let loose a scream that startled the two animals, causing them to rear.

She lost her seating and tumbled to the ground. Had the man not pulled her away, the horses surely would have trampled her with their enormous hooves. At least they looked enormous from her vantage point on the ground, headed straight for her head.

The Indian male continued grumbling after he latched onto her arm and hauled her out of harm's way. His hand remained firmly latched while Skips Along The Water soothed the animals, his look daring her to scream again.

She returned the glare, trying to convince herself it was worth whatever punishment he meted to cry out again; but though her brain was ready to make the effort, her mouth remained firmly sealed, the memory of his speed and sharp smacks too fresh.

When the animals had settled, Skips Along The Water came to stand next to her. If not for the brother, Cara would have launched herself on the smaller female and finished what Rankle started. As if sensing her intent, Skips Along The Water's brother latched onto her other arm, and pulled her back flush up against his body.

"Do you mind?" She snarled, trying to put some distance between them, but she heard a low rumble from his chest, which escaped his lips as a chuckle. She stopped struggling, satisfied with the few inches she'd managed to put between them.

"Will you stop fighting now?" Skips Along The Water asked.

"Not in this lifetime," Cara stated resolute, and pierced the young Indian maid with what she hoped was her most intimidating glower. If she couldn't free herself, she could at least make the girl feel guilty. It didn't work.

"Again, I will say I am sorry," she whispered, "but you must listen and do as you are told. You will not be harmed unless you cause the harm yourself."

"I helped you," Cara snapped accusingly. "Why are you doing this to me?"

"I knew my brother would come for me and I was right. I found him and the warriors preparing to attack your people. If had had not stopped them, your people would be dead," Skips Along The Water explained.

"So instead of attacking them, you told them to kidnap me? Do I need to remind you that I helped you?" Cara snapped again.

Skips Along The Water asked her brother a question in their native tongue. Cara presumed it was to do with her own query, but hoped not when her brother's response made Skips Along The Water grow pale.

"What? What did he say?"

"He said that you will be punished as payment for your people harming me," she replied softly.

"But we didn't harm you, Rankle did! Tell him that!"

Skips Along The Water quickly explained all that had befallen her after being abducted by Rankle. The warriors grip loosened slightly and for a moment Cara thought he'd release her; but then his grip suddenly tightened again.

"What? Didn't you tell him?" Cara squealed, but Skips Along The Water was already talking to her brother again. When he responded, she paled again.

"Now what? Why isn't your brother letting me go?"

"We will keep you with the people until your man brings to us the man named Rankle," she explained, but didn't seem happy over that decision; and neither was Cara. She started struggling in earnest, kicking and squirming even more than before.

"Please stop," Skips Along The Water implore. "Your foolish behavior will only anger my brother."

"My foolish behavior?" Cara screeched. "You're abducting the person who came to your aid, so who is the one being foolish here?"

Skips Along The Water sighed, "I am sorry..."

"So you keep saying," Cara retorted.

"…but it is necessary for you to come with us. It is the only way we have to make your Mr. Scott help us find the man who took me from my home."

"Casey knows you have me?" Cara asked, suddenly hopeful.

"We have left our braves with him to explain and to help him track the man down. When the man that hurt me is found and brought to us, you will be released to your Mr. Scott."

"Why don't you just go after him yourself? Why do you need Casey? He's not a tracker. Your braves would do a far better job at locating him than Casey would?"

"I believe that only the three of us know what the man who took me looks like …"

"Then *you* go after him," Cara interjected snappishly, too angry to realize the flaw in her reasoning. If she'd been thinking clearly, she would have been able to argue that the warrior who kept watch over the village would have recognized Rankle, potentially, so would have been able to track the man down without need of Casey; without need of kidnapping herself. However, her anger was prohibiting rational thought.

"He must be made to pay for what he did," Skips Along The Water said patiently, ignoring her comment. "By taking you with us, your Mr. Scott will work very hard to find him and bring him to our people. Your Mr. Scott loves you very much, so it should not take long."

"And what am I supposed to do in the meantime?"

"You will be my guest."

"And what happens if Casey and your men can't find Rankle?"

Skips Along The Water looked at her brother as if seeking the answer, and then blanched slightly when it was given.

"Lyuno asgaya nadvne nasgi nigesvna vgalutsv udalulv itsula anagisdi aquatseli gola owenvsv nasgi ageyv wili adanelv saquu aquatseli tsulitsvyasdi usdayvhvsgi."

"What did he say?" Cara demanded. "Surely I'm not meant to be harmed if Casey doesn't deliver your abductor. You can't very well blame us for what the man did to you."

"Nasgi iyulisdodi?" Skips Along The Water responded, again ignoring Cara.

"Gilo asiyvwi wili wha ganohalidasdi nasginai nasgi ageyv. Wili nasgi nigesvna aduladi hnadvga asequui."

"Vv, nihi duyugodv," she replied, and then looked back to Cara. "I am sorry."

"The last time you said that to me in that tone, I ended kidnapped."

Skips Along The Water sighed heavily, "My brother has said that if your Mr. Scott does not return before my people move to their winter home, then you will be given to one of our braves as wife."

"What?" Cara's eyes bulged. She wanted to rail a rejoinder, but she couldn't form words past the shock.

"He is right," she continued doggedly. "If your man does not return, then you will need to be cared for, hunted for, and no warrior will wish to do this for a woman that is not his. Maybe my brother will have you."

The brother snorted, and Cara twisted her head so she could glare up at him. All she saw was his chin, which was thrust forward arrogantly. Still, not being able to stare him down wasn't going to deter her from having her say.

"I wouldn't have you either, and don't pretend any more that you don't speak English because I can tell you do," Cara snapped at him and was surprised to see a grin form. She turned back to Skips Along The Water, "I will not concede to this madness," she declared resolutely.

"My brother has spoken and it will be as he says," Skips Along The Water said softly, "but be comforted in knowing that we will not begin our move to our winter home until the month you call October."

Oddly enough, it did provide a modicum of relief knowing that Casey had a good two months to find Rankle. Surely between Casey and the Indian trackers, they would be able to find Rankle and turn him over to the Arapaho people long before then. Still, she wasn't pleased with having to remain captive during that time.

"I am sorry," Skips Along The Water whispered.

"If you say I'm sorry to me once more, you truly will..." Cara started, but her tirade was cut short when Skips Along The Water's brother hauled her from the ground and tossed her onto his mount's back. Skips Along The Water watched the spectacle and then moved to where her horse awaited her.

"Must you be so pushy?" Cara snapped at him over her shoulder when he mounted behind her.

"Must you speak so much?" He replied.

"You do know that I *helped* your sister, right?" Cara snapped. "I'm not the enemy here."

"You are all my enemy," he said quietly.

"Are you always this pleasant?" Cara goaded.

"Always."

"Let me guess, your Indian name translates to He Who Always Sulks," Cara said sarcastically.

"No, I am called ..."

"You're going to say it in English, right?" Cara interrupted, not wishing to play another game of charades just to know the name of a man whom she really didn't care to know at all.

He laughed, "I should not, but I will. I am called River Runner."

"I'd say it's a pleasure to meet you, but under the circumstances, and considering the fact that you view me as an enemy, despite the fact that I rescued your sister from being whipped to death, I'd have to say I'd rather not have met you at all."

To her surprise, he laughed again, "Perhaps I *will* consider taking you as my wife."

"Why in heaven's name would you want an enemy as a wife?" Cara said, not really taking his proposition seriously.

"Because you are very funny."

"Trust me, it is completely unintentional," Cara muttered, not wishing to encourage him, in the event he was serious.

"And you have good hips," River Runner continued.

"What in heaven's name above do my hips have to do with anything?" Cara snapped, unable to prevent rising to his provocation.

"Good hips means easy birth; strong babies," River Runner replied.

"Well then," Cara sighed heavily, "I guess now would be a good time to begin that diet I've been meaning to start."

"What is this diet?" River Runner asked.

"A way to make my hips smaller," Cara said, non-joking. "That way I'm less appealing and no one will want me."

"Hmm. I will have to have Skips Along The Water watch you closely to make sure you eat."

"Why would you care?"

"I do not wish my woman to have small hips," River Runner replied.

"I'm not your woman, I'm Casey's woman."

"If he does not return, you will by my woman," River Runner whispered against her ear.

"I wouldn't count on it," Cara said sharply, leaning forward out of reach of his hot breath. "With the help of your trackers, Casey should find Harold Rankle and be around to pick me up within a matter of weeks."

"Hmm. Perhaps he will trade you for horses," River Runner persisted. "How many horses do you think he will want for you?"

"None," Cara snapped.

"None? Then you not only will give me strong babies, but you will come to me free. That's a good bargain. If he loved you, as you say, he would offer many horses," River Runner was joking with her because he found her outrage humorous, but the more he joked and the more she countered, the more he liked her. *Perhaps I will consider keeping her*, he thought.

"If you haven't figured it out yet," Cara retorted combatively, "I am not joking. I will never be your wife."

"We will see."

"Your mother should have named you He Who Does Not Listen," Cara muttered. As they sat there on the horse, Cara realized that they seemed in no hurry to depart the area. "Why are we still sitting here?"

"I am waiting on my warrior to return to tell me that the white men understand not to fight; to tell your man what he must do."

Before Cara could reply, a warrior broke through the trees and walked up to where she and River Runner sat atop his mount. They broke into that language Cara could not understand, but something in their tone made her wish she could.

"The white men are secured?" River Runner asked.

"They did not fight back," the warrior responded.

"And you have explained to the one called Casey Scott what it is we wish him to do?"

"Yes, I told him that he will travel with me to find the white man; that his woman would be returned when the white man is caught and brought to you, as you instructed. The anger on his face shows he wishes to kill us all, but he said he would willingly help us; that you do not need to keep his woman captive," the warrior replied. He was confused over the instructions given by their chief also, but knew not to question his orders. Still, did their chief not trust his warriors to track a single man? Why would they need a lowly white man to help them? "Do you have more for me to do?"

River Runner's lips pursed in thought and he waged a war within his mind at the change in instruction that he was about to give his warrior; an instruction that would likely cause Casey Scott to wage war with his people; however, after speaking with the white woman, he felt compelled. Initially, he and his warriors were set to kill all of the white men, or to take the white woman to punish her for what happened to his sister; but his sister stopped him, explaining that these people had helped her. He'd already captured the woman, so then he thought only to use her to enlist the white man's cooperation in finding the man who'd harmed his sister; but now.... When he issued the new instruction, the warrior's eyes widened.

"Do you think that is wise, my chief? I thought we were only to hold her..."

"I know, I just..." River Runner paused and his gaze traveled from the top of Cara's hair, golden in the waning light, to the curve of her hips;

to her legs straddled across his stallion's mount. He drew in a deep breath and nodded. "It is what I wish."

The warrior nodded in acceptance, but his expression showed he was not pleased with the changes, "I will tell him what you have said, but it will not be easy to stop him coming after you."

"Tell Runs With Deer to ride ahead to try to locate the man Rankle. He will know what he looks like, since he was there and watched him from outside the town. Tell him what I wish him to do. Keep the white men secure until the sun rises. That will give Runs With Deer the time he needs."

The warrior drew in a deep breath and nodded, "The white man will be very angry. He will want to fight."

River Runner nodded, "I know, but I trust my warriors will prevent this. I must go now. Do as I ask," River Runner concluded, and kicked his horse into a gallop. His warrior was right—the decision he'd made was likely to anger the white man greatly and it was wise to put as much distance as was possible between them.

Cara held onto the pommel as if her life depended on it. They were moving faster than she'd ever ridden a horse before and the blur of ground rushing past made her nauseated. It wasn't until hours later, when they'd slowed to a walk that she was able to ask a question; to appease a curiosity that had been rattling around in her brain.

"How did you know?"

She heard him release his breath slowly, "I have had one of my braves nearby to your town since my sister was taken, and to other towns," he said softly. "He saw you stand to protect her before riding to let me know he'd found my sister. For this, I will say thank you."

"Why didn't he come to protect her?" She asked, but she knew the answer before she finished the question.

"He would have been harmed," River Runner replied, "and then he could not have been free to tell me my sister was alive."

"So, instead of just taking your sister home; you show your gratitude by kidnapping me."

"It is the only way."

"Maybe in your head, but in my head, you could have done things far differently."

"In my head, I know any other way would not have worked," River Runner replied, though in his head he was thinking about the change in orders. He hoped his decision would not cause them to go to war.

"Then you need to have your head examined."

"It is time for you to be silent now," River Runner sighed, worried he'd made a mistake. He was allowing his heart to overrule his head, something a chief should never do.

"Yeah, that may be for the best," Cara murmured, shaking her head in frustration.

CHAPTER 9

Casey paced.

He could think of nothing, short of murdering the Indians, to do. It angered him that they repaid his kindness with treachery. It infuriated him that he had allowed Cara to talk him into making such a dangerous journey. It galled him that he had not predicted such a turn of events, but mostly he was scared and worried, especially when he heard her scream.

"She is unharmed, but will not remain so if you attempt to retrieve her," one of the warriors stated, reading Casey's intent very clearly. He wanted to kill the warrior and bolt after Cara. It would have been foolish, since the other warriors would have assaulted him—but he would have her here, now, by his side, safe. Instead, she was on her way to somewhere foreign to her, her safety in question. "We ask you to stay here and do not fight us."

Casey had boldly stated that nothing, absolutely nothing, could keep him from protecting his own woman, but something had—warriors from the Arapaho. They were detaining him, in his own camp by his own incompetence.

His men moved to settle on nearby logs and rocks, all appearing sullen and angry; mirroring his own disposition. The Arapaho had overtaken them without the slightest resistance; and to make matters worse, those in the company of these warriors had abducted his fiancé beneath his very nose.

As soon as all of Casey's men were secure, the head warrior returned to speak with Casey before departing to go confer with his chief. The conversation still resonated in Casey's head.

"My chief wishes you to come with me to find the man who harmed our maiden. When this is done, your woman will be returned to you."

"I'll gladly assist you. You don't have to take Cara. Let her go..."

"This is not what my chief wishes, but I will go speak with him and tell him what you ask."

Now fifteen minutes later, he was still waiting—hoping -- Cara would walk through the woods, returned to him. His nerves were so taut, he was barely staying inside his own skin. He turned toward the direction the brave departed, but was immediately cut off by two fierce-looking warriors, "I just want to know what's going on," he said, but either the remaining warriors didn't speak English or were disinclined to respond.

Just as he was preparing himself, mentally, to charge and go after Cara, the English-speaking warrior returned. He spoke with one of the other warriors, who immediately mounted his horse and rode off. Then he settled onto a nearby tree stump; completely ignoring Casey and his men.

Casey strolled over and sat in front of him, "I just need to know what's going on. Why isn't Cara here? Did you tell him what I said?" He asked softly, trying to keep the pleading tone to a minimum.

"I will tell you what you need to know, in time," the warrior responded, and then crossed his arms over his chest, effectively ending the conversation.

By the time the sun rose over the horizon, Casey was heartsick, but not nearly as heartsick as he was angry. After the warrior refused his queries, he began to pace and didn't stop all night—until the English speaker approached again. As agitated as he was, he'd give anything to take a swing at the man, but knew the action wouldn't help Cara, his men, or himself.

The warrior stopped a few feet away, as if sensing the murderous rage emanating from Casey. Yet despite the anger aimed in his direction, the warrior's expression was strangely sardonic which made Casey even more irate. He certainly failed to see the humor in this particular situation.

"It is time for your men to return home," the warrior said, speaking for the first time in over eight hours.

"Why?" Casey asked, "And where is my fiancé? Where have your men taken her?"

"I will answer all of your questions soon," the warrior said patiently, "but first your men need to gather their things and go. My men will escort them to see that we are not followed."

"So, I'm still going with you," Casey said tersely.

The warrior merely nodded, and then turned to face his own men, issuing curt instructions.

Casey turned and walked toward his men, who stood hastily at his approach. He rubbed his thumb thoughtfully across his forehead, uncertain what to say, or even where to begin. They were more at a loss regarding what had transpired than even he, and it didn't help that he was about to send them packing. He scratched his chin and then took a deep breath, "I can't tell you for certain what's going on here, fellas, but it's probably for the best if we follow their instructions, for Cara's sake."

"So they do have her then?"

"Yeah," Casey said, cracking the tension out of his neck. "They took her last night. That must have been the scream we heard. The whys are still unclear. I haven't gotten much in the way of answers."

"Maybe they don't want us going after her," Murphy suggested.

"That's my notion," Casey sighed. "Otherwise there wouldn't be so many warriors here detaining us."

"So, now what?" Carl asked, eyeing the warriors warily.

"Now, you all go home," Casey said, running a hand tiredly through his already disheveled hair.

"Home?" Murphy exclaimed. "Why in Hell would we want to be doing that?"

"Because that's the instructions I've been given," Casey explained, trying to maintain control of his frazzled nerves.

"And what about you?" George asked.

"I'm going with 'em."

"You don't really expect us to leave you out here alone, do you, Casey?" Murphy asked.

"What choice do we have, Murph?" Casey replied in exasperation. "These people have Cara, and my help before they'll let me have her back."

"That's a big assumption," Carter interjected. "For all you know they hold you responsible for what happened to their squaw."

"Yeah, Casey," Luke added, nodding his agreement. "Cara could be dead and you could be next."

"Don't even say that," Casey snapped, and then sighed heavily. "I have to believe that if they wanted us dead, they could have done it without us blinking an eyelid—all of us—but they didn't. They detained us. Now they want you to go home and me to accompany one of their warriors."

"You thinking this might be about Rankle?" Murphy asked.

"That's what I was told, yes."

"Okay, so we leave and then we backtrack and stay on your trail," Murphy said. "Make sure you're safe."

"I'd like nothing better, Murph," Casey smiled humorlessly, cracking more kinks from his neck. "It won't be possible though. The warriors intend to accompany you most of the way, to ensure that y'all don't do that very thing."

"Damnation!" George said, stomping his foot. "I ain't never felt so dadblasted helpless in all my born days!"

"Me too," Casey said softly. "Now imagine how Cara feels and you can see why it's so important for us to listen and do what they say."

"Okay, so what do we do when we get back home? Just sit and wait for your return?" Murphy asked. "And how, exactly, are we supposed to explain to the governor that we lost his daughter and her fiancé?"

"Just tell him the truth as far as you know it," Casey said, clasping his friend's shoulder reassuringly. "I'll try to send a wire now and again to keep you posted—that is if my own captor hasn't any objection."

"This is madness," Murphy said quietly, "You know that, don't you?"

"I can't recall ever being in a hairier situation," Casey admitted, "but I can't risk getting Cara hurt, so I'll do as they ask."

They stopped their conversation when the warriors approached.

"It is time for your men to leave," the lead warrior said, and then turned to address Casey's men. "I want you to know that we do not wish any harm on your friend or his woman."

"Why in Hell should we believe you?" George blurted, but a hand on his arm prevented any further provoking outbursts. The Indians, however, did not seem to mind the question, even when angrily asked.

"Because his woman saved the life of our Chief's sister," the warrior answered. "All we ask is for help in finding the man who harmed her, so that we may bring him to justice."

"By kidnapping Casey's woman?" Murphy exclaimed.

"It is the only way we know to make sure we find this man," the warrior continued patiently. "Once he is found, your friend and his woman will be brought home. We wish you to tell this to her people so that they do not do something foolish."

"Like a retaliatory attack?" Murphy asked.

"We mean them no harm," the lead warrior repeated firmly.

Casey stepped forward and shook Murphy's hand, "Make sure her dad knows, okay? We don't need a full-scale war over something that should not have happened in the first place."

"Damn Rankle to Hell and back," George exclaimed.

"I think that's what the Arapaho have in mind, George," Casey said, "but I'm fairly certain that they don't want him to come back from Hell. They want to send him that direction, permanent-like."

"Go with God, my friend," Murphy said softly.

"You too, and try to keep the business running as usual."

Murphy nodded, and then all of his men headed toward their horses, followed closely by the warriors. Casey watched until his friends vanished over a distant hill before turning to face the lone warrior who stood behind him, patiently waiting.

"So, what do we do now?"

"We begin the hunt for our enemy."

CHAPTER 10

Cara was tired. She'd never worked so hard in her life; never worked a day in life, really. She was privileged, and with that privilege came servants. Now she was working harder than any servant had ever worked. She looked down at her hands and cringed. Calluses were already forming beneath newly formed blisters.

"Have some water," Skips Along The Water said, kneeling beside her.

"I've asked you repeatedly this last month," Cara said menacing, not bothering to look at the proffered water skin, "not to talk to me. I have nothing to say to you—ever!" Cara had learned something about herself in the last month—she knew how to hold a grudge; a trait she no doubt would never have discovered had she not been abducted.

"Since I am one of the few who speak your language, and you refuse to learn ours, it is a good thing that I have not heeded your request."

"If I get thirsty, I'll find my own water. Did you want something, besides the water?" Cara asked wearily, trying not to snap again.

"When you are done here, you are needed to help with the skins," Skips Along The Water said, laying the skin full of water next to her.

"You know, when you told me I'd be a guest here, I didn't think that equated to becoming a slave," Cara said, reaching for the water, her thirst overpowering her continued indignation.

"It is important that you know what is required of you, so when you marry one of our warriors ..."

"That is *not* going to happen," Cara interrupted.

"...you will be a suitable wife," Skips Along The Water continued undeterred.

"Suitable slave, you mean," Cara muttered, returning the skin to Skips Along The Water.

Skips Along The Water sighed, "It is best for you if you accept what the Great Spirit has willed. Your man has been gone with our warrior for over a month of your time. He has only three of your weeks left before we leave this place. Perhaps it is best if you accept my brother as your husband, or another..."

"No!" Cara snapped, leaping to her feet, trying desperately to contain the urge to punch this girl in the face.

"I think my brother is willing to have you," Skips Along The Water tried again.

"No and no and no," Cara said through clenched teeth. "I am here as a guest. I may have to wear the clothes you've given me, I may have to do the chores you assign to me, but that does *not* mean I have to marry your brother, or anyone else for that matter! And it doesn't matter where you move me, Casey will come for me."

"Three weeks, that is all, Cara," Skips Along The Water said softly, "I am sorry."

"Oooooh," Cara sputtered, "I am so sick of your apologies, I could scream."

Skips Along The Water sighed and shook her head, "It is all I know how to say to express …

"Try saying 'you're free'", Cara suggested, her tone dripping with sarcasm.

"We are not a bad people," Skips Along The Water said gently.

"No, you are a determined people," Cara rejoined, "who have met an equally determined woman. I'm not trifling with you when I say I will not marry your brother. If Casey fails to bring Rankle back, I will find a way to leave and return home."

"Why do you simply not go then?" Skips Along The Water asked. Her tone held such a smirking quality that Cara had to close her eyes and draw in deep breaths to prevent gouging her eyes out.

After a few minutes, she let go of her breath and responded in a secure tone, "Because I believe that Casey will triumph, that's why. And since he's coming for me, I will honor him and give him time to do as has been requested of him." It wasn't an honest reply; not completely, but she couldn't tell this girl that she was too afraid to strike out on her own; too afraid she'd never be able to find her way home.

"I think that you know our warriors will simply return you, which is what they will do anytime you try to leave," Skips Along The Water said. "Think carefully on those words before you try to go away."

Victim of Love Barbara Woster

Skips Along The Water turned and left Cara to her thoughts and her tears. She'd cried, unseen, every day of the past month and then fervently prayed as the sun rose and set each of those days that Casey would ride into camp, Rankle in tow. Each day she prayed and each day would end with no sight of her fiancé. And again, her day would end on her knees, renewing her faith and her hope, and then wither as the new day, laborious, dragged on.

She kept telling herself that a weaker woman could not survive, and then thanked God that He'd given her an inner strength that many women of her acquaintance didn't possess.

"Oh, Casey," she said softly, looking to the horizon, "please come for me."

"Perhaps he cannot or does not wish to do so," a voice said behind her, startling her.

Cara spun on her heel, clenched her teeth, picked up the basket of maize, and started toward camp, saying not a word to the intruder.

River Runner grinned and then yelled at her retreating back, "You will have to speak to me when we are man and wife!" His grin turned to laughter when he saw her head raise a notch. *She is a stubborn one*, he thought, strangely pleased.

CHAPTER 11

Casey was frustrated. Somehow, Rankle seemed to know he was on his trail and had managed to stay one step ahead of him. At least that was the only explanation he could conjure as to why they'd not captured him yet.

The tracker that accompanied him did the best he could, but it was never enough. He sensed someone was willing him to fail, but he couldn't fathom who or why? Rankle was a burr in the saddle of life, and needed to be removed—something the Arapaho was more than willing to do; something he was willing to do. But who could want him alive so badly as to hinder Casey from finding him?

Casey sighed aloud realizing that his frustration was simply supplying stories to his brain, because he could imagine no one wanting Rankle to live, therefore his inability to capture him was a simple matter of ineptitude.

"Are you sure he came this way?" Casey asked, unable to discern the slightest clue from his surroundings. He wasn't a tracker and realized, after day one, that this was why an Arapaho accompanied him on this trek. He'd come to admire the warrior's ability and wished he had that same ability. At least if he did, he wouldn't have to rely so much on someone else. He watched and questioned in hopes of developing that ability, so that sometime soon, he'd be able to ditch his companion and strike out after Cara, but the warrior seemed disinclined to teach him. Probably because he knew that Casey would ditch him and head out after Cara, if he knew how to track the tribe.

"There is a town ahead," the warrior said. "Perhaps he is there."

"Let's hope so," Casey said, sighing, "because I'm tired of chasing down his filthy hide."

"I will wait for you here and make camp," the warrior said.

"As usual," Casey responded sarcastically, and then spurred his horse into a gallop. It was a reasonable decision for the warrior to remain hidden in the woods, because most little towns didn't welcome red skins with open arms. Still, it would have been nice to have someone watching his back when he went into a town. There were too many ways for a man on the hunt to be gunned down from a criminal in hiding.

That thought had the hairs on his arms rising, as he rounded the bend and rode beneath the sign welcoming him to Twin Springs. Instinctively, his gaze began scanning every window in every building, his nerves keenly alert to any threat.

While his eyes remained busily scanning everything in sight, his brain began formulating his next move if Rankle wasn't here. He hoped that this would be the town Rankle was hunkered down in; hoped that this would be the day, for every day that passed, haunted him.

He still recalled the day when he agreed to accompany the scout. The day when that scout told him what would happen to his beloved Cara should he fail. That was the day when God tested his patience beyond all measure, and he had to mentally, and physically restrain his reaction—for Cara's sake. What he wanted to do was strangle the life out of the warrior, hunt down Rankle and hang him up by his entrails. Then he wanted to storm the Arapaho village and slaughter every single person before freeing Cara from their conniving grasp.

Cara was the only thing stopping his outrage. Would they really take her life, kill her, for what Rankle had done to their chief's sister, just to ensure his compliance? The warrior's words echoed in his head daily:

You will find the man who harmed our chief's sister, or your woman will die.

Initially, the warrior told him that Cara would only be held until Rankle was found and returned to the people; at which time, she would be released to return home with Casey. It wasn't until after the warrior left to consult with Cara's captors that something changed; that the threat became more real. That releasing Cara had changed to them killing her if Casey failed in his task. He closed his eyes against the memory and prayed it didn't come to that. He mentally ticked off the days as he did every time he was close to catching Rankle, and by his estimation, he had only three more weeks to find the son-of-a-bitch and get him back. Three weeks before his Cara was murdered. So little time. Of course, he thought two months hadn't been a great amount of time to begin with, but felt confident he could pull it off, especially with an experienced tracker on his side. Now, as time ticked away, so his hopes continued to sink, as if mired in quicksand, and it was getting harder to maintain any level of optimism.

When he approached the first of the buildings on the edge of town, his first sense was that the place was a ghost town, so dilapidated were the buildings. If not for the people walking the seasoned boardwalks, he would think this stop a waste of time.

In addition to scanning the windows and doors of every building, he also ran his gaze over the people's faces. It was a lot for his eyes to take in quickly, but if he didn't pay attention to everything, Rankle could walk right by him unseen; or he could put a bullet in his back.

The first time he entered a town, his brain provided positive scenarios which had him smiling: Rankle walking unmindful down the boardwalk; that Casey would see his smirking countenance, lasso his ugly rear end, and put an end to his and Cara's misery. However, as was his luck of late, he had no such luck. Rankle was never seen, anywhere. Now, after so long on the hunt, instead of positive scenarios, his brain had started supplying tortuous ones: His beloved Cara being tied down in the heat of the prairie, left to die a slow, agonizing death; fodder for the creatures that roamed the night.

He shook his head hard and had to latch onto the pommel as the violent shaking nearly toppled him. He sighed heavily, then sighed again when he spotted one of the signs he was looking for: Telegraph Office.

He turned his mount toward the building and pulled on his reins with a quiet, "Whoa", when he reached the front of the building. The horse immediately complied. He dismounted and wrapped the reins around the hitching post, and then stepped onto the boardwalk. He needed to let the governor know what was happening. He despised these intermittent dispatches; hated having to tell Cara's father that he was no closer to returning his daughter than he was on day one. He could only imagine the governor's opinion of him now—incompetent, unreliable, and completely unworthy of his daughter's hand. At his request, he never received a reply to his telegrams, partly because he never knew where he'd be from day-to-day and partly because he didn't want to receive a dispatch from the governor telling him the engagement was off.

When the latest report was on its way, Casey left the telegraph office and walked down the boardwalk to the saloon. Perhaps he'd get lucky today and Rankle would be sitting at a table, drinking a lukewarm beer, laughing it up with some acquaintances; not alert to the fact that someone could be hunting him down. It was a hope he'd clung to for the first few weeks; a hope that was fading with every passing day after.

He stopped before the swinging doors a moment and lowered his head in prayer. Once his supplications were sent on their way with a sighed "Amen", he pushed the doors open.

He stood just inside for a moment while his eyes adjusted. The room was dark and a heavy film of smoke clouded the air, but it didn't prevent him seeing a sudden movement to his right. Instinctively, he knew movement of that sort meant a gun was being drawn and he reacted as instinctively as if he were a gunslinger with a bounty on his head. He dove to the ground, yanking his pistol free from its holster. He landed on his side, slammed back the hammer on his gun, and aimed for the corner. Before he could fire, a bullet whistled through the air above his head, striking the wood behind him. He fired in the general vicinity from which the bullet came, but it was too late. As the smoke from the gunpowder cleared his vision, he spotted two men running out of the back door. He leapt to his feet, spun on his heel, jumped off the boardwalk, and shot around the side of the alley heading to the rear of the building. As he rounded the corner at the back, an enormous black, and extremely familiar, stallion nearly trampled him.

"Rankle!" He yelled at the retreating animal.

"Go to Hell, Scott," Rankle yelled over his shoulder, digging in his heels and spurring the horse to faster speeds.

Casey heard the next set of hoofs a split second before being trampled a second time. He leapt and rolled out of the way as a Pinto shot past him—carrying an Indian brave.

"Son-of-a-bitch!"

CHAPTER 12

Casey jumped up and ran back down the alley, mounted his horse, and spurred the stallion down the street, in pursuit of Rankle, and whoever it was that was with him, or in pursuit of him. He had questions and he was damned sure going to get answers.

It was a moment more before he realized that he was heading back the way he'd come, which meant that Rankle was sure to encounter his guide. A grin split his lips. Rankle's running had finally ended. It was over. If he didn't catch up to him, then his Indian guide would certainly be able to stop him, and that meant he could finally drag that sorry ass back to the Arapaho, collect his woman, and head home. He still had questions as to who the other rider was—the Indian—but all he could surmise was that another tribe, not the Arapaho, was after Rankle too. It wouldn't surprise him. After all, if Rankle could abduct and whip one Indian maiden half to death, he could easily have done it before. The only issue he had with that was convincing the other Indian to let him take possession of Rankle; allow him to escort Rankle back to the Arapaho.

The relief at knowing Rankle was within grasp released so much stress, so rapidly, that he felt near hysteria. He began to laugh. The first genuine laughter he'd had in a month. He leaned over his mount's neck, "Let's get 'em boy," he whispered, spurring his horse into a faster pace as he passed under the town's archway.

He spotted the two mounts he was in pursuit of, just as they entered the far woods and laughed again. Just as he thought, they were headed straight for where his scout was camped, which meant that Rankle was as good as caught.

"It's the end of the road for you, Rankle," he said to himself as his horse bounded across the open expanse. A few minutes later, he slowed his horse as he approached the woods, turning his mount toward the worn path through the maze of trees. A gust of wind rustled the limbs overhead, and he imagined them guiding him, whispering encouragement.

In his mind, he could see the scout in camp alerted to the approach of intruders. The seasoned warrior would no doubt grab his bow and arrow, find a secluded spot to lay in wait, and when Rankle broke into the clearing, he would step from his hiding spot and put a well-deserved arrow in his thick, moronic hide. He imagined Rankle writhing about on the ground in pain, begging for mercy. He laughed again, relieved that his mind was once more supplying positive, uplifting scenarios.

What he didn't imagine when he reached the location in which he left his guide, was what actually awaited him.

"What the devil is going on here?" He exclaimed, as his gaze scanned an empty clearing. There was no sign of anyone, including his guide.

CHAPTER 13

Rankle kept riding, Hell-bent, despite the calls from behind that it was safe to slow. He didn't stop for another hour, and probably wouldn't have then had his horse not started to slow on its own accord. He heard the sound of rushing water nearby and steered his exhausted mount toward the welcoming sound. When he reached the bank, he leapt from his horse's back and stomped toward the two Indians nearing his location.

"You said he wouldn't catch me! Damn your red-skinned hides!" He yelled, moving threateningly toward his constant companion of the past month. The only thing that prevented him from attempting to strangle the warrior was the second warrior that had taken up with the first in their race to get away from Casey.

Both natives leapt from their horses and approached, equally angry. "It was not to happen, and though we rode fast, he is probably not too far behind," Crazy Beaver said in a barely-controlled calm, "but Runs With Deer said that you slowed him many times these past many days because of your need to drink. If you had not stopped in every saloon, then perhaps he would not have gotten so close."

"A man can't go without something to quench his thirst," Rankle asserted, shrugging his shoulders. "And it shouldn't matter how many times I stopped, y'all were supposed to ensure he didn't get close; which he did."

Crazy Beaver snorted, "Because of your foolish behavior, the man named Casey Scott will think that we have helped you, instead of believing that I was helping him track you."

"You *have* been helping me, but who in Hell gives a damn?" Rankle yelled. "It's not as if he can do anything about it now anyway."

Rankle stormed toward the bank of the river, slapping angrily at the branches overhead, his mind wandering back to a month ago when he'd wakened to find a warrior bending over him, a knife pressed to his throat.

You will stay with me or you will die.

Rankle had a dozen questions but wasn't about to argue with a man with his life in his hands. Over the course of the next month, the Indian reluctantly explained that he was there to keep him from Casey Scott.

The truth was more involved, but never revealed, which is perhaps why Rankle remained in a state of confusion; however, as the weeks passed, and the Indian had indeed kept him out of Casey's clutches, he began to rely on the Indian more; all the while hoping that Casey would quit searching for him—eventually—although his brain never quite comprehended what would happen to him if Casey *did* stop searching.

"We have helped you, but Casey Scott does not know this," Crazy Beaver supplied. "Still, if he finds out my people helped you, he may do something foolish."

"Yeah, like get his future daddy-in-law to send an army to wallop your asses," Rankle said, laughing.

Runs With Deer muttered something, pulling his knife from its scabbard. He started toward Rankle, but Crazy Beaver raised his hand, "Be still, Brother," he murmured.

"The pig needs to die," Runs With Deer said, his tone filled with disdain. "I still do not understand why we had to play this game."

"It is not for us to question, Brother. For now, we need to think how to proceed. Perhaps Casey Scott will merely think that I am in pursuit," Crazy Beaver said thoughtfully.

"It is possible, but I do not see this, Brother," Runs With Deer said. "If you return without Rankle, he will not believe that you could not catch this worm; and he saw *me*."

Crazy Beaver sighed heavily, "This is not going the way it is supposed to go. We were simply to keep Casey Scott away from this man until the people moved to their winter hunting grounds. That was not to be hard to do."

"What I don't get," Rankle said, "and maybe you can explain it me, is why we had to lead the man on a merry chase to begin with? I mean, I never did quite understand why Scott would want to take me into custody, as you said. All I did was threaten Casey and his fiancé, but you guys...well, I mean, I whipped one of your squaws...that is to say, if anyone wants me, well...I mean, don't get me wrong," he grinned, "I'm mighty happy that you guys decided to let me live, but what I don't get is why? I've been wanting to ask that for some time now, actually. You found me easily and could have taken me back to your people, unless of course, I found a way to whip your..."

"When we took the woman," Crazy Beaver interrupted, "we only wanted to be sure that the white man had nothing to do with what you had done; and to tell us where to find you. We secured the woman to ensure they helped us find you."

"Wait! This guy tracked me down without problem," Rankle interjected, pointing at Runs With Deer, "so your explanation still isn't making sense." He didn't know why he cared about their machinations, but those machinations had kept him alive when he could easily have been dealt with long ago. He'd enjoyed whipping that squaw, but was questioning the wisdom of his actions since the Arapaho found out about it.

"Our chief..."

"Is it wise to tell him, Brother?" Runs With Deer interjected.

"There is no need for this to be secret," Crazy Beaver said. "The game is over anyway."

"Game?" Rankle asked, his curiosity piqued.

"We were coming in search of the man who'd harmed our maiden..."

"Yeah, I got that much," Rankle muttered, still angered he'd been found out.

Crazy Beaver sighed at the interruption, but simply continued, giving a very brief accounting of what had transpired, "When we came across the white man, River Runner spotted our maiden with them and grew angrier. He was about to have us attack and kill all of the white men when he saw the white woman with them. He changed his mind then and was just going to take her to punish her as you had done our maiden."

"She certainly would have deserved it," Rankle snapped, recalling her interference which ended up getting him fired from a job he liked.

"After we captured the white woman, our maiden talked our chief into not harming her, but said that we should use her to make the white man help in our hunt for you."

"Yeah, but you didn't need the help," Rankle said, rolling his eyes. "Or have you forgotten that I have been with your warrior for over a month now?"

"She, nor our chief, knew it would be easy to find you."

"Yeah, but it was," Rankle retorted, angry that he'd been found so easily. "All you had to do," he said to Runs With Deer, "was take me back to your tribe and the white woman could have gone home. Not that I'm not grateful again, mind you..."

"The night that we took the white woman from Casey Scott, our chief decided he liked her and wanted to keep her."

"You've got to be kidding me!" Rankle started laughing. "You're telling me," he said between bouts of laughter, "that someone would actually be attracted to that pestering shrew? Well, Casey was, I suppose. Wait, wait, wait, the light of understanding is getting brighter here. You wanted Casey's help to find me, not because you needed the help but because your chief wanted a reason to keep Casey's woman, which Casey would never have allowed if he'd known the truth. What did your chief hope to accomplish? That Cara would suddenly fall in love with your chief and forget about Casey altogether? That Casey would simply go back to Martin's Landing and willing give Cara to savages?"

"Let me kill the maggot sperm," Runs With Deer whispered, his agitation growing, not at Rankle, but because what he said was true. None of it made sense to him. He'd only done what his chief commanded because he had to; and to hear this white man speak the words his own confused mind couldn't make sense of, made him angrier than he already was. That anger, simmering inside, would having him drawing his knife at night when Rankle was asleep, positioning it just above his throat, imagining the blade slicing through the heavy layer of skin, imagining the blood slowly oozing until his life was gone. Only this morbid ritual sustained him through the following day—the torturing month.

"At first, we intended for you to die for what you did to our chief's sister. That was all we sought to do, but what our chief wanted changed many times in the time after we found the white man returning our maiden."

"Yeah, because your chief decided he wanted a white man's woman," Rankle laughed.

"After capturing the woman and speaking with her, our chief changed his mind. River Runner decided he wanted to keep the woman. To do this, he needed to make Casey Scott believe that she would die."

"Huh? What's that got to do with the price of corn in China?"

"I do not understand..." Crazy Beaver's brow knitted in confusion over the unfamiliar phrase.

"I just mean, what's any of that got to do with me?" Rankle interrupted irritably.

"Instead of killing you, River Runner decided that we were to make Casey Scott believe we needed him to find you; so we could bring you back to River Runner. River Runner gave him until the people moved to our winter hunting grounds to find you and bring you to him. The longer we kept him away from you, the closer it got that our tribe would move and Casey Scott would not be able to find you. Once that time arrived, Casey Scott would believe that our chief killed his woman in retaliation for his failure."

"Hmm, but if all he wanted was Scott's woman, why not simply kill him and take her? Massacre the lot of them like your chief intended when he first found them?" Rankle asked, swatting at a fly buzzing around his head.

"We did not want to kill the men who had done our people no harm. It is not our way," Crazy Beaver said softly.

"Bullshit!" Rankle coughed.

"If we had killed Casey Scott, then there would have been trouble that we did not want," Crazy Beaver said. "It was better to make him think that his woman would only be harmed unless he found you. To stop him, we made sure that he stayed one step behind."

"Seems like an awful lot of trouble just to keep a woman that no man in his right mind would want anyway, but then again ..." Rankle said, then stopped when he saw the murderous rage on the face of the man who'd escorted him across hill and dale for the past month. "What?" He snapped, tired of the looks the man was always sending his way. If he hadn't been certain that his life would end quickly had he dared fight the man, he would have attempted to take him out the first week in his company. Then he could have been a truly free man—free to go wherever he chose, not where this redskin led him.

"Whether you think the decision to keep you alive was wise or not, it was not for you to decide," Crazy Beaver said shortly, tired of the discussion. "My chief made a decision, but now the game is over."

"You keep repeating that, but you haven't explained what you mean by it," Rankle asked, growing concerned over the looks he was getting. "After all, Scott still hasn't caught up with us; so all you have to do is sit here, wait for him, and make him believe that I outrode you."

Runs With Deer snorted, "You would never..."

"Brother, it is unnecessary to argue further," Crazy Beaver interjected. "Casey Scott will know that something is wrong when I do not return with you," Crazy Beaver explained slowly. "Therefore, we do not need to stay with you more. We do not think that Casey Scott will be able to find you without help and return you to the people in the time remaining."

"So, what then? You're going to leave me here now? I'm free to go? Your chief won't mind?"

Crazy Beaver continued speaking as if Rankle hadn't interrupted him, "It is our hope that he will return home; that he will think his woman died because of his failure."

"Son-of-a-bitch! And I thought I was a cold, unfeeling bastard," Rankle declared with a short laugh. "You know, I don't think you crazies have thought this through very well. I mean, if you think about it, you've contradicted yourselves. You stayed with me to throw Casey off the trail, but if you really wanted him to fail, you could have just set him after me on his own. He's no tracker. I could have easily stayed one step ahead of him. He'd have never found me."

"He needed to believe we were helping," Crazy Beaver explained again.

"Yeah, I got that—so that the army wouldn't attack your people over the abduction. You're dumber than a mule if you think he'll believe that y'all were helping now. You're even more dumb if you think he'll buy that y'all killed his woman; and you're the stupidest redskins on the planet if you think he'll stop looking for her just because you gave him a deadline."

"We must do this. Scott will get here soon," Runs With Deer muttered near his brother's ear. "This conversation has passed necessary."

Crazy Beaver nodded, and sighed. There was nothing to be done now but to hope that Casey would believe his woman was killed and return to his home. Just as it was time for them to return to their home. River Runner would be angry that they killed Rankle before the time set; but they had to take the chance that he would understand the reason they needed to do it.

With deadly intent, Crazy Beaver drew his knife from its scabbard, just as Runs With Deer hurled his knife at Rankle.

"Son-of-a-bitch," Rankle squealed, as the knife landed in his shoulder. As he was trying to pull the knife free, Crazy Beaver's knife hit the back of his hand. He screamed in outraged pain. Forgetting about the knife in his shoulder, he pulled at the knife in the back of his hand. Before he could rid himself of the daggers painfully penetrating his flesh, the two warriors rammed into him, knocking him to the ground; leaving him temporarily winded.

Runs With Deer moved to stand next to Rankle and bent over with a grin, wickedly wrenching free his knife from Rankle's shoulder. Rankle moaned and placed a hand over the oozing wound. He had no time to react before he heard an ear-piercing war cry. His gaze went wide as he watched Runs With Deer leap onto his stomach. He screamed again when the warrior thrust the blade deep into his chest.

Rankle screeched and bucked, knocking Runs With Deer onto the ground. He tried to roll to his feet, but a sharp pain startled him. He looked up to see Crazy Beaver pulling the knife free that was lodged in his hand. The pain was as sharp as when it penetrated, and Rankle let out another bellow. He desperately tried to pull himself onto his knees, but Crazy Beaver kicked him in the rear, knocking him face-first into the dirt. Before the stars could clear from before his eyes, from the pain swimming about in his head, Crazy Beaver knelt down on his back, brutally yanked his head back, and moved the blade slowly around so that Rankle could view the instrument of his imminent demise; then stabbed him deep in his throat. Crazy Beaver stood and smiled in satisfaction.

Rankle's eyes bulged, and he fell to his side, struggling to draw breath, which immediately took on a gurgling sound; a sound of desperation that drew no sympathy from the two warriors. He reached up for the knife protruding from his throat, but was too weak to pull it out. Seeing his attempts, both Arapaho leaned over, and, without compassion, pulled their knives free, the action causing Rankle to close his eyes in renewed agony. The blood dripped from their blades as they watched Rankle fight to hold onto life, which was draining as fast as the blood from his wounds.

The sound of distant hooves pounding against the ground startled them, and they quickly rolled Rankle's body over the embankment into the river below.

"We should have killed him when I first found him," Runs With Deer declared. "Scott is not a tracker. He would never have found Rankle—dead or alive."

"You know we needed the white man to believe we were helping."

"Well, it does not matter now. Scott will not find his body before we move to our winter camp, because the river will carry it far away."

"And if he does find our camp and asks why we left him?"

"We tell him we chased Rankle many days and found him dead, so returned to the people."

Crazy Beaver nodded. "And the woman?"

"We will tell him we released her as promised," Runs With Deer replied, confident they would easily be able to trick a stupid white man.

Crazy Beaver was less confident, but he was tired and ready to return home. He hoped that this would be the end and that the white man would let go of the woman. He certainly did not want to go to war over a woman. "Let us go," he said tiredly, and then went to retrieve his stallion. He latched onto the reins of Rankle's stallion, leapt onto his own horse, and spurred both into a gallop.

"So long, maggot," Runs With Deer called toward Rankle's body, drifting along with the river current. He watched the body bob along for a second more, then spat on the ground, mounted his horse, and then took off after his brother.

CHAPTER 14

Runs With Deer need not have been concerned that Casey would catch up to them quickly, because he was lost in the woods, trying to find his way out. For two days, he rode around in what he thought was the general direction of the riders, but he kept passing familiar landmarks, which had him convinced he was traveling in circles.

He tried to put into practice the tracking skills that Crazy Beaver had demonstrated, but either he was the poorest observer in the world, or looking at rocks was not the way to find someone.

"I have a feeling that Crazy Beaver didn't want me to learn to track," Casey said to himself. He'd done a lot of talking to himself over the last two days—mainly about how big a dupe he was. He was also questioning how he was to locate Rankle and get to the tribe if 1) he had no clue where Rankle was; 2) he had no clue where *he* was; and 3) he had no idea where the Arapaho's winter camp was. A camp the Arapaho would be moving to in less than three weeks. If all of that wasn't frustrating enough, Scott's horse chose that precise moment to get a stone in its shoe.

"Damnation!" He shouted, pulling his limping horse to a halt next to the river. He leapt from its back and pulled his knife free from its scabbard. "Okay, boy, let's take a look. Hopefully, it didn't cause any damage to your foot, or we're going to be in a world of hurt."

Scott rubbed his hand along the back of the horse's leg, gently coaxing it to lift its foot. The horse complied. Scott's examination was quick, as the pebble was readily viewable. He placed the tip of the blade gently beneath the stone and popped it free; then set about inspecting the foot for swelling or bleeding. He sighed when he spied neither.

"Well, that's one thing we can thank our lucky stars for," he whispered, rubbing the horse along the flank. "I'm glad you're unhurt, boy—for both our sakes; and, for both our sakes, I need to find a way to get to that river and retrieve some water. We both could use a drink."

The horse whinnied, as if in understanding, and Scott smiled, "Yeah, you more than me, I know." He leaned over the embankment, "It's a ways down. Looks muddy and slick. We might do better to move to a different..." He stopped his one-sided conversation when he spied something large snagged on one of the downed trees. The sight of boot heels floating above the water was his first clue that the something large was a man.

He repositioned himself along the bank until he could see the body better through the thick brush. It wasn't easy to get a clear glimpse, but even an unclear glimpse was enough to convince him that it could be Rankle. It had to be Rankle; he prayed it was Rankle. Still, the only way to know for certain was to climb down to see for himself.

His brow knitted, as he returned to his horse for some rope, as to how Rankle—if it was Rankle—had ended dead in the river. His mind, minus all of the facts, began to make up its own scenario—as always: *The guide caught up to Rankle, got into a scuffle, and Rankle was killed. His body just happened to fall over the side...No, too much bramble; it would have gotten hung up, not be in the river. So that means the scuffle took place further upriver and was washed down here. But would Crazy Beaver really kill him so readily when his chief wanted Rankle returned? Was it even Crazy Beaver who killed him? What about the Indian that was with Rankle? Could it have been him that killed Rankle?*

He shook his head to dislodge the rampage of questions. Whatever the reasons for Rankle potentially ending up in the drink, he was grateful. Dead or alive—he possibly had Rankle in his grasp; which left only two of his hurdles. The two hurdles he still had to face were enormous, but having to deal with a dead Rankle was far preferable than dealing with a live one. It eliminated the need to accost the man, struggle to get and keep him bound, and then listen to him curse and complain the entire length of the journey to the Arapaho camp.

"Of course, I'm basing all of these assumptions on that being Rankle down there. I sure in Hell hope it is. I'll still get you some water, boy. Promise, but if it's Rankle, that promise will have to be put on hold a short while."

The horse whinnied, bobbing its head sharply.

"Protest noted," Scott laughed, his spirits hitting a high note. He reached for the rope attached to the saddle and headed for the embankment. "Whew, this looks treacherous."

The horse whinnied again.

"Laugh it up, Chuckles. Just remember, if I don't return, you don't get that water."

Casey slung the rope over his saddle's pommel, wrapped the other end about his own waist, and then grabbed onto the nearest branch. He took a step over the edge, and his boot immediately slid out from under him, causing him to do an uncomfortable split, "Damnation!"

Instead of trying to return to the bank, he decided it was best to go over the edge and just hold on tight when his other foot slipped out from beneath him. He closed his eyes at the startling effect of his feet slipping and sliding, while he held on for dear life to the branch over his head. It was a battle of man over nature. Fortunately, Casey won. He lifted a booted heel and jammed it hard into the mud, securing himself against the sloping ground, and then secured his other foot. When he felt locked in place, he sat down, released his feet and started the too-fast slippery slide down the slope, slapping his heels against the ground in an effort to maintain control over his descent. The last thing he wanted—or needed—was to tumble head-over-heels into the rapidly-moving, glacial river below.

He was breathing hard by the time he reached the bank by the river and sloshed over to where Rankle was lodged on a downed tree, but he couldn't afford time to rest. He leaned down and tugged on the dead man's shirt, pulling the weight with all his might. The shirt rent in two and Casey started swearing up a blue streak. He closed his eyes and drew in a deep, calming breath, then reached over and got a better grip on the man's shoulder. With a final wrench, he fell on his rear, the body rolling over onto the muddy bank.

Casey's breathing, already shallow, threatened to stop altogether, when he saw the condition of the body. He'd seen firsthand what Indians could do to an enemy, and this was proof they could be brutal. However, the gaping hole in the throat was a new sight and Casey had to turn his head to prevent his retching from turning into hurling. Combined with the bluish bloated skin from being submerged in icy water and the man looked as if he was dressed up for a morbid Halloween party[1]. Even though he looked the worse for wear, it was still obvious who it was. Casey's plea that it be Rankle had come to fruition; and though the body was a mess, he still looked enough like Rankle that the Arapaho chief would have to release Cara—once—*if*—he found his way there.

Casey couldn't focus on that, however. All he could think about right now was finding a way of getting back to the top of the bank and getting the body secured for transport.

Casey untied the rope from around his waist, looped it under Rankle's arms, keeping his gaze as averted as possible. He was a strong man, but his stomach seemed to have developed cowardly tendencies. He glanced up the embankment and sighed loudly, "So much underbrush to get hung up on," he moaned. "This is going to be a feat."

He bent back to his task, making certain the knot he'd fashioned would hold. Holding firmly to the rope, he began the long, slippery climb back to the top of the bank. Nearly half-hour passed before his hands reached up and grabbed hold of the grassy overhang.

He rolled onto the bank, his chest gasping in great gulps of air. He used to think he was in decent shape. Now, however, he began to wonder whether too many nights sitting on a barstool was taking its toll on him. He vowed to hire out on somebody's ranch until he managed to start his own. Ranch work would whip him back into shape in a heartbeat—if his heart managed to survive today's exertions.

After another fifteen minutes of rest, he rolled to his feet, and walked over to where he'd left the stallion. The equine appeared completely oblivious to its owner's exhausting work or his presence, until Casey

---

[1] Celebration of Halloween was extremely limited in colonial New England because of the rigid Protestant belief systems there. Halloween was much more common in Maryland and the southern colonies. As the beliefs and customs of different European ethnic groups as well as the American Indians meshed, a distinctly American version of Halloween began to emerge. The first celebrations included "play parties," public events held to celebrate the harvest, where neighbors would share stories of the dead, tell each other's fortunes, dance and sing. Colonial Halloween festivities also featured the telling of ghost stories and mischief-making of all kinds.... In the second half of the nineteenth century, America was flooded with new immigrants. These new immigrants, especially the millions of Irish fleeing Ireland's potato famine of 1846, helped to popularize the celebration of Halloween nationally. (History.com)

made it clear that he wasn't the only one that was going to do any exertions. "Okay, boy," he said, "I need you to haul that carcass up for me."

The horse whinnied, and bobbed its head sharply.

"No arguing. We're both in this together, so pull."

The horse whinnied in protest, but then started walking backwards.

"That's it, boy! Keep it going," Casey said, walking next to his steed. He looked behind the horse to ensure he wouldn't walk into anything, and then continued his encouragements. As feared, the horse's momentum jerked to a halt. The body had snagged.

"Lord Almighty, give me patience," Casey sighed and then moved to see where the hang up was. Rankle was snagged on some bramble, which meant that Casey was going to have to slide back down to free it. "Dear sweet Lord, I really need that patience!"

He sat down on his bottom and grabbed hold of the rope; grateful that rope was still attached to a thousand pounds of horseflesh. He slid over the ledge and used his feet, and his hold on the rope, to slow his decent, slapping the heels of his boot against the muddy ground repeatedly to keep from picking up speed. When he reached the body, he slammed his heels hard into the ground to stop his momentum, silently thanking God it didn't cause him to tumble. When he felt secure enough, he reached around to grasp hold of Rankle's head, the closest part of the body within reach.

"Sorry for the morose method, but I don't have time for niceties, and...well...it's not as if you can feel this." He pulled hard on Rankle's head, praying it didn't break free of his shoulders. When he heard the fabric rip free of the brambles, he sighed, but continued to pull until he was certain it wouldn't snag in the thickets again.

"If this weren't a matter of someone else's life and death," he breathed hard in Rankle's direction, "I'd just forget about you altogether." Casey fell back, completely spent. It was a few minutes until he felt physically able to continue, then began to pull himself back up, stopping his ascent as quickly as he started it. He looked up to see if there was anything else the body could snare on, otherwise, he was going to be heading back down again, which was something he'd rather avoid. He'd promised he'd go back down to bring up water for his stallion, but that promise would just have to wait until he found a place less treacherous. His horse would just have to forgive him.

Other than a whole hell of a lot of brush, it looked clear, so Casey snagged hold of some tree roots and tugged. This time he jammed the toes of his boots down as hard as he could, anything to gain a modicum of traction. After a short while, he pulled himself over the embankment and flopped onto his back, staring up at the clouds in the sky. His mind tried to convince him to stay there, that the cloud formations were an interesting sight, but then one started to look like Cara's face, which startled him, causing him to leap to his feet faster than his body was ready for. He shook the stars away that formed in front of his eyes, and on shaky legs, moved back to where his horse stood, waiting for the command to continue pulling.

"Okay, boy," Casey breathed, "we should be able to get this done now."

The horse whinnied again, bobbed its head, and started the slow-step backwards. A few minutes later, the body came into sight, and then rolled onto the embankment.

"Whoa! Good boy," Casey praised. "Now, if only you could lift that stinking mass and throw it across your own back; that would make my life so much easier."

The horse whinnied and Casey laughed shortly. "Yeah, you're right. I wouldn't want that thing riding on me either. I think perhaps I'd better fashion a litter. If I have to walk all the way to Arapaho territory, we'll never make it. And I'd certainly never make it with a corpse riding double."

It took several more hours to create a workable litter using what branches he could find; and was sundown when he finally mounted his horse and headed out. Using dependence on his stallion's sense of step, he headed off into the darkness, pulling Rankle along behind him.

It was half-hour later when he found a suitable place in which to let his horse quench its thirst, and for him to refill his canteen. While he stood, staring at the stars above, his mind began formulating his next course of action: how to find the Arapaho.

He decided to follow the river, since he'd heard that tribes tended to make their homes next to a water source. He located the North Star, remounted, and headed as northerly as was able. If he were wrong in his estimations, he could end up in New Mexico before realizing his mistake. If he were right…"I've got to be right."

CHAPTER 15

Crazy Beaver and Runs With Deer returned to the people a week later, to the astonishment of their chief.

"What has happened?" River Runner asked, the moment they dismounted.

"There was a problem," Runs With Deer said, turning the horses over to the two young braves who had come to meet them. Their women were also running to meet them, eager to return to the teepees to show them how much they'd been missed. Yet each wife knew that, until their men reported to their chief, there would be no reunion. After a quick hug and a promise to be brief in their meeting, Crazy Beaver and Runs With Deer followed River Runner to his teepee.

"What has happened?" River Runner repeated, the moment he pulled the door flap closed.

"The man named Casey Scott found us," Runs With Deer said. "Because Rankle could not stop stopping to fill his need for the white man's whiskey," he said with disdain.

"Then why has Casey Scott not returned with him?" River Runner asked, and though he wanted the answer he was relieved that he would not be releasing Cara from the tribe.

"Rankle took off on his horse. We gave chase, but Casey Scott fell behind."

River Runner's gaze narrowed but he said nothing, rather sat and waited patiently for the full explanation. It was not like his warriors to be so careless. Still, if the white man, Rankle, needed to stop so often, he would not blame his warriors.

"We caught up with Rankle. He was tired of running and attacked us," Runs With Deer lied. Crazy Beaver didn't approve of his brother's deceit and interrupted, thinking it best to just provide the final details than weave a web of lies.

"Rankle is dead."

"So you killed the man?" He said, his anger rising. "You were supposed to keep him alive so that Casey Scott would continue his chase until we moved to the winter camp. If the man is dead, then Casey Scott will come here and demand...why are you doing that?" River Runner snapped when Crazy Beaver began shaking his head.

"Since Casey Scott does not know that Rankle is dead, he will continue to search for him. The time you set will come and go and he will have failed; and because he thinks his woman will die if he fails, he will return to his people. He will be saddened, but he will think we helped him and will not seek to find us further or send their army to attack our people."

"Could he still have the army attack us for killing his woman?" River Runner asked more rhetorically, thoughtfully to himself, wondering again whether his decision in threatening to kill her was wise; but Runs With Deer responded nonetheless.

"I do not see this. Casey Scott will see the failure as his. You gave him time and told him what would happen if he did not bring Rankle to you. To him, you are a man of honor. If he thinks you killed his woman, he will blame himself."

River Runner nodded approval, "Possible. Still, I would have been more pleased if Rankle was with you. It would have given me much satisfaction to kill the worm myself."

"If Rankle came with us, you would have needed to release the woman," Crazy Beaver assured his chief.

"We are sorry that you did not get to drive your own blade deep into his heart, but it was necessary," Runs With Deer added.

River Runner's brow knitted suddenly, "Rankle may be dead, but the time given Casey Scott has not passed. If Casey Scott should find Rankle, and then find us?"

"Soon, we will begin the move to the winter camp, and you will be able to make the white woman yours," Runs With Deer said in a confident, soothing tone. "It is your wish, is it not? That is why we did all we did?"

River Runner smiled, but the smile slipped, "I will not relax until the time is passed. Until then, there is a chance that Casey Scott will come here and try to take the woman home."

"I do not fear this, for Casey Scott is not a tracker," Crazy Beaver grinned. "He will not find Rankle and he could never find the people."

"And, we would not let him take the woman away, even if he did come," Runs With Deer added. "And even if he comes, he would have failed in his bargain because he would not have Rankle with him. You do not have to let the white woman go, if he fails."

River Runner nodded again, feeling more confident that the white woman would become his soon. "It is done then," he sighed, his words filled with relief. "You may go now, my friends, to greet your women. They have eagerly awaited your return."

Both men nodded, stood, and headed out of the tepee. River Runner lay down on his bedding and stared at the ceiling, his mind envisioning the night when he would take the white woman as his own.

His smile widened. She was untouched, he was certain, which meant that she would know only him. He felt himself responding to thoughts of taking her, of filling her with his seed; and that thought spurred him from his skins, headed to the river. If he allowed himself to dwell on the woman, he would take her this night. He needed to douse his flames in the cold water, now.

He made his way down to the riverbank, and, without slowing his step, walked straight in up to his waist. He closed his eyes against the onslaught of cold, breathing in and out heavily through his nostrils; refusing to move until..."Ah," he breathed, when he felt his erection lower.

He was about to move from the water, when he spotted Cara walking toward his sister's teepee. He felt himself harden again as his gaze traveled along the length of her body, stopping to admire the sway of her hips. "Arrgghh, I will freeze to death before my body is disciplined against the thought of her."

She turned, as if instinctively, and her gaze met his; hers as glacial as the water in which he stood. There was no acknowledgement of his presence. She simply turned her face away and continued her short trek.

"Bedding her is going to take determination," he murmured, "for she will not come willingly into my arms."

Sensing her hostility and dealing with her antagonistic words slung at him during her stay with his people, he worried that he'd made a rash decision; that she would not grow fond of him and live with him willingly. He suddenly envied Casey Scott for having such a passionate female in his life. Not a listless, brainless woman but a vibrant, passionate mate. He wondered whether he should hold out hope that, in time, he could win over her affection; that she would come to care for him as she does now the man for whom she waits.

He sloshed over to the bank, ignoring the icy coldness jabbing at his muscles and walked over to his sister's teepee. He stopped outside the wall next to where he knew Cara slept and pressed his ear against soft hide of the teepee. He closed his eyes against the onslaught of guilt and rage that settled in his heart as he listened to her soft sobs drift through the thin wall. He'd made this a weekly ritual, since she first arrived. The first time he heard her crying he knew it was a reaction to being taken from her people; abruptly removed from the company of the man she loved. As time passed, he wished that the crying would cease and that, after a hard day's labor, she would find solace in the warmth provided by her temporary shelter and sleep peacefully through the night. His hope had proved in vain.

He turned, ready to leave and seek his own shelter to sleep, but after the day's events he was too restless. He moved around to the flap covering the front of the teepee and as quietly as was possible, lifted it and stepped inside. This was something he would never do normally— enter the home of a woman unbidden. Still, he justified his intrusion by reminding himself that this was his sister's home and she would not be offended at his presence. As for the white woman, she was not of his people yet, so was not aware of his breach of conduct.

With silent steps, he moved to stand next to Cara's mat. She was lying on her side, eyes closed tight, tears streaming over the bridge of her nose and falling to soak the skins upon which she lay.

River Runner knelt and watched her for a moment, trying to control the aching in his heart. He had come to care for this woman and it hurt him to know that she was so unhappy. His hand reached out for her, as if willed on its own, and he quickly withdrew it; closing his own eyes against the knowledge that, had he touched her, she would have likely screamed and drawn attention to his presence. Still, there were things he needed to talk to her about, and he wished to do so while it was fresh in his mind.

Before he could talk himself out of his actions, he lowered his hand and placed it against her mouth.

Her eyes flew open and grew wide with fright, but instead of bucking in outrage in an attempt to dislodge his hand, the fear in her eyes dissipated, replaced by a sad indifference. She relaxed, breathing slowly through her nostrils.

"I think you understand," River Runner whispered, "that I am not here to hurt you."

Cara blinked, but made no other attempt to acknowledge or assent.

"Will you come with me?"

Cara shook her head slightly, a movement made difficult by the restrictive pressure upon her mouth and the mat beneath her head. Still River Runner translated the movement easily enough. She didn't want to. He sighed.

"Perhaps I should not have asked," he said, and felt her jaw clench. He sighed again and removed his hand, silently beseeching the Great Spirit to keep her quiet. "There are things we need to speak on, and I will have you come with me now."

Without seeking further permission, he reached for her hand and tugged, surprised when she acquiesced, allowing him to draw her to her feet. His gaze narrowed as he waited for her to snap at him or to scream out a warning, but she did neither; rather her gaze remained steady on his, a resignation in their depths that worried him. He drew in a deep breath and moved from the teepee, leading her along behind him. Without stopping, he moved through the encampment, weaving around the other teepees, until he reached his own, situated on the outskirts. He lifted the flap and stepped inside, pulling her along behind him.

"Stand over there," he instructed. "I must shed these leggings before my legs turn to ice."

Cara quickly turned her back to him, unwilling to watch him disrobe even something as innocuous as his leggings. She closed her eyes against the fear racing through her veins. She'd tried to affect a disinterest in him in the hopes that he would lose interest in her; in the hopes he'd leave her alone, especially since her quips toward his person, no matter how barbed, always resulted in the same outcome—more interest. Though her sudden melancholy affectation seemed to distress him greatly, it had not deterred him from removing her from her sleeping quarters and taking her to his. Now she stood with a man, disrobing in part, worried that he'd concluded his waiting and would now force his attention upon her person. What was she to do now? If she fought against him, she'd lose, and he could very well end up hurting her a great deal—either in anger or in an attempt to stop her struggles. If she acquiesced to his attentions, she'd lose, because he'd assume she'd accepted her fate. There simply was no positive outcome that her brain could formulate. She was truly in a no-win situation.

She jumped slightly when he laid his hands on her shoulders, "Come, sit with me a while," he said against her hair and she felt goose bumps rise on her arms. She drew in a shaky breath and made to turn toward him, but his hands on her shoulders prevented her. Apparently, though he wanted to speak to her, he wasn't ready to release her. She felt his lips press against her hair and stiffened. The action must have been pronounced, for he sighed heavily and lowered his hands.

"Come, we will sit and talk."

She turned and followed him the short distance to his sleeping skins. He sat down on them, but Cara stopped short of doing so. He closed his eyes against her continued defiance and then patted the skins, "We will talk," he said again, more firmly.

Cara clenched her teeth and moved to settle on the skins. There was not enough room afforded to allow her to situate herself far from him, but she did her best to distance herself in the space allowed.

River Runner closed his eyes and shook his head in agitation, but before he could speak, Cara found her voice.

"My time isn't up yet," she said confidently, hoping that by reminding him of the agreement he'd made with her fiancé, he'd not assault her tonight.

River Runner nodded.

Cara saw the acknowledged nod, but sensed a 'but' coming and braced herself.

"You know how the white people think of us, and of those who spend time in our teepees," River Runner said softly, thoughtfully.

Cara nodded stiffly.

"Perhaps knowing this, you would be willing to remain here with me?" He asked softly.

Cara didn't miss the hopeful tone in his voice, but refused to accept his offer—despite her knowledge of how white people treated redskins, and those white people who'd been in the company of a redskin. She lowered her gaze in shame, precisely aware of most whites opinion of the native people, but she didn't consider herself the same as most of her peers. Of the opinion of women removed from redskin clutches, she'd only heard rumor; never met any; however, from those who had, the opinion was no better than that reserved for prostitutes in local whorehouses; a place in which many rescued white women found themselves, since no respecting white man would lie with a woman who'd kept company with a savage. Her circumstance would be different she didn't doubt, convinced she'd not be shunned. She certainly hadn't been shunned for being an Indian sympathizer. Of course, it was a stance she'd not vocalized too loudly. It was a stance she was reconsidering after spending time, unwillingly, in their company.

"My family will not turn their back on me. As for how white people treat your people, I'm not most white people," she said softly, "or have you forgotten what I did for your sister? I placed my reputation on the line..."

"I have not forgotten," River Runner interjected, "and I do see that you are not the same as many of your kind. This is why I have come to respect you as I do."

That caused Cara to blink rapidly, uncertain her ears had heard correctly—the chief of one of the Arapaho admitting respect for a lowly white woman? Certainly this was unprecedented.

"It is why I wish to speak to you now," River Runner said, his gaze remaining firmly on the ground in front of him. "I have held out hope that Casey Scott would not find the man who harmed my sister, because I wish you to be mine. You are...," River Runner started and then paused, "I do not know the words I wish to say because I have never felt it important to convey words of affection before to a woman."

"I'm not certain I'd want to hear them," Cara admitted.

River Runner smiled pensively, looking at Cara for the first time since they settled down to talk. "You fascinate me," he confessed, lifting a hand to stroke her cheek. Cara wanted to pull away but was fearful that he'd seek retribution against her for rejecting his advancements; after all, the white man wasn't the only one with a cruel reputation. The stories she'd heard related to those white women taken captive were not pleasant—accounts of rape and abuse, brutal treatment to which she preferred not to be subjected. She shuddered.

"I certainly am not trying to," she stated breathless, praying he'd keep his hands to himself from that point on.

River Runner laughed softly, "I am aware." He lowered his hand and the smiled vanished from his face, "My warriors returned today," he continued, suddenly somber.

"I don't understand," Cara replied immediately aware of the shift in his mood; the tone in his voice worrisome. What did the return of his warriors mean for her?

"They brought news of the man who harmed my sister."

Cara's eyes widened; the concern over her future intensifying with each word he spoke. If not for his tone, she'd think this joyous news for her.

"The man, Rankle, is dead," River Runner concluded. "Your Casey Scott failed to bring him to me, and has now returned to your people..."

"No!" Cara interjected, throwing her hands over her ears. She didn't want to hear anymore. It wasn't possible that Casey had failed. It wasn't possible that he'd leave her in the possession of this man. It wasn't possible that he wasn't coming for her as River Runner stated so callously.

"He and I agreed, if he did not come to me with the man who harmed my sister that he would give you to me as payment..."

"No! He would never!" Cara repeated firmly, closing her eyes against the onslaught of reminders of her circumstances; tears streaming down her cheeks. "Please, no."

River Runner fell silent, watching the battle of emotions rage on Cara's countenance. He did not feel it was necessary to speak further. He'd accomplished what he wanted—to give her the awareness that she would now belong to him. He needed her to realize that she no longer had a choice but to submit. He was sorry that he had not been completely honest—after all, her man still had time to locate her—but he knew that it wasn't likely to happen. Not without a tracker to assist and not after what he'd been told.

Casey had been informed that his Cara would die if he failed, and since it was unlikely he would succeed, River Runner assumed he would simply return to his home, thinking she'd been killed. And by telling Cara that her love wouldn't come for her, River Runner hoped her love for Casey would sour; that she would now forget him and that she would turn to him for comfort. She was strong, and he knew, in time, she would adjust to her new life as his wife.

CHAPTER 16

She wasn't adjusting—at least not as fast as he wanted.

River Runner watched Cara from a distance. She was skinning hides as if her life depended on it. He shook his head and sighed. She was literally working herself into exhaustion every day, so that, come nightfall, she fell onto the skins and was asleep the moment her head hit the ground. It had been a week since he'd informed her that her life was now as a member of the people, and she'd stubbornly refused to accept it as fact. She'd even stopped talking altogether. He was growing concerned.

He walked over to a small boy who was playing nearby with some sticks; needing a distraction from the growing frustration over his woman.

"What are you building?" He asked in his native tongue, a smile on his face at the thought of one day having a son of his own.

"My own teepee."

River Runner was stunned by the vehemence with which the words were uttered and the frown lining the boy's face.

"What has angered you so that you wish your own place away from the love of your family?"

"My brother hits me," the little boy whined, fighting back the tears that threatened.

"Truly? And you sit there and allow it to happen?" River Runner asked, startling the little boy with the question. "Do you not defend yourself against attack?"

The boy sniffled loudly, "I do not know how."

River Runner's brow knitted wondering where his father was and why he was not teaching the boy that which he needed to survive. Initially he'd called him over to request a favor of him, but now his need was temporarily set aside, as was his thoughts of Cara.

"Take me to your teepee," he commanded, taking the boy's hand.

The boy's eyes grew wide, but he quickly led River Runner across the encampment to where his mother was sitting outside the familial home, fashioning a pair of moccasins. From the size of the shoes, and the size of her belly, they appeared to be for her unborn child.

She saw her chief approaching and made to stand, but he waved her back down, "Do not. Stay seated," he said, his tone brooking no argument. "Where is you man?" He asked brusquely.

The woman lowered her gaze, "He left a week past to go hunting. The party has not returned."

River Runner's eyes widened. He'd been so involved with his wants and needs that he had not even realized his warriors had left the people to go hunting. He would have to correct this soon, or his people would grow jealous of his Cara and call for her banishment or worse.

"Your son is not being taught to fight against attack?" River Runner asked, attempting to keep his tone from being accusatory. "He says that his brother is constantly hitting him; so much so that he was attempting to build his own teepee. No boy should..." River Runner stopped talking when he saw tears slapping the ground beneath the woman's lowered head. "Is this entire family unhappy? What have I not seen or been told? Speak now!"

The woman swiped at the tears and lifted her head, drawing in several ragged breaths before she was able to speak. When she did, her voice was broken, but it became stronger as anger replaced shame. "I was given to Little Bear last year when my husband was killed by the buffalo," the woman began but River Runner's eyes widened at the mention of the warrior's name. He was not a warrior with whom he would entrust the safety of his own sister, much less a daughter—if he had one. The woman continued. "He spends much of his time smoking his sage. When he is not smoking, he is bedding me to prove his prowess or hitting my children..."

"It is his child you carry," River Runner stated.

The woman nodded, "His first child."

"You do not wish to remain with him?" River Runner asked.

The woman shook her head.

"I was told of Little Bear's problems which is why he remained a single warrior so long. Why would your family give you to him? Was there no other that would take you as wife?" River Runner asked, scanning her features. She was pleasing to look upon, so he didn't see why no other warrior would have her. Why would Little Bear take her when he was not able to provide for a family?

"My father thought he would treat me good since I would be his first wife and have proven able to birth strong sons, but Little Bear only agreed if my father paid him three horses."

River Runner sighed heavily, "Pack up your belongings and collect your children. You are no longer Little Bear's wife. I will find a husband for you." Just as he finished speaking, a scrappy boy about ten walked around the side of the teepee, covered head-to-toe with mud. "Your son?"

The woman nodded.

"You will never strike your brother again. We do not harm family," River Runner said harshly. The boy's eyes grew wide, but he nodded, not daring to defy their chief. "Help your mother pack and then bring your belongings to me." He ruffled the littlest boy's hair and then turned to head back to his teepee, stopping abruptly when he saw Cara leaning against a nearby tree, eyeing him curiously.

He smiled at her, but she didn't acknowledge, merely turned around and strolled off.

"It's time to change things," he murmured, following after her.

CHAPTER 17

Casey hit the tree, closing his eyes against the sharp pain that shot up his arm. A quick glance at his knuckles made him instantly regret his decision to take his anger out on the closest pine. He reached for his canteen and inhaled sharply through his nostrils as he poured the tepid water over the damaged flesh, rinsing away dirt and blood.

He spotted the moss growing on the side and determined he needed to shift his direction slightly in order to continue his trek north. His next glance fell on Rankle's body, slowly decomposing on the litter he'd fashioned over a week ago. Most of the time the smell of rot remained far away from his nostrils, but only when the wind was in his favor, keeping the stench downwind. On those days when the wind was his enemy, he would gag incessantly; the handkerchief over his nose and mouth doing little to ward off the putrid odor. He'd willingly keep company with a skunk at this point.

He snorted at the irony that he smelled almost as bad as a skunk, as he caught a whiff of his unwashed pits. If finding the Arapaho weren't the highest priority in his life right now, he would be offended at his lack of attention to his own hygiene; something he normally took very seriously.

Added to the discomfort of traveling with a quickly decomposing corpse, and his own quickly deteriorating body odor, was his rising anger at having made little progress in locating the Arapaho. Hence his assault on the local plant life.

"How can a major tribal unit be so elusive?" He asked his horse, as he remounted and prepared to continue his quest. "Apparently as elusive as townships out here."

His horse snorted and bobbed its head, stepping gingerly into the stream.

"Easy boy, step lightly," Casey encouraged when his horse slipped slightly. The horse whinnied, regained its footing and maneuvered the remaining distance without incident. "Good boy."

As the afternoon wore on, Casey felt the daily bout of hopelessness threaten. Being in the wilderness alone with nothing but a horse and a dead body for companionship was taking its toll; and knowing that his beloved Cara would soon be moving with the Arapaho even further away than she was now…or would they kill her prior to moving to their winter camp?

As he'd done so often over the last couple of days, the thought of losing Cara elevated his temper so rapidly that he leapt from his horse and headed for the nearest tree—this time kicking it repeatedly. His horse slowed on its own accord and then set to munching on some nearby grass.

"Cara!" Casey screamed at the top of his lungs, scaring some pheasant from their hiding place in the nearby grass; and startling his stallion into galloping a short distance away. Casey quickly whistled, drawing the horse to a stop, then whistled again to bring it back. "Jesus!" he murmured to himself, "I better watch my temper or I'm going to find myself out here alone and on foot."

When his horse returned to his side, he reached up to stroke its flank gently, calming, "I'm sorry, boy. I'm not used to feeling so desperately out of control. I'll try harder to keep control of my emotions. No more outbursts. My word of honor."

His stallion whinnied and he smiled, then reached into the saddlebag to retrieve some jerky.

"I'm running low on supplies," he murmured, taking a swig from his canteen. "I certainly hope I run into a town soon. If this is going to take longer than intended, I'm going to need to find provisions soon." He finished his jerky and then remounted. The stars were starting to appear as the sun lowered and he hoped it would be a clear night. That would make it easier to follow the northern star.

"Okay boy, I've gotten the latest agitation out of my system, so let's see how far we can get before my mind causes me distress again, shall we?" He gently kicked his stallion's side and the horse leapt into motion, quickly settling into a steady canter. Within an hour, he left the confines of the trees and moved onto a vast, flat landscape; just as the sun sank completely over the horizon, throwing everything around him into blackness. He let loose a nervous breath, hating having to continue moving after nightfall, but thus far his horse hadn't let him down by stepping into a prairie dog hole. He took a deep breath and prayed tonight would pass with the same lack of misadventures. The blackness was always unsettling and he felt mildly guilty making his horse travel at a time when he would usually never consider doing so himself.

Something in the far distance caught his attention and he pulled his stallion to a halt, "What...?" He started to question his horse, but stopped when he spotted it again. "That's either people or...well, I'd rather not consider an alternative. Let's check it out."

Without thought, he spurred his horse into a gallop. A few minutes later a loud thump sounded behind him, startling him—and his horse. The horse whinnied loudly and reared, nearly unseating him.

"Whoa boy, easy now," Casey soothed, hanging on for dear life. After a moment the horse settled and Casey looked to his rear, unable to see what had caused the loud bang, worried at what he might find when he did discover the source. He dismounted and pulled the matches from his pocket and then ran his hands along the horses flank until it bumped into his saddlebag. His hands slid over the bag and knocked against his lantern. He untied it from the bag, laid it on the ground, and felt his way along the circular exterior until he located the latch; then he struck a match and lit the wick. Light filled the area around him and he groaned when he saw the source of the fright.

"Son of a bitch," he murmured.

The rope attaching the litter to the pommel had loosened during the gallop across the bumpy terrain, sending the litter tossing and flipping into the air only to return to the ground with a loud thump, which had startled him and his horse. The unwrapped, decaying body hadn't handled the disruption well, falling apart at certain seams—namely the arms—which lay a few feet away. Still cursing a blue streak, he untied the handkerchief from around his neck and picked up the first arm, tossing it on the corpse's abdomen, then the other. He nearly lost the jerky in his stomach when he moved past the body and the light fell on Rankle's face, tissue slashed and falling away from being slapped and dragged against the ground.

Casey quickly looked away and retraced his steps to his horse, but the sight wouldn't leave his mind and the roiling in his stomach wouldn't abate. He turned away and hurled the jerky before he could stop himself. After a few minutes, the heaving ceased and he managed to return to an upright position. He wiped his mouth across his sleeve and turned on unsteady legs to remount his steed.

As soon as he gathered his composure, he re-tied the litter to the pommel and led the horse back to where the body lay. With a mighty heave, he rolled the body back onto the litter, which ended face down. That was fine by his estimation, as he didn't fancy staring at a rotting face again anytime soon.

"If you weren't already dead, I'd kill you for all of the grief you're causing me," Casey huffed, then turned back to his horse.

As soon as he remounted, his gaze sought out the distant source which had garnered his attention earlier. After a few minutes searching, he spotted what he was now certain were the flickering lights from lanterns. He was about to spur his horse into a gallop again, but the recall from his last blunder slammed into his brain and he stopped himself.

"Let's take this a little slower, shall we, boy? I don't think that whoever it is out there is moving at this time of night. We'll get there in one piece…damn," he swore, reminded of the fact that Rankle was no longer in one piece.

With a light touch of his spurs, he sent the horse into a canter. Forty-five minutes passed before the light was big and bright enough to distinguish clearly, outlining several Conestoga wagons pulled into the typical circle, meant to secure those camped inside from the hostility of the local natives, should any be inclined to attack in the middle of the night.

When he was within earshot, he slowed his horse to a walk, "I'm a friend; may I approach?" He called loudly, stopping his advancement altogether while he awaited a reply. Several minutes passed before several men—armed and carrying lanterns—moved around one of the wagons.

"I'm a friend," Casey repeated, lifting his hands into the air. "I was hoping to impose upon your kindness for a meal, if you can spare it?"

The men looked at each other as if seeking mental agreement before finally lowering their weapon.

"Ye're welcome," the elder man said, and then all three men turned to return to their campfire.

Casey dismounted and moved cautiously around the wagon, ensuring the welcome was indeed friendly and not a tactic to put him at ease so they could rob and murder him. He spied the three men sitting next to the fire, along with two other younger men; teens perhaps, but there were no women to be seen. The men probably shooed them to the wagons as soon as he'd made his presence known.

"Come settle over," the elder man called. "We've beans to spare, and coffee."

Casey sighed. He'd lived on hardtack, gruel, and jerky for over a week now and the thought of beans and coffee made his mouth water. He was salivating so heavily in fact that he needed to wipe his mouth on his sleeve to prevent an embarrassing display of drool.

"I apologize for my foul manner," Casey said, settling on the ground next to the fire, "but I've been on the trail for a while and haven't come across a stream to bathe." He had in fact passed a dozen streams, but his urgency to locate Cara took precedence over his need to be clean.

"Not to worry," the elder said, passing a tin plate piled with beans over to Casey followed by a tin cup brimming with steaming black, and very bitter, coffee.

"Y'all headed west?" Casey asked politely between large bites.

"Yep," was the only reply. Casey cast a quick glance at all of the men, but none seemed inclined to look him in the eye or converse with him. He knew he smelled something awful, but not to where he'd be mistaken for a destitute; certainly not enough to warrant being shunned. He decided it best to brush it off and eat his food since it wouldn't be polite to mention their haughtiness when they'd given him nourishment. He'd only just scraped the last of the beans into his mouth when all the men stood, as if cued, and headed toward their wagons. The elder man held out a hand and took the plate, wiping it down with ashes before setting it aside to be washed at a later time.

"Ye're welcome to bed down by the fire and sup with us come morn. I'll bid ye good eve."

Before Casey could reply, the elder turned and headed to his own wagon. Casey couldn't help but shake his head in disbelief at the polite dismissal. As much as he wanted to take the old man up on his offer and sleep the night away, he swore he wouldn't rest a full night again until he had Cara safe and sound back home, preferring to take snatches while in the saddle. The fact that he hadn't fallen off the saddle during a quick catnap was another thing Casey felt grateful for; something that could easily cause himself as much physical damage as his horse stepping into a prairie dog hole.

He stood and stretched and then made his way languidly back toward his horse. It took a minute for his eyes to adjust from bright firelight to pitch black nightfall, but when they did he didn't see his horse anywhere. Panic settled in, and he started forward, ready to whistle as loud as he could, caring less if he disturbed everyone's sleep. He puckered his lips, ready to let loose a piercing shrill when he stumbled over a protrusion on the ground.

"Damnation!' He whispered. He knelt to feel his way over the protrusion, and then realized it was his horse's leg. The stallion had bedded down in the grass and was sound asleep, not even budging at Casey's unintentional assault on its leg. If not for the rise and fall of the horse's chest, Casey would have thought the steed dead. He sighed in resignation.

"I guess we both could do with a good night's sleep. I only hope Cara will forgive me for wasting precious time." Casey's words emerged slurred as a man who'd had one too many whiskeys, exhaustion clouding his brain and enveloping his body. He laid his head on his horse and was asleep instantaneously.

CHAPTER 18

"This isn't right," Cara murmured.

"I feared you would never speak again," River Runner said, sincerely surprised at the utterance. After enduring her silence for a week, he began to wonder if she would ever talk to him again.

Cara didn't want to speak to him again, because it seemed to please him no end when she did; however, she couldn't convince him that what he was doing was wrong if she remained silent. It was a definite conundrum, and the only way to extricate herself from this predicament was to select the option which would serve her best—speaking.

"This isn't right," she repeated softly, keeping her gaze averted. "You're forcing me to choose you sooner than I should have to. Casey still has...how long before your people move?"

"We begin readying in a few days."

Cara's eyes widened in fear and disbelief.

"Do you see why I brought you to me now? You need a husband to care for you, to hunt for you, to shelter you," River Runner said softly. In reality, he was tired of waiting for her to accept what was to be inevitable; was tired of the silence and the hostile glances. In reality, he knew that for her to learn to be a part of the people, he was going to have to force her to become a part of the people. Only then would she accept her fate.

Cara closed her eyes and shook her head slowly, "I can't be your wife when I'm engaged to Casey," she whispered, the pain in the words evidence of her unwillingness to relinquish hope, "and it isn't right for you to tell me that I must bed with you before the time passes that you gave him to complete his task. Since you were willing to have your warriors help him before, why have you not sent warriors to find my fiancé, to help him bring Rankle back here…"

"Rankle is dead," River Runner interjected.

"Yes, you said that before, but dead or alive, if my fiancé keeps his word and brings him here, you are supposed to let me go!" Cara stated fiercely. "And if your warriors knew that Rankle was dead, why didn't they bring him back, why not help Casey bring him…" Cara stopped, sucking in a large breath, filled with disbelief and rage. "You! You manipulative…! You planned this whole thing, didn't you? Oh, why didn't I see this the first time when you told me your warriors had returned with news that Rankle was dead?" Cara asked vehemently, rhetorically. She stood and began pacing the small confines in short, clipped steps; the reality of her circumstances crashing through her brain like giant boulders. "You told me that you sent warriors to assist Casey in locating Rankle, because Casey was the only man who knew what Rankle looked like, and you had me to made certain he found him. You told me that, if Casey brought Rankle back, I'd be released; free to return home. Yet your warriors found Rankle, dead. They both returned without his dead body *and* without my fiancé. Did they kill Casey also?" Cara asked suddenly, turning on River Runner as speedy as a viper. "You said Casey knew he'd failed and returned home, but Casey couldn't have failed. Dead or alive, he would have brought that man to you. So, did you kill my fiancé to prevent him coming for me?"

"Yes," River Runner answered impulsively.

Cara hadn't been certain what her spontaneous query would result in, but she certainly never expected him to admit to murder.

Oh my God! Casey! Cara cried in her mind, sinking to the ground as her legs gave way in her distress.

River Runner stood, reached down, and pulled her brusquely to her feet, "It is time for you to forget about him and accept your place as my wife. You are my wife now, but I will give you until the next full moon to mourn and then you will come to my bed willingly." He released her arm abruptly and she fell back to her knees, the tears and pain making it impossible for her to remain upright. She felt as if a huge weight were pushing down on her shoulders and she was helpless to shake it free.

River Runner stood over her and watched her wallowing in grief for a moment more and then left the tent—angry with himself for causing her pain and angry with her for her rejection. When he exited the tent, he stopped, uncertain where he needed to be at that moment. It was nearing dusk, which meant it was nearing mealtime. His sister took care of his needs currently, ensuring that he remained healthy and fed, but he hoped that Cara would take over tending to his needs, as he fully intended to see to hers.

River Runner approached his sister's tent, knocking on the door frame respectfully before entering. He pulled aside the door covering and walked over to where his sister knelt near the boiling sack which held their deer meat. She was roasting ears of maize over the open flame.

"Hello Brother, why is your face so sour?" Skips Along The Water asked. Ever since her brother determined to keep the white woman for his own, he rarely smiled. She wanted to tell him that it would be better for him to let her go, because she knew all too well what obsession could do to a man. The man who kidnapped her from her family had been obsessed with her and it nearly cost her life. "I think it has to do with a white woman, yes?"

"She is now my wife," River Runner said as he flopped down beside the fire, but his tone did not reflect joy over the news he imparted. His sister didn't miss the misery in his tone either.

"She is now giving herself to you willingly?" Skips Along The Water asked sardonically.

River Runner arched his brow and scowled, "No, but I have given her time to mourn the loss of her other man before I take her to my bed. Hopefully, during that time, she will come to see the wisdom of allowing me to care for her."

"Hmm," his sister snorted. "I think it will take much longer than the cycle of a moon for her to stop her mourning. I saw them together, and there was much love between them…"

"Be silent, Sister! You are not being helpful!" River Runner snapped, his scowl deepening. "I am hungry. Feed me."

"When it is ready, you will eat," Skips Along The Water snapped back, slapping at his hand when he reached to remove the boiling sack. She grinned when he flopped back like a child reprimanded by his mother. She checked the progress of the food, "It will only be a minute more. So, when do you wish for your new wife to learn her duties and cook for you?"

"Now," River Runner stated strongly, standing.

"What do you mean, now? Where are you going?" Skips Along The Water asked as River Runner ducked from her teepee.

"To get my woman!" She heard him yell and shook her head. Her brother had never been married before and for him, the challenge was more than he thought it could ever be. Of course, had he married a woman of the tribe, she thought, there would be no disharmony. She heard the shuffle of feet outside far sooner than anticipated and grinned wider.

"Come in," she called, not even waiting for the knock upon her mantle.

River Runner pulled the covering aside sharply, and entered, tugging a resistant Cara behind him. With little ceremony, he shoved her in front of him, and then slung her toward where his sister knelt.

Skips Along The Water had never seen her brother behave so brusquely toward any woman and wondered why Cara's rejection would cause him so much anger as to treat her so poorly.

"Brother," she whispered softly.

River Runner closed his eyes and drew in a deep, calming breath, "I will say I am sorry for my treatment of you, Cara," he whispered, kneeling before the fire. "But you must now learn to cook for our family and my sister will teach you. Tonight, we will eat together; to welcome you as my wife."

Cara closed her eyes, refusing to look at either River Runner or his sister, "I'm not..."

"Do not speak!" River Runner snapped, unwilling to listen further to her complaints about her circumstances. "Only do!"

Skips Along The Water's eyes widened slightly, but she didn't dare interfere. She knew things for River Runner had been difficult since he had Cara brought among the people, but witnessing her distress and defiance in the presence of their chief was shocking. No one dared defy her brother. No wonder he was so angry; no wonder his smile left him.

"Is the food ready?" He asked, softening his tone when he spoke to his sister.

She nodded, pulling the boiling sack down, "Would you kindly remove the maize from the fire, Brother? I will take this outside and empty the water."

Skips Along The Water returned a moment later and finished cutting the boiling sack open. She spread the bag open and the contents of deer meat wafted into the air.

"Hmm, that smells satisfying," River Runner sighed. "I have not eaten much today and my stomach is yelling its protest." He looked over at Cara who had not moved since being forced into their company. He sighed again, "My sister will show you the manner in which you will serve me food. After tonight, you will remain with her while you mourn, and she will teach you how to gather supplies and cook our meals. You will do this," he continued rapidly, before she could utter a single protest, "with her help, but in time, you will do it on your own—as it should be done."

He nodded at his sister, who moved to where Cara knelt, "Come, we will serve our chief," she said softly.

Cara didn't budge, "He is not my chief."

"By the Great Spirit, I will stand no more!" River Runner snapped loudly, standing abruptly. He reached down and yanked Cara to her feet, pulling her along behind him. "For every moment you defy me, it will be a moment you will regret," he said sharply, moving toward to the bank of the river. Without slowing, he picked her up and threw her into the frigid water, then began rooting around the river's edge in search of a sturdy switch.

Cara surfaced, kicking and sputtering; struggling to find her footing. When her feet landed on the sandy bottom, she started straining and pushing against the currents in an attempt to reach the bank, her water-logged clothing acting as a deterrent to her efforts.

"You will stay!" River Runner snapped at her, as she drew nearer. "Until I tell you otherwise!"

"I'll catch my death in this water!" Cara cried out, continuing toward the bank.

"If you step foot onto the bank, I will beat you, and then toss you back."

"You wouldn't!" Cara cried incredulous.

"You will learn obedience," River Runner said with no regard to her discomfort. "You will cease defying me, or you will not return to the people. You will stay in the river."

The raucous noise drew attention, and soon the bank was crowded with wide-eyed spectators; people unused to seeing their chief behave in an uncontrolled manner. Many found the spectacle amusing, while others, including Skips Along The Water, were taken aback, distressed at the show of hostility.

Skips Along The Water moved to stand next to her brother and placed a hand on his arm. Instinctively, he reacted, yanking his arm away and turning on her, ready to strike out. When he realized how aggressive his reaction was to his own sister, he dropped to his knees and bowed his head, silently seeking her forgiveness.

She knelt in front of him, and placed a hand upon his head, then whispered her concerns so that none of the people would hear, "You are a good man, Brother, but you have forgotten what this woman did for me. You have forgotten that she was to be our guest. Would you become the same as the man who kidnapped me; who forced me to be to him that which I did not wish to be?"

River Runner lifted his head, the only indication of a reaction to her comment was the widening of his gaze. He drew in a deep breath through his nostrils and then nodded slightly. He realized that he behaved poorly and knew he needed to make amends, but at the same time, he could not have the white woman behaving unmanageably toward him without consequence. It would make him look bad in the eyes of his people.

He stood.

"Remove yourself from the water," he said to Cara, his tone unforgiving. He then turned to face his sister, speaking in soft tones. "Thank you, but you know she must face what is to be. I will leave her to you. You will teach her. I will leave her alone and allow her to mourn, but in time, she will need to accept her place."

"I will do my best to mold her into a good wife," Skips Along The Water said, turning to face Cara, who was making her way onto the bank—her teeth chattering and her body quivering uncontrollably. River Runner glanced over at her and then turned and strolled away.

"I...hate...that...man!" Cara stammered, each word a challenge to utter between the quivers and quakes.

"It does not matter," Skips Along The Water said, unsympathetic, "he *will* be your husband, so you *will* learn to respect and obey, even if you do not learn to love him. Now come to my teepee. You will dry and we will eat. You will take food to my brother and serve him, or you will be treated badly each time you do not."

Before Cara could reply, Skips Along The Water turned and headed back to her teepee. The food would be barely palatable now that it had been sitting, but they would eat it, for her people did not believe in waste.

Cara trudged along after, dripping puddles with each step, shivering uncontrollably in the cool fall air. When she reached the teepee, her first instinct was to head straight in and soak the entire living area with the frigid water drenching her clothes; however, her upbringing wouldn't allow it.

"I cannot enter soaking wet," Cara called through the door covering, her tone contrite. "It would be rude."

Skips Along The Water stopped serving the food and stood, pulling the covering aside brusquely. She was about to snap at Cara again for holding up their dinner, but the sheer misery on the girl's face made her rethink her own disposition.

"Thank you for being kind, even though I would understand if you were not," Skips Along The Water replied softly. "But you cannot change your wet clothes outside for all to see, so just step here," she said, pointing to a spot just inside. "I will bring you clothes to change into," she offered, and then sighed as she turned to collect another of her own attire to share with Cara. "That is another thing we must teach you soon—to make your own clothes. You must learn these things because I cannot keep sharing what is mine with you."

When she'd collected the clothing, she turned back and stopped short. Cara was standing inside her doorway, unclothed, covering her shivering body, as much as was she able, with her hands. Tears were streaming unchecked down her face, adding to the puddle forming at her feet. Her shoulders were hunched and shaking in despair. Yet she made not one sound.

Skips Along The Water closed her eyes and felt tears sting her own eyes. She slowly made her way over and then wrapped Cara into her embrace, hugging her tight; trying to supply both comfort and warmth. For Cara, the display of kindness was her undoing and she started sobbing loudly, uncontrollably. She placed her head on the maiden's shoulder and allowed all of her anger, bitterness, and grief to flow, emptying her mind from all of the pain she'd endured of late.

After a while, the flow dried up and she sniffled loudly, repeatedly. She pulled away from Skips Along The Water and nodded, swiping at her eyes, "I am fine now. Thank you for your kindness."

"I realize now that it is not right for us to fight, Sister," Skips Along The Water whispered. The endearment startled Cara and she was stunned into silence. "I will try to be kind. Please, I ask that you dress now. Our food probably does not taste good, but we still must eat. And I ask that you please kindly take his food with grace."

While Skips Along The Water continued her monologue, Cara quickly slipped the buckskin dress over her head. She and Skips Along The Water were similar in size, except in height, so she felt half-dressed when wearing one of her borrowed dresses. She was going to need to learn to make her own clothes soon.

"Tomorrow, we will begin to sew you clothes. Although you are not very tall, I am still not as tall as you are, and my clothes do not fit you well," Skips Along The Water continued, placing food upon the wooden plates, echoing Cara's own thoughts about the clothes she was wearing. "With winter coming, you will need clothes that fit you better. You do know how to sew, I hope?" Skips Along The Water asked as she passed Cara a plate of food. Cara nodded as she dug into the food. Skips Along The Water was correct, it was not very palatable, but her stomach could have filled with grass and she would have been grateful.

"Good, then we will get that done quickly. After you have several clothes made, I will begin to teach you to cook food. You have learned other things already so those things you will continue to do on your own. You will collect berries, maize, fish, and clean the animals brought by your husband." Skips Along The Water took her plate and handed her another.

Cara waved the plate away, "I cannot eat another plate full, but thank you."

Skips Along The Water sighed heavily, "This is for my brother. You will serve him now that you have filled your own belly; or do you not believe he deserves to eat a meal because he threw you in the river?"

Cara's face turned a deep red and she reached contritely for the plate.

"When you return, we will sleep. We will be up early so I can show you what your day will become soon. We must learn quickly for in two days we will begin to tear down to move to our winter home."

Cara stood reluctantly. She didn't want to face River Runner. For one, she feared her own self-control. Her instinct was to toss the food in his face and run off—neither action, however, would lead to a positive outcome. Still, the impulse was so great she could nearly see the devil with the pitchfork sitting on her shoulder taunting her to act upon that impulse. She glanced at the other shoulder but didn't see the angel, which made her shake her head and sigh.

The walk across camp was all too quick and she soon found herself standing before River Runner's door flap. She closed her eyes and tapped, before she could talk herself out of it.

"Come," he called and she ducked inside. She kept her gaze lowered, not in deference, but because she knew if she looked at him she would react; and despite the taunting from the devil, her brain still had enough sense left to realize she couldn't react.

Instead, she kept her gaze lowered and simply held out the plate, waiting for him to stand and collect his meal. He took far too long as far as she was concerned. When she saw his feet beneath her gaze, her nerves jumped.

"You will sit there in the corner and wait for me to finish. Then you may return to my sister after you have washed the plate at the river," River Runner instructed softly, his tone surprisingly calm and kind.

Cara scrunched her eyes closed at his instruction, not wishing to spend any time in his company, but it would not bode well at this point to defy him further. She silently moved to the corner of his teepee but refused to sit. She stood with her back to him and waited tensely for him to finish, which he didn't seem in a hurry to do. If he were as hungry as intimated by his sister, he'd have wolfed down his meal as fast as she did.

She shifted her weight a few times as the standing began to cause an ache in her feet. It had been a long day and she would like nothing more than to return to her assigned teepee and bed down for the night.

She heard movement behind her and, again, her neck and back muscles tightened painfully with tension. Although he'd said he'd give her time to mourn, she couldn't trust his word. She closed her eyes as tears threatened again. Being in his company was a reminder that he'd killed her Casey; that she would forever be a prisoner of the Arapaho.

His hands laid again on her shoulders and she felt his lips press against her hair. Instead of moving away again when she tensed, he remained.

Victim of Love Barbara Woster

"I will say to you that I am sorry for all that has happened," he whispered. "I would not hurt you if it were possible. I did not expect to happen what happened, but know that I am willing to take care of you. I will let no harm come to you."

Despite her discomfort at his nearness, Cara could not maintain her tense stance and relaxed her body. River Runner took it as a sign of submission and turned her into his embrace. He wrapped his arms around her and squeezed her tight against him.

"I am sorry," he whispered again, and then moved back a step. He reached up and cupped her face in his hands and before he could stop himself, and before she could utter a protest, he leaned down and kissed her. It was a mere lips meeting lips but Cara was at a loss on how to respond. Again, she felt at war with herself. If she acquiesced, he could take her now to his bed. If she fought, his anger could flare again and she could end in a worse situation than being tossed into the river. Her mind was in turmoil.

When he lifted his head, she decided to remain calm and hope he released her, "Perhaps I should take your plate now," she whispered, her gaze lowered.

River Runner laid his forehead against hers for a moment and then sighed, "Yes, it is best you return to my sister." Without another word, he released her and moved to where he'd left his plate. He picked it up and carried it over to her, then took her elbow and led her from his teepee.

Cara breathed a sigh of relief as she stepped into the cool evening air, but the relief was short-lived when River Runner maintained his clasp on her arm. She looked up at him and wished she hadn't. In his gaze she read hope and desire and longing—emotions she felt uncomfortable seeing. Then his glance lowered to her lips and she felt a shudder run through her body. If he changed his mind about giving her a month to mourn, she would never be strong enough to fight him off.

"Goodnight, Cara," he whispered after a moment longer. He released her elbow and turned; ducking back into his teepee. Cara's knees were so weakened by the encounter that she wasn't certain they would carry her to the river and back to her sleeping quarters. She remained planted for several minutes more in the hopes she'd regain strength in her legs, but when she started toward the riverbank, her knees collapsed and she fell. Her mind, so unnerved by the encounter slowly shut down, and she passed out.

CHAPTER 19

River Runner stood just inside his teepee watching Cara's shadow. He knew he'd distressed her greatly with his actions, but she hadn't fought against him, and that had given him hope, but as she remained rooted in place that hope began to waver. Was she standing outside his teepee deciding whether to join him in his bed, or was she too afraid to move?

When she turned away, he sighed—both in sadness and relief. Sad that she was walking away; relieved that she was not too afraid to walk away. Little could she know that she was causing as much devastation upon his emotions as he was on hers. Never had a woman created such turmoil within his heart and mind.

He was about to turn toward his bed when the shadow collapsed. He raced outside and bent to check on an unconscious Cara; her breathing shallow. Without second thought, he scooped her up and carried her inside, laying her carefully upon his mat.

A moment later, a soft knock sounded on his door flap. Without awaiting an invitation, his sister ducked in.

"I was coming to check on Cara and saw what happened," she said immediately. "Is she okay?"

River Runner nodded, "I think she is just too tired and fainted. A lot happened for her today. She will stay here with me tonight, Sister. I wish to make sure that she will be fine."

"Very well. I will come for her in the morning. Sleep well, my brother."

"You also, my sister."

River Runner stood over Cara only a moment more, then shed his clothing and crawled onto the mat. Gently, he slid Cara's dress up over her hips, then lifted her limp body to a sitting position, so he could slip it over her head.

She must be truly tired if she is not protesting, River Runner thought, trying to keep his thoughts pure and his hands puritanical. Neither of which were easy when his gaze raked along her naked form. She was so pale, such a contrast to his people.

He closed his eyes against the onslaught of desire, then scooted to his sleeping place, determined to remain immune. He lay down next to Cara, slid his arm beneath her, and scooted her body against his, molding her form to his; her hips cupping his. *Just keep her safe so she may rest,* he told himself, but could not stop the erection that occurred. Still, he knew it would be wrong to take advantage of an unconscious female; and he was grateful that Cara appeared not to notice. She remained oblivious to anything and everything around her. Only her steady breathing assurance to him that she was still a member of the living. She may have fainted from the stresses of the day, but she remained asleep because of exhaustion. He could empathize. He too was beyond tired. He'd never fought against anyone so hard—even an enemy.

He yawned deeply, snuggled closer to Cara and closed his eyes. His last thought before his brain closed down for the night was how nice she felt in his arms.

CHAPTER 20

Cara's breath caught in her chest when she felt the weight across her abdomen. She kept her eyes tightly closed for fear of what she would see if she opened them. The light filtering through the crack of the door flap pierced her eyelids, so she knew it was morning. She wasn't unsure of where she was or whose arm was lying on her body. That, in and of itself, wasn't as unnerving as she thought it would be. That which unnerved her more was her state of undress. She was naked, which meant it likely that River Runner had undressed her; which meant that he was likely nude also. Her heartbeat started thumping loudly in her chest and her breathing became more rapid. She squeezed her eyes closed, trying to get control of the panic welling within her; worried that River Runner would feel the tension streaming through her body and waken.

After calming her breathing, Cara slowly opened her eyes and cautiously turned her head. River Runner lie next to her, his face so close that if she moved even an inch in his direction, her head would bump his. She looked at him, in repose, and wondered why she wasn't angry or distraught over being in his bed. Her gaze wandered his features, relaxed in sleep, and had to admit that he was a very handsome man—for a savage.

Would he make a good husband? Do I even have a choice in the matter now?

She felt tears prick at the reminder that her life was taking a very disagreeable turn and she was completely unable to control her own destiny. Questions surrounding her fate started slamming into her head: *If she were to accept River Runner as her husband, would that mean accepting defeat? Should she try to escape and return to her people? Would she be accepted now that Casey was dead? Would she be rejected and end up living her days as a whore as she'd heard was what happened to others who'd lived with savages? Would her life among the Arapaho be better? They made her work hard, but was that so bad?*

The questions stopped abruptly and she turned her head again to look at River Runner, sucking in a deep breath when her gaze met his. He was watching her intently, warily.

He's probably wondering when the explosion is going to come? She thought sardonically.

"You are untouched," he whispered, his breath caressing her skin with its warmth.

Cara closed her eyes and drew in a deep breath through her nostrils. The tears started flowing then and she was helpless to stop them. River Runner shifted his position slightly and then pulled Cara into his embrace, holding her close as she cried; her tears soaking his chest.

It was some time before the tears turned to sniffling shudders. Only then did River Runner loosen his hold. He stroked her hair softly, comfortingly.

"I need to leave now," Cara whispered once she was able to find her voice.

River Runner closed his eyes against the pain in his heart. His mind knew she meant that she needed to leave his bed and return to his sister's teepee, but his heart heard, *I need to return to the white man.*

In a sudden movement that caused Cara to squeal, River Runner shifted position, placing himself in elevation above her. He held himself erect with his elbows locked, his legs on either side of her own. For several minutes he did nothing but peruse her face; his gaze so intense that it caused her blood to start pounding through her veins and her flesh to tinge pink with embarrassed uncertainty.

"River Runner…"

"Shhhhh, speak not," he commanded softly. "I will allow you to leave my bed," he continued, his nostrils flaring as he too tried to gain control of his runaway breathing, "but I am having difficulty letting you go. No!" He said sharply when it looked as if Cara was going to say something further. His gaze traversed to her lips and stayed there, as if fascinated by them; her breath blowing heavily through their slightly-parted fullness. Her tongue shot out to moisten them and it was his undoing.

He lowered his head and then pinned her with a gaze so penetrating that she no longer felt herself capable of breathing, "I will release you from my bed as soon as I have bid you a proper good morning."

Victim of Love Barbara Woster

Cara could not have protested had she wanted to; so stunned and frightened at the prospect of what was coming; of what he meant by 'a proper good morning'.

He lowered his head slowly, telling himself that he was giving her every opportunity to protest, to stop him; although he wondered whether she would after being told not to speak. *She could always turn her head away, but will that even deter me at this point?* He wondered, but the question was quickly answered when his lips touched hers and she remained absolutely still.

Her lips, still slightly parted, afforded him access and he took full advantage, slipping his tongue inside.

Cara had been kissed before, so for her, it was nothing new; except that it wasn't Casey kissing her; however, what startled her was that River Runner seemed as adept in stirring passion within her gut as Casey had been. That made her wonder what sort of person she was, but then her mind backtracked. Perhaps it didn't matter who was doing the kissing, perhaps kissing just caused butterflies in the belly all of the time. She simply didn't have enough experience to answer the troubling questions swirling about in her head, nor the ability to stop her body responding to River Runner's touch.

Instinctively, her head tilted slightly, and her body relaxed. River Runner groaned, deepening the kiss until all breath was stolen from Cara's chest. She felt the hardness of his body as he lowered himself against her; but it wasn't until she felt another hardness that she stiffened.

River Runner felt the change immediately and broke contact, rolling to the side. He lay on his back, staring at the ceiling, trying to regain control of his breathing and his body. He could hear Cara beside him breathing hard also, and wondered what had caused her to tense. Had thoughts of her fiancé caused her to pull away in guilt? Had she felt his desire and been startled by the knowledge that he was more than ready to claim her as his own?

"I will not stop you from leaving now," he breathed heavily, and Cara hesitated not a second. She leaned over and grabbed her dress, pulling it over her head in desperate haste. When she was certain she was decently covered, she rolled off the mat and stood, heading straight for the door flap without looking back.

"Cara," River Runner whispered, stopping her in her tracks. She stopped but didn't look back.

"Yes?"

"Good morning."

Cara nodded slightly and then ducked outside and collided with Skips Along The Water.

CHAPTER 21

"Oh!" Skips Along The Water exclaimed as she worked to regain her footing; to prevent toppling over when Cara ran headlong into her. "I was just on my way to retrieve you," she said, ignoring Cara's flushed demeanor. "We have much to do today, and we have no time to waste. I must teach you how to make clothing for you to wear first. We are moving tomorrow and I will need all of my clothing." She kept talking rapidly, heading toward her teepee; expecting that Cara would follow behind.

Cara did follow, reactively, because she wanted to get her mind off of River Runner and working with his sister was the perfect way in which to keep preoccupied; to keep from dwelling on River Runner's actions. He'd kissed her in a way that only Casey had done prior; in a way that made her body feel alive. The difference was, she loved Casey and felt nothing but anger and contempt for River Runner, the man who took her fiancé away from her. How was she supposed to contend with that, knowing that, after tomorrow, he would be her husband; the man with whom she would spend the rest of her life?

Tears began to slowly fall down her cheeks as she watched Skips Along The Water instruct her on how to fashion clothing from the skins she'd been working on since her arrival. The clothing was so simplistic, that within a few hours, she'd sewn three winter dresses and two pair of moccasins. The whole time she worked, she cried—off and on—the pain in her heart more than she could bear.

"You will need to keep one of the skins to wear to keep you warm," Skips Along The Water stated, and Cara realized that there was a nip in the air and before too many months more there would be a few feet of snow on the ground. "And you must stop allowing your tears to flow. It is time to put the past behind you and know your place here, as River Runner's wife. Now, let us put these clothes away; we must prepare our evening meal. River Runner will have eaten what he could find since we were very busy, but we cannot allow him to go hungry forever—or us either."

Cara sniffled and wiped at another flow of tears that started at Skips Along The Water's chastisement. Although gently spoken, it was meant as a reprimand for clinging to what was, when she needed to see what would be; what had to be. At least that's the way Skips Along The Water saw things. Cara, on the other hand, couldn't see past the angry bitterness over being forced into a life not of her choosing.

"Can I ask you a question?" Cara asked softly, swiping tears away as they cut up the deer meat to place in the boiling sack.

Skips Along The Water nodded.

"You were with Rankle six months. Did you accept what your life was to be? No, you didn't," Cara continued quickly, answering the question for Skips Along The Water, because she knew what her response would be. She, herself, had stated how she'd tired of Rankle and attacked him the last night with him, which made him take her out to whip her. "Would you expect any less of me then, than to fight against my own abduction; my own circumstance of being forced to lie with a man for whom I care little at all?"

"It is different," Skips Along The Water said, but her tone held no conviction.

"Do you really believe that, or are you just saying it because you think that I have no choice?"

"It is different because Rankle was cruel to me. He treated me as not a person. My brother would be kind to you, and because you are the wife of our chief, you would be respected among the people. I was not respected."

"Have you forgotten that your brother threw me in a freezing river and would have left me there..."

"He did so because you continued to defy him..."

"And did you not defy Rankle? Isn't that why he decided to whip you? What's to stop your brother..."

"My brother is not the same as Rankle!" Skips Along The Water shouted, standing and taking a defensive posture.

Cara stood, her voice raising in pitch also, "Well, I certainly do not know what he's capable of; and you know as well as I do that our circumstance *is* the same. I am no more than a slave to your brother and he would have already taken me to his mat..."

"But he didn't!" Skips Along The Water yelled. "That's why he is different. Rankle gave me no choice. He forced his way into my bed and took what he was not to take. My brother has not done this. He is giving you time to mourn the loss of your man, even though that man was not your husband and a period of mourning should not be granted. My brother has affection for you too, something that Rankle did not have for me. My brother is a man of honor and courage. Do not ever think to compare Rankle to my brother again, or I will throw you in the river myself!"

Cara stood fuming but could think of nothing to say to that threat. She was well aware that Skips Along The Water could not throw her anywhere, but the threat was real nonetheless. Cara had maligned her brother's character, and Skips Along The Water was having none of it.

Skips Along The Water sat abruptly and returned to cooking, "I can see now why my brother threw you in the river; why his smile has left him. You are a very difficult woman. Now no more talk. I cannot listen to you complain further. Let us cook."

Cara drew in several deep breaths to calm her runaway temper. It took longer than she thought it would, and it was several minutes more before she was able to return to tending to the evening meal. She sat sulking, not wanting to speak further; and decided it best to just focus on learning to cook. Just like with the sewing, cooking among these people was easy and it didn't take Cara long to become adept. Soon the teepee filled with the aroma of deer meat.

A ruckus outside startled them and they quickly stood and ducked outside. There was a man, unsteady on his feet, who appeared to be challenging River Runner.

"What's going on?" Cara whispered.

"River Runner took the man's wife from him to give to another. The man has just returned from hunting to find his woman gone. The woman was with his child."

Cara's eyes widened as she remembered River Runner speaking to a pregnant woman with two young boys. Her eyes scanned the people who'd come to witness the confrontation, and found the woman in question. She held to her rotund belly protectively. There was a man standing in front of her, a spear gripped firmly in his hand. *The woman's new husband*, Cara thought.

"What are they saying?" Cara asked, her curiosity piqued.

Skips Along The Water sighed heavily. When she spoke, her tone was laced with impatience, "I will be glad when you have learned our tongue, then I can listen and not explain. My brother is telling our war chief..."

"War chief? I though River Runner was chief."

"River Runner is chief over all. Little Bear is the war chief of our people. Our chief is telling Little Bear that he was given the woman as wife by mistake and that he is much too busy as our war chief to be burdened with a wife and children."

"Does he really believe that or is he just..."

"He is saying what is necessary to keep Little Bear calm. Little Bear has been smoking and it does not seem he is behaving well. River Runner will see this and try to keep him from becoming violent."

Cara was about to ask another question when her gaze met Little Bear's. He had shifted his attention from River Runner to her. His gaze narrowed and before anyone knew what he was doing, Little Bear headed toward her at a fast clip.

Skips Along The Water instinctively stepped between the warrior and Cara, but her endeavor at defense was unnecessary since River Runner, seeing Little Bear's destination, ran to place himself between the two women.

"Why do you move toward my wife?" River Runner asked, the patience in his tone forced.

"You took my woman from me, so it is only right you share yours with me. Our people share with each other, so why not your woman? Share with me and it will be returned to you multiplied many times over. My seed is strong. She will bear a strong son, or maybe two sons," Little Bear announced smug, his words slightly slurred.

Cara tapped Skips Along The Water on the shoulder, waiting for an interpretation, especially since she didn't like the look their war chief was giving her; but Skips Along The Water seemed not to notice. She stood very tense and her features were devoid of emotion. Cara knew it was deliberate, to prevent showing that she was affected by the confrontation. Still, Cara didn't like being left in the dark.

Little Bear stopped speaking and it was River Runner's turn, "I thank you for the offer to give my wife many strong sons, but this is a woman that I wish to keep for myself."

"Then why did you take my woman from me, if you are not willing to give me yours?" Little Bear asked, his tone dripping with disdain.

"You are our war chief. Your mind needs to be clear to lead our warriors into battle," River Runner replied. "The woman given you was not for you. She already had two sons, and you are too important and too busy as our war chief, to take time to teach them to be warriors."

Little Bear snorted, but his face displayed pride at the words. River Runner sighed inwardly. As chief, it was his job to maintain peace among the people. He had acted impulsively, removing Little Bear's wife, but Little Bear was not meant to be a husband.

"How will I fill my need, now that I have no woman?" Little Bear asked, again his gaze raking over Cara.

Before River Runner could respond, a young woman stepped forward, "I will be Little Bear's woman," she said shyly and River Runner arched a brow in her direction. She was young, no more than sixteen; but she was homely and he knew it would be hard to find her a willing mate.

Perhaps since Little Bear was always drinking and smoking, he would not notice that she was not fair to look upon. Still, he wanted to make certain that she would not be mistreated.

"Step forward," River Runner said. "Where is your father?"

An older man stepped forward, his chin jutted in defensiveness, resignation in his gaze. River Runner read the body demeanor quickly—the old man would not interfere with his daughter moving to be Little Bear's woman because he understood her choices would be limited. River Runner nodded at the old man and then took the young girl's hand.

"Little Bear, will you promise to care for this girl? She is willing to give herself to you."

"Does she come with horses?" He replied without even looking at the girl.

"She comes without horses, but I will give you one of mine," River Runner replied, "but first I will speak with her in private." He took the girl's hand and led her away from the group, "Do you understand what it is you are doing? Little Bear is not a provider..."

"I have hunted for my food since I could hold a bow. My father taught me. I think he knew that I would not attract a man and would need these skills. If Little Bear does not provide deer, I can hunt for rabbit and I know how to catch fish. I know how to take care of myself. Perhaps I will take care of him."

River Runner smiled slightly, "You are braver than many men that I know. Hold your head high. Still, I want you to come to me if you ever need anything. I will not have your harmed."

The girl nodded.

"What are you called?" River Runner asked.

"Broken Dove," the girl replied softly.

River Runner drew in a deep breath. He shook his head in dismay over the callousness of some parents; still, as chief he had the power to affect change. "You will no longer bear that name. I name you Brave Dove," he replied and the girl's eyes misted over. "Hold your head high and be proud." River Runner led her back to stand beside Little Bear,

"Brave Dove is now your wife. Care for her and she will bear you many sons. It is done. Now everyone will depart to eat their meals."

River Runner watched as Brave Dove followed Little Bear to his teepee. He hoped that it was a good decision and that he would be good to her.

"She made her choice," Skips Along The Water said, moving to stand beside her brother. "It is not a good choice, but she is a strong girl and she will make it work."

River Runner nodded.

"Come brother, your wife has made you food to eat."

River Runner's eyebrow arched and he looked at his sister with humor in his gaze.

"Truly?" He asked, casting a quick glance at Cara. "Is it food I will die if I eat?"

Skips Along The Water smacked her brother on the arm, "Do not be mean, Brother. She has done well."

River Runner smiled and that made his sister happy. He had not smiled in a long while. *Perhaps the winds were changing*, she thought as they all ducked into the teepee to eat.

CHAPTER 22

The winds had changed. They were howling so strong that Casey had to duck over his horse's head to prevent being unseated. The horse too was having difficulty maintaining its footing against the gale-force gusts, keeping its head ducked low. Casey knew that a strong storm would follow the winds soon and he would need to seek shelter or neither he nor his horse would escape unscathed. He was surprised that the litter hadn't been blown to smithereens, and could only surmise that the horse's body was acting as a shield against the stronger blasts of air.

A movement to his right caught his attention and his breath caught in his throat. A wall of rain was clearly visible in the distance, but what frightened him more was the twister forming.

"Dear sweet Jesus!" He exclaimed. "We have to get to the tree line boy, or that twister's going to toss us about like a rag doll!" He yelled into his horse's ear. The horse whinnied, put its head down, and pushed toward the tree line with all its might. Somehow they remained just ahead of the wall of water, but it was approaching fast. Getting wet wasn't as big a concern as getting picked up by a twister, but he sure hoped he could avoid either of those occurrences.

He shot a quick glance over his shoulder at the funnel, still well away from them. It appeared to be moving in a direction other than theirs.

"We may just make it, boy!" Casey called as they entered the stand of trees. Just as he dismounted, the wall of rain hit with as much force as the preceding winds.

"Get down!" Casey yelled, pulling on the horse's reins. The horse neighed and then hunkered down, lowering its head to protect its eyes from being speared by the needle-sharp raindrops. Casey pulled the litter beneath a pine and then sloshed over to lie as close to his horse's body as he could, pulling his Stetson down low over his forehead. He may have preferred the rain to a twister, but getting too wet in the middle of fall weather was a recipe for getting sick; and getting sick was something he could ill-afford to do.

An hour passed before the wall of rain reduced to a mere drizzle. Casey lifted his head and promptly sneezed, followed by a lung-hacking cough. When he caught his breath and made to stand, he groaned, every muscle and bone in his body fighting against him. The cold and excessive exertions, combined with not-so-healthy food consumption had weakened him considerably. He may not be able to afford getting sick, but his body seemed to have a mind of its own on the matter.

"If we don't find the tribe soon," he moaned to his horse, "I may die from exposure." The horse stood and shook the water from its mane, showering Casey with water. "Thanks a lot!"

Wearily, Casey moved to reattach the litter and then mounted, fighting to control the shivers wracking his body.

"You know, I can't hardly recognize that mush of flesh back there," he confided to his horse, his teeth chattering. "Hopefully, the Arapaho won't fight against me when I bring the body in; that they'll take my word that it's Rankle. After the Hell I've been through, getting my woman back should go smooth. God owes me that much."

It was several hours more before the sun started to dry out Casey's clothing, and just as long for the shivers to subside. He reached into his pack and pulled out some jerky, realizing that his teeth ached with every pull and chew. He was getting sick, and he knew it.

He topped a small hill and spotted a wagon train moving slowing along, and spurred his horse toward the group. He hoped they had something to eat other than jerky and hoped they maybe had news of any tribes nearby. He glanced behind him and suddenly worried over the reaction that they may have over his pulling a decaying corpse along behind him; but he couldn't worry too much. He needed sustenance.

"Ho the wagons!" He called loudly, as he approached. The lead wagon pulled to a stop, and a young man leaned around the schooner, waving his hat in response.

Casey glanced behind once more and changed his mind about subjecting the wagon members to a corpse. He dismounted quickly and removed the litter. He'd pick it up again after he'd eaten.

"It's not as if anyone would steal it," he quipped, remounting. He spurred his horse into a canter and soon met up with the train.

"Ho, friend," the young man said as he approached.

"It's good to encounter a friendly face," Casey replied. "I was wondering if you had a bit of food to spare. I have travelled long and hard and am in need of supplies."

The man nodded, jumping down from his schooner, "We have not long since finished our noonday sup and have a bit of food spared. You are welcome to it, friend."

"God bless you," Casey said, his tone full of sincere gratitude.

The man walked around to the back of the wagon and spoke shortly to someone who Casey couldn't see. A few minutes later, a kerchief was passed from the rear along with a plate full of rice. The man whispered something more and then moved over to Casey, who quickly dismounted at his approach.

"The rice is for now. My wife has placed some supplies in the kerchief for you to consume at a later time," the man said, passing the food over to Casey. He was so hungry, he did no more than nod his thanks before diving into the plate full of rice. The man smiled and turned to walk back to his wagon.

"Wait!" Casey mumbled through a mouthful, rice sputtering onto the ground.

The man arched his brow, but returned, "Is there more that I can do for you, sir?"

Casey nodded, working to swallow the mouthful of rice before speaking again, "Have you, by chance, passed by any tribes recently?"

The man's eyes widened slightly with latent fear and he drew in a deep breath before responding, "A day's ride north. We saw a tribe in the distance. They were tearing down their housing. We stayed well away, but several of their warriors still moved in our direction with ill-intent. We can only assume that they wanted to make certain we were harmless to them. We ended giving them a few trinkets so they would be appeased."

"Arapaho?" Casey asked with bated breath, as he scraped the last of the rice from the plate.

The man shook his head, "We do not know. Why do you search out the savages, friend?"

"They took my fiancé," Casey admitted. Normally it would be unwise to admit to anyone that a white woman had been taken by savages; her reputation would not withstand the backlash. Casey knew, however, he was unlikely to ever encounter this man again, nor did this man know Cara, so could not damage her reputation with ill gossip.

The man's gaze widened and Casey saw the contempt clouding his gaze, though he tried to prevent it showing. Casey had encountered such looks before and they generally followed with comments on why the man would search out tainted goods. In the eyes of those who abhorred the natives, the women stolen by them were not worthy to live among the civilized whites any longer.

This man, however, chose to keep such opinions to himself. Instead, he retrieved the outstretched plate and murmured, "God go with you," before turning back to his wagon.

"And you," Casey called back, and for only the second time since setting out after Rankle, Casey felt a spring of joy in his step as he latched onto his stallion's reins and headed back to where he left his corpsified companion. His body still ached as he worked to reattach the litter, but the elevation in his spirits helped to push the discomfort aside.

"I hope we can put this whole ordeal behind us soon, boy, because I am going to need to see a doctor before much longer. I feel a fever coming on." Casey mounted and then headed in the direction the young man indicated. He thanked God that he'd been headed in the right direction all along, but was flabbergasted at how far the tribe had travelled to retrieve their abducted maiden. *Then again, it may only seem a great distance, because I've been riding all over God's creation the last couple of months,* Casey thought. Either way, he could see an end to his journeys and sighed with relief.

Victim of Love Barbara Woster

His mind tried to convince him that he could now rest for the night, as the sun lowered on the horizon, but Casey fought off the urge to stop; he wouldn't abandon the pursuit now, not when he was so close to reaching his Cara. As night fell and darkness settled over the land, Casey wrapped the reins about his waist and tied it to the cheek strap, then leaned over his horse's neck, "Get us there safely, boy. I'm counting on you," and then promptly fell asleep.

CHAPTER 23

Cara walked along beside Skips Along The Water. River Runner rode nearby, keeping a close eye on her. Ever since their encounter with Little Bear, a couple of days before, neither had left her alone.

"Surely you don't think he'd harm me?" Cara asked when River Runner insisted that she would now bed down with him.

"He would, and my sister would not be able to protect or defend you; nor would you be able to defend yourself. You will bed with me," River Runner stated emphatically. "I will honor my word and not touch you as my wife, but you will lie with me now, so that I can keep you safe."

His tone brooked no argument and the night before they tore down to move, Cara had spent an uneasy night lying next to River Runner. It was hours before she was able to sleep and when first light arrived, she awoke to River Runner's arm across her abdomen, much as it had been the first night in his bed.

She wondered, when he woke, whether he would attempt to bid her good morning with a kiss, as he had before, but when his eyes finally opened, he merely smiled and then rolled from the mat, "Come," he said, reaching to help her up, "we have much to do today."

And he had not exaggerated. With swift efficiency, the men and women worked to tear down their teepees and close up their life in this part of the prairie. They would move to where the buffalo were headed at this time of year. There they would spend the winter months before packing up and heading back to the plains the following year.

Cara did what she could to assist Skips Along The Water, but she was unfamiliar with their ways and ended up mostly in the way.

"Just watch and learn," Skips Along The Water finally told her, "but stay near," she added as Little Bear strolled by, eyeing Cara possessively.

"Why does he keep doing that?" Cara asked frustrated. "Surely he wouldn't dare anger your brother? I've seen your brother mad, and it's not a pretty sight."

Skips Along The Water laughed, "No, it is not, but Little Bear does not fear much, and his mind is always fogged with the sage, so he does not think much either. That makes him stupid and dangerous."

"Great. Just what I need," Cara muttered, sidestepping quickly when the poles to the teepee toppled, nearly popping her on the head. "And I don't need to be rendered unconscious either."

"How are things going?" River Runner asked, leading his laden stallion over to where they were working. "Can I help? I am done with my work."

"If you are done, you can help. Cara is of no use," Skips Along The Water teased.

"Hey, it's not as if I didn't try!" Cara defended and River Runner laughed.

"It is okay. I do not expect a white woman to know how to work. You will learn in time," he said, stroking her cheek before moving to assist his sister.

Cara's breath caught in her throat at the display of affection, and at the beauty of his smile. Her skin tingled where his fingers contacted her flesh and she again questioned the rightness of those feelings. *What am I feeling?* She thought, as she watched River Runner work. *Surely I cannot be accepting of this man? Surely I cannot allow myself to feel for him after what he's done?*

Those questions swirled within her as she followed River Runner and his sister out of the area, walking briskly behind. The first night on the trail, Cara didn't know what to expect, but after a quick meal of Pemmican, River Runner took her hand, and led her to a space away from the horses.

Without a word, he laid out a blanket and lie down. When she just stood there, he reached up a hand to her, "I am tired, Cara. Come, sleep."

Cara took his hand and allowed him to pull her down next to him.

Without speaking further, he drew her into his embrace, wrapped the blanket around them, and then pulled her tight against him. He placed a light kiss on her hair.

"Goodnight wife," he murmured and then fell asleep.

Victim of Love Barbara Woster

Cara was too tired to protest and soon fell asleep against the gentle rise and fall of his chest.

CHAPTER 24

It was their second day walking. Cara didn't speak much, too deep in thought over her relationship with River Runner. She was also fighting a constant fatigue. She wasn't used to walking this much and her mind barely remained alert enough to keep placing one foot in front of the other.

She tripped and landed against Skips Along The Water, who latched hold of her arm to try to assist in steadying her. It didn't work, and they both tumbled to the ground.

River Runner dismounted and shook his head in bemusement, "Come, Cara, you must remain strong," he said, pulling her to her feet. "Are you alright, Sister?" He asked, unable to hide the laughter in his tone.

"I am as well as one can be who has been squashed," she snapped, but the glint in her eyes revealed she was not angry. "Can she not ride with you, Brother? If only to spare her falling on top of me again?"

"Why can't we ride? Why only the men?" Cara asked, blushing when the questions escaped on a yawn.

"Perhaps you can explain, Sister. I must return to my mount now; and Cara, we will stop soon to hunt. After you cook our meal and eat, you will be able to sleep long before you start walking again tomorrow."

"Oh, joy!" Cara replied sarcastically and River Runner laughed. An actual laugh out loud laugh that she hadn't heard since … well, ever. She'd heard him chuckle, but never laugh like this. It startled her.

"Perhaps we should stop now, before my wife becomes too disagreeable," River Runner said to his sister, who nodded with a grin. He mounted and rode back along the line, letting everyone know they would begin to hunt for their meal. The men didn't hesitate, quickly grabbing their bows and quivers. The women began chatting amiably among themselves preparing for when the men returned.

Some began sharpening the tools needed for skinning whatever animals the men returned with. Others started collecting wood for fires over which to cook the meat. This fascinated Cara and she told Skips Along The Water as much.

"Why does this fascinate you?"

"I don't know. I just didn't think that you roasted meat. You always seem to be boiling it in those bags you make."

Skips Along The Water grinned as she leaned over to pick up another stick. "We do not roast the meat in our teepees because it could cause trouble," she explained. "The boiling bag keeps the animals away because it holds the smells while cooking. It also means that the fat from the animal does not…hmm…what is the way to say it will make the teepee to burn?"

"Oh, if the animal fat splatters," Cara clarified.

"Yes, but out here, there is no teepee to burn."

"Well, that makes sense…so you never did tell me why we can't ride the horses."

"If we are attacked, the warriors must be free to fight and we must be free to run."

"And they can't fight if we're on the horses with them?"

"They would lose time while we got off of the horses; time they need to ride and fight."

"Ah, I see. Makes sense, but it still doesn't make it easier," Cara said, her arms now laden with small sticks and branches. "Where do we take these?"

"River Runner likes it quiet when we move, so we will start our fire here, away from the others."

"Oh, I thought we'd be making a giant community fire," Cara said lamely.

Skips Along The Water laughed, "Sometimes we do, but not out here. We keep fires small. Less attention is given that way."

"Why, do you think the animals will smell the smoke and come running for dinner?" Cara replied sardonically.

"No, but tribes not friendly to the Arapaho may come, or the white man's soldier."

Victim of Love Barbara Woster

The reminder of the white man took away the uplifted spirit that had temporarily wrapped about Cara, snatching it away as a heavy wind an autumn leaf. She shivered.

Skips Along The Water sensed the change in her mood, and understood quickly what had caused it, "You are of the people now, Sister. It is best not to dwell on the things that were and look to the things that are. Even if your white soldier came, he would not see you as white. He would take you away from the people, from your husband, but he would not welcome you home. You know this to be true."

Cara shook her head, "Let's just get things ready for dinner. I don't feel much like talking right now."

"Perhaps it is for the best," Skips Along The Water sighed. "Do you know how to start a fire?"

Cara shook her head disinterestedly.

"I will not show you this time. This time, you will do as I tell you how. You need to put your mind somewhere else or you will never stop the tears from flowing."

Cara reached up and felt the tears sliding down her cheek. She'd been so consumed with the sadness over hearing of her fate once more, that she didn't even realize she'd started to cry.

Skips Along The Water pulled two rocks from her pouch and handed them to Cara, "Take these and bang them together. They will cause a fire to start. It is the easy way to begin a fire. I see the men returning, so we must prepare quicker."

Cara did as instructed, her movements sad and stilted. Still, it did not take long for the sparks to light the sticks that they'd fashioned and soon there was a warm flame going. Cara was so used to feeling numb from the cool autumn air that the warmth from the fire was startling; however, it did little to alleviate the chill in her heart and River Runner was quick to notice the change in her demeanor when he rode up.

"What has happened?" He asked his sister in his native tongue. He dismounted and pulled two rabbits from his pouch, placing them on the ground. "Why is Cara saddened again?"

"I spoke of the white man," Skips Along The Water sighed. "I am sorry, Brother. I told her that she must stop the tears and learn that she is Arapaho now."

River Runner nodded, looking at Cara's profile while his sister spoke.

"Can you prepare our food tonight, Sister? I wish to take Cara to walk."

Skips Along The Water huffed, "I am used to feeding you by myself, Brother. It is a good thing I am not yet married or I would not have time to feed my family too."

"Well, that will change very soon, Sister," River Runner grinned. "Soaring Eagle has asked to make you his wife."

Skips Along The Water lowered her gaze and hid the grin that formed on her face. She liked Soaring Eagle. He was handsome and strong, and she felt pleased that he would choose her from those women still seeking mates, "And did you agree, Brother?" She asked softly.

"I will, now that I know you like him," River Runner laughed softly. "Perhaps when you are done cooking our meal, you can take some food to him. His family is big and he eats too little. He will welcome the extra food. If you want, you may stay with him and become his wife."

Skips Along The Water smiled wide, wrapping her arms around her brother's neck, "Thank you, Brother. I have longed hoped to find a husband, and you have given me a good one. I will stay with him. Besides, it will give you time alone with Cara," she grinned, pulling back and casting a glance at the woman who had not moved, nor glanced their way since their conversation began. "Perhaps you can persuade her to accept her place?" She said softly, collecting the rabbits for cleaning. "I know you promised her time, but perhaps it is best you take her now. It will help her forget faster. I will cook. You go walk with her."

It didn't take a soothsayer for River Runner to read his sister's meaning. Until he made Cara his woman, she would never accept her place. He looked at Cara's despondent countenance and sighed heavily, "Cara?"

She closed her eyes, forcing herself not to react to her name on his lips. If she accepted her place as his wife, she would never be able to return home; to find a Christian husband, as she should have. If she lie with River Runner, her chances of being accepted back in the white world would go from slim to no chance at all. She shuddered at the thought. She would not treat him or his sister poorly, but she would not succumb to his charms.

"Cara?" River Runner said again, his tone soft and questioning.

"I am fine, River Runner," she replied. "I will help get dinner ready now."

She stood and River Runner did also. He clasped her hand and drew her away from his sister, "She will tend to the meal. I will have you walk with me for a while."

"But..."

"No, Cara, you will not argue; you will come with me."

He held her hand as they crossed the short distance to the tree line.

"Be careful not to let the branches hit you," he said, as he pulled her along behind him into the thick stand of trees. Soon, the light from the waning sun began to fade and it grew darker.

"Do we have to go so far? It's scary in here."

River Runner stopped and turned to face her. He placed his hands on her shoulders and gently moved her back until her back bumped into the nearest pine, "I did not want the people to hear us," he whispered, stepping so close to her that only an inch separated her breasts from his chest.

"I don't under..."

"Shhh. You will understand soon," River Runner whispered, his mouth moving closer to hers, his breath caressing her skin. "You are my wife, Cara, and it is time for us to become one."

Cara's head moved side-to-side, "No, River Runner, you promised..."

River Runner placed his mouth on hers to silence her outburst. When she fell quiet, he moved back, gazing at her flushed features, "You cannot forget where you came from if you do not know where you belong now. You belong to me, Cara, and I will hear you say it before we return to the people."

His gaze held that same intensity as the morning when he kissed her for the first time, and Cara knew that he fully intended to kiss her again. This time, however, there was no pause. He took possession of her mouth as a hawk after a mouse, devouring her with his passion and his strength, and Cara knew he intended to overwhelm her into submission; and she knew she would never be able to fight against him.

The kiss deepened and he leaned into her, pressing his body into hers, until she was crushed between two hard surfaces and barely able to draw breath. He wasn't giving her an inch to fight him.

His hands slid along the sides of her body, skimming her breasts, causing her to shiver. He reached her hem and tugged, groaning when his hands slid beneath her dress and he cupped her bottom, pulling her tight against his erection. She moaned against his mouth, fear gripping her when his fingers began kneading the flesh of her rear. Still, his mouth clung to hers, sapping her strength. She felt her legs weakening, and if not for his chest pressed against her, his mouth clinging to her own, and his hands gripping her rear, she would not have been able to remain standing.

One hand continued to knead her bottom, but the other began to slide around to the front, caressing her skin along the way. Another shiver ran through her body and she felt tears prick her eyes. Fear waged with desire, anger with want, but it wasn't until his hand moved between her legs and his finger slid into her, that the flashes of electric shock fired in her mind, and she reached up to clasp hold of his arms. She pushed against them, but her efforts were no match for his strength and determination.

His finger moved in and out, around and around, and she cried out against his mouth.

He released her mouth then and she gasped for air.

"Say you belong to me," he breathed heavily, plunging his finger deeper inside her. She cried out again, and he pulled his finger back. "Say you belong to me," he whispered again, his voice thick with desire, his finger continuing to make love to her.

"I...oh..." Cara couldn't have formed that many words just then had her life depended on it. River Runner grinned at her reaction and took possession of her mouth again, kissing her deeply, while his finger continued to caress inside her.

After a few minutes more, he released her again and she sucked in a deep breath, her head feeling loose upon her shoulders.

"Since you cannot speak, nod if you belong to me," he breathed against her mouth. He was determined she acquiesce before filling her with his seed, and if that meant driving her to the brink of madness, then he would. Of course, he too risked falling into the abyss with her, and he would if she didn't nod soon. When she remained motionless, her breathing ragged, he pulled his finger back, then opened the lips of her womanhood wider, and slid two fingers inside, pushing them deep into her until she cried out in agonized yearning and pain, he knew, as he felt her barrier give way; but to him that was good, because she would not feel the same pain again when he joined with her.

"Nod if you belong to me," he demanded, pushing his fingers deeper still. Cara's head was thrashing wildly, her brain shutting down from the flashes rapidly firing around in her head. She could take no more and finally her head fell down against his chest.

"Yes," she breathed, "yes."

River Runner closed his eyes in relief and stilled the movement of his fingers. He lie his head down atop hers and remained there while he brought his heartbeat and breathing under control. He also wanted to give Cara time to regain a modicum of composure. She'd said yes, but he wanted her to say the words.

"Say you belong to me," he whispered against her hair.

"I belong to you," Cara replied, the words escaping on a jagged breath.

River Runner clasped hold of her arms and slowly turned her to face the tree. She lie her head against the truck, her breathing ragged, her body a bowl of aspic. He lowered his head and nipped at the exposed flesh along her neck and shoulder, while his hands, again, began to caress her bottom, sliding between her legs to push them aside.

His member was pounding with need and he worked to slide his pants down so that he could ease the hunger welling within him. Cara didn't fight, struggle, or resist; instead hugging tightly to the tree in an effort to remain upright, but within a moment, his body was removed from hers and she could no longer stand, sliding down to form a puddle at the base of the tree.

At first she did not know what caused him to stop, but then the sound of voices reached her ears. Someone was calling for him—urgently.

He started muttering in his native tongue, his anger at being interrupted palpable. Cara would have gladly remained put while he went to investigate, but River Runner reached down and latched onto her upper arm, pulling her upright and along behind him. When they reached the clearing, he let go and she instantly fell. He didn't seem to notice, rather started yelling.

Skips Along The Water came running, followed closely by several warriors—two of whom had been responsible for keeping Casey Scott away from the people.

"Stay with her here," River Runner said brusquely and then walked away with his warriors. Skips Along The Water immediately took in Cara's disheveled appearance and flushed skin and smiled. *Perhaps now she would accept what is to be*, she thought, kneeling next to her sister.

"What has happened?" River Runner asked, as soon as they'd put some distance between he and Cara.

"It is Casey Scott," Crazy Beaver responded. "Our scouts have seen him coming this way. He is moving slow, but he will be here very soon."

River Runner's gaze widened and he drew in a deep breath filled with concern.

"I do not see this as a problem," Runs With Deer interjected quickly.

River Runner arched his brow and waited for his warrior to explain. How could it not be a problem? If Casey Scott discovered Cara among the people, he would demand her release, and River Runner was unwilling to let her go. Not now, not ever. The only option he could see was to kill him and leave his body to rot on the plains, but if the army were to miss him and send men to look for him, they could blame his people and massacre them.

"Crazy Beaver will go out to meet him. He knows Crazy Beaver and will not feel worry. Crazy Beaver will then..."

CHAPTER 25

Casey lifted his head wearily from his mount's neck and breathed a sigh of relief when he spied a tribe stopped along the edge of the woods. He was still too far away to determine if it were the Arapaho, but he was beyond caring, and too sick, at this point to feel much concern. It could be Apache and he'd ride straight into the midst of them, if it meant there was a chance of locating his Cara.

He sat up straighter when he saw a lone rider headed his direction. Hopefully, the warrior wasn't there to put a spear in his hide, because he was in no shape to defend against an attack. Still, he didn't want the warrior to spy any signs of weakness, so he sat up as straight as was possible and stiffened his spine. The action caused his head to spin and he nearly toppled from his horse as stars erupted in his vision. He blinked slowly, continuously, until the stars subsided. When his vision cleared, the rider was upon him.

He recognized the warrior immediately as the one who'd ridden with him, tracked with him, for the two months they searched for Rankle.

Without waiting, Casey declared, "I have brought Rankle. I know I am later than I am supposed to be, but please tell me your chief has not killed Cara."

Crazy Beaver spied the rotting flesh in men's clothing upon the litter and his eyes widened, both in recognition and astonishment. He never would have thought it possible for this man to have accomplished what they thought was impossible; yet here he sat upon his mount, the man his chief sought in his possession. Crazy Beaver knew what he had to do, but his respect for Casey Scott became great at that moment.

"Your woman lives, as far as I know," Crazy Beaver said slowly.

"What do you mean, 'as far as I know'?" Casey asked, his brow furrowing with growing concern. "Where is Cara?"

"I found the man, Rankle," Crazy Beaver explained. "He was killed by another warrior."

"The man I saw racing after him?"

Crazy Beaver nodded. "When I found him, he was dead and in the river. There was nothing more to do, so I returned to my people to tell my chief. I could not find you again to tell you. Because Rankle had died, he paid for what he did to my chief's sister, so there was no reason more to keep the white woman among the people."

"What are you trying to tell me? Are you telling me you just let her go?"

Crazy Beaver shook his head, "A warrior took her back to your people many moons ago. That is why we are surprised to see you here now. We thought you returned to your people too."

"Wait a minute," Casey stated, trying to make sense of what he was hearing. He shook his head to clear his thoughts and immediately regretted the motion, because his vision blurred and he passed out, sliding from his horse and hitting the ground with a loud thud.

Crazy Beaver slid from his stallion's back and walked over, leaning down to run his hand along Casey's face, feeling for his breath. "You are very ill," he murmured. He stood, remounted, and headed back to where River Runner and the other warriors waited.

All of them were mounted, should the need for support arise. When Crazy Beaver drew near, Runs With Deer was the first to question him.

"We saw the white man fall. Did you kill him then?"

River Runner's face clouded with anger at the thought, "It is not what was to be done..."

"I did not," Crazy Beaver interjected quickly before River Runner put a spear in his gut for disobeying his orders. "He fell. He is very sick."

Little Bear spoke up then, "Then we should leave him to die. He will become bear food."

River Runner nodded, "We could, but we know that he is important to his people. If they send people to find him, they may not know why he died. They may blame the Arapaho for his death since we took the white woman away. We have kept peace with the white man and do not need their men with guns to come..."

"The white woman has been trouble since you brought her among the people," Little Bear snapped. "We should send her away. Give her to the white man; then we would not worry over the white man and his guns."

"Perhaps Little Bear is correct," Runs With Deer interjected. "We know that you want to keep the white woman, but maybe we should give her back to the white man."

"He showed himself very brave in his quest to return Rankle to the people..."

"But he did not do so," River Runner interjected sharply, not liking the direction in which the conversation turned.

"But he did," Crazy Beaver replied quickly. "Rankle is dead, but Casey Scott still placed his body on a litter and brought him here."

"What?" River Runner was incredulous. Surely he did not hear his warrior correctly. "The body?"

Crazy Beaver nodded, "He found the dead body and brought it back here. It does not look like a man any longer, though it is the man, I am sure. He wanted to make sure we returned his woman. He wanted to make sure that you knew the man who took your sister was dead. He has shown himself to be honorable."

River Runner was not liking the tone of approval in his warrior's tone. If the man, Casey Scott, had the respect of his people, then River Runner would have to relinquish his prize and he did not wish to relinquish the white woman, "What did you tell him before he fell from his horse?"

"I told him that we returned the white woman to his people many moons ago because the man, Rankle, was dead."

"Then he does not know we still have the woman here among the people," River Runner said thoughtfully.

"He does not."

River Runner nodded, "Go and carry the man, Casey Scott, home to his people..."

"But River Runner, he would not survive the many days travel back to the white man's home," Crazy Beaver objected.

"Take a healer with you. She will tend to the white man on the way. If his people sees that we have healed the man, Casey Scott, and returned him to his home safely, it will keep the white man our ally. It is what is to be done."

"And the white woman? Why do you keep her when she is a danger to the people?" Little Bear snapped. "We will be allies with the white man until he knows she is here. Then the white man with guns will come to take her away. Why is she so important to you?"

River Runner looked at each of his warriors, his gaze flinty, "She is different," he replied finally, "and she will bear me strong sons."

"She is trouble," Little Bear persisted.

"Oh stop your cawing, Little Bear," Crazy Beaver snapped. "You are just jealous that our chief snatched a valuable prize. You are just angry that he took away your woman and gave you Broken Dove. Do not cause the people trouble because of your anger."

Little Bear huffed, "I will not be taking the white man back, so I do not need to stay here," he snapped, then turned his stallion's nose toward camp and rode away.

"The sage is making his mind crazy," Runs With Deer stated. "I fear he will cause trouble."

River Runner nodded thoughtfully, "Crazy Beaver, select a warrior and go get Crow Woman also. You will see to Casey Scott. Make certain you tell the white man that we helped him. Runs With Deer, call together the council. We will discuss finding a new war chief and what is to be done about Little Bear."

The warriors dispersed, but River Runner's mind would not find peace. He rode out to where Casey Scott lay, still unconscious. He slid from his stallion and knelt beside the inert body. Casey moaned, startling River Runner, but he was even more disconcerted when Casey opened his eyes.

"Cara," Casey whispered hoarsely. "Where's my Cara?"

River Runner's jaw clenched and his breathing intensified, "She is no longer your Cara. She is mine. We will take you back to your people, and you will never return."

"Cara," Casey murmured, his eyes closing again as he slipped back into a fevered sleep.

"You will never have her back," River Runner whispered harshly. "She is now my woman, and if you ever come for her again, I will drive my spear into your chest."

River Runner stood and remounted, heading back to his camp. It was time for him to make Cara his; time to finish what he started in the woods. As soon as she was with child, the sooner she would be his and no one would be able to take her away.

As he drew nearer, he was met by Little Bear and Brave Dove.

"We are leaving," Little Bear stated. "We will not stay to watch you destroy the people. We will begin a people of our own; or maybe join our Cheyenne brothers."

River Runner nodded and was about to ride past when he noticed Brave Dove looking at him oddly, "Do you wish to speak, Brave Dove?"

"She has nothing to say," Little Bear snapped, pulling on Brave Dove's reins, he continued on their way.

River Runner's gaze narrowed. He was about to turn away when he saw Brave Dove turn. She tried to sign something, but the look on her face revealed she was having difficulty with some words. After a few minutes, she pointed to River Runner, then to herself, and then ran her hands along her hair. River Runner determined she was speaking about Cara. He nodded and she nodded in return. Then she pointed to Little Bear and then her mouth. She made the sign of words leaving the mouth.

It was all that was needed. River Runner knew that Little Bear had spoken to Cara. That was why he packed to leave so quickly, because he knew River Runner would kill him if he caused trouble for him and his woman.

His first instinct was to ride after Little Bear to confront him, but he knew that it would be pointless. If Brave Dove was correct, and Little Bear had spoken to Cara, then the damage was done and going after Little Bear would not undo it.

He glanced once more at Brave Dove, wondering if he'd done her a kindness, giving her to Little Bear. Her eyes were wide and she was pointing frantically behind him. River Runner glanced over his shoulder and started cursing in his native tongue.

Cara was running in his general direction with Skips Along The Water running behind. There were tears streaming down her face and he knew she was crying for her white man. She didn't even look his way; instead her gaze was pinned to the white man's stallion and she was calling out for Casey.

River Runner closed his eyes against the pain that slammed into his belly. He slid from his horse to intercept her. He would not allow her to see the man, Casey Scott. He would not allow her to continue crying for him.

He moved into her path, but she didn't stop running; instead she speared him with a hostile stare, and picked up speed. He knew she was going to ram him and planted his feet firmly on the ground. As soon as she was close, he reached out and latched onto her arms, gripping them tightly.

She was thrashing wildly, kicking at his shins, "Liar! You lied! You told me Casey was dead! You told me he was dead!" She continued fighting against his restraint until she exhausted her efforts and stilled. "Let me go," she whispered harshly. "I will go to him, so let me go!"

"No! You belong to me and will return to our camp," River Runner stated firmly.

"I will never belong to you," she hissed, piercing him with a deadly stare. "I belong to Casey. The only reason I remained with you was because you lied to me. You told me he was dead."

"My warriors told me he'd been killed. I had no reason to doubt them," River Runner explained, wondering why he cared whether she thought ill of him or not.

"You said they killed him on your order," she accused.

"*You* said I had him killed. I saw no reason to make you think otherwise. I will see to Casey Scott and make sure he returns to his people safely. I do not wish you to grieve further. He will be unharmed. Now return."

"No! I won't. I want to go home!" Cara cried, her gaze returning to where Casey's horse stood. "Where is he? What have you done to him?"

"He fell from his horse. He is ill."

"No! Casey!" Cara started to struggle against River Runner's grip again, but he held fast, refusing to let her go. It was several minutes more before she tired enough to stop her struggles again.

River Runner forced her to turn, "See? I have not lied to you. My warriors are coming to see him home; and I have asked our medicine woman to go with them, to tend to him so that he will live."

"No, I should be there. I should be tending to him. Please," Cara pleaded. "Let me go."

"I cannot," River Runner replied.

"Brother," Skips Along The Water intervened, her tone soft, pleading. She spoke in their tongue, to prevent Cara knowing what she was saying. It would not be good if the white woman thought her an ally against her own brother. "She knows that her man lives. There will be no joy for her here now. Let her go home."

"I cannot," River Runner admitted, closing his eyes against the pain flowing through his body.

"It would be the right thing to do," his sister persisted. "She will no longer come to your bed willingly. Do you want to never smile again, as you did when she first came among our people?"

"Enough!" River Runner yelled. "I will not release her. She will accept her place in time."

His sister sighed, "I fear she will not." Without waiting for another outburst from her brother, Skips Along The Water turned and headed back to camp to another dinner that would be no longer good to eat. If she had her way, it would be the last dinner that would be ruined because of a white woman and her brother's stubborn pride.

She heard Cara screaming and glanced over her shoulder. River Runner had slung Cara over his shoulder and was moving toward his stallion who was rearing at the commotion. She grinned without humor. "It will do him good if the horse kicks him in the head."

CHAPTER 26

Dinner was a morbid affair. River Runner gulped his barely edible food down in sulking silence, while Cara lay, bound hand-to-foot on their blanket, weeping silently.

"I am leaving to go be with my new husband now," Skips Along The Water stated after she'd consumed her food. "I will not feed him from this, since it is not good to eat. I wish you well in taming your wife, Brother. I will not help further. She will cook for you or you will starve."

River Runner drew in a disgruntled breath through his nose, but didn't stop his sister leaving. She had the right to happiness and he would not hold up her life just because he was currently going over deadly rapids.

"I wish you many strong sons, Sister," he whispered.

"And you, Brother."

Skips Along The Water turned and left his campfire. River Runner tossed aside the rabbit bones and then stood, kicking dirt over the fire. He moved to the blanket he shared with Cara and knelt beside her. "I will unbind you, but you will not fight me."

Cara didn't respond, nor acknowledge his presence. She just lie there, staring into the distance. Her tears had finally subsided, only to be replaced by a stony depression.

River Runner reached out and untied the leather straps, then stretched out onto the blanket, pulling an uncharacteristically pliant Cara into his embrace. He placed a kiss on her hair and then whispered in her ear, "If you try to leave, my warriors will return you."

Cara closed her eyes knowing that what he said was true. He'd laid claim to her and had made it clear that he would not let her go. She was trapped. She wanted to rant, to threaten, to make him sorry for keeping her against her will, but she was exhausted and she also knew it would be futile. She'd worried when she first arrived that he could simply overpower her if she fought, and thus far he'd proven that thought true more than once. He'd abducted her with ease, despite her struggles; he'd tossed her in the river for defying him; had overpowered her in the woods, stealing her virtue against the trunk of a tree; and had prevented her going to Casey, all with only his hands upon her arms. She was no match for his strength and determination and it sickened her in the pit of her stomach.

She lie awake long after she felt the steady rise and fall of his chest. Her mind wandered to Casey. Would he be okay? Would the medicine woman heal him with her herbs? Would the warriors truly return him safely to Martin's Landing, or was it all a ruse to put her mind at ease over his well being? There had been too many different stories told to her for her to know whether anything was true. Although she knew it would be pointless, she wanted to run away. Now that she knew that Casey was alive, she wanted to run back to him. If she could get to him, he would keep her safe; would protect her against River Runner.

He wouldn't be able to protect me until he got better, she thought. *Until then, the warriors with him would easily be able to fight him and win. They could kill him because of my foolishness.* She sighed out loud causing River Runner to groan in his sleep. His hand slid from her shoulder, freeing her from his grasp.

If I could move away without him waking, she thought, testing her ability to at least roll away by slowing shifting onto her side; silently willing him to remain asleep. She moved slowly, carefully, until she was lying on her side, her body free from contact with his. Most nights, they both slept so soundly that she didn't know whether she'd be able to move around or not. All she knew for fact was that, whenever she awakened, River Runner's arm was lying across her abdomen.

She shifted slightly and realized that her head was still lying on his arm, which meant she wasn't completely apart from him. She moved cautiously and sat up, sighing when he remained deep asleep. It was a small triumph, and it brought her a modicum of peace, knowing that she had a small measure of free will remaining.

A sound nearby drifted to her ear and she squinted into the blackness trying to see what it was. For all she knew, they could be attacked by a wolf; which for her would not necessarily be a bad thing—if the wolf got a hold of River Runner and not herself. If he were dead or injured, he couldn't stop her leaving. She sighed softly, feeling guilty for wishing ill-will against another human being.

"Shh."

The whispered sound issued near her face, and had Cara not recognized Skips Along The Water's scent, she would have cried out in fear. A hand reached out and skimmed her shoulder, and she jerked reflexively.

"Shh." The command came again, as the hand slid down and latched hold of her hand. Skips Along The Water tugged, until Cara stood. It was too dark to see the girl and her lack of speech only served to make her nerves jump nervously. What if her assumption that it was River Runner's sister was incorrect?

Still, the person was leading her away from River Runner and that made him or her a friend—currently.

"How can you see where we're going?" Cara whispered.

"Shh."

Cara tripped and nearly fell, but quickly regained her footing. For fifteen minutes, the two moved quickly away from the camp, in darkness and in silence. The sound of a horse neighing nearby caused Cara's heart to flutter. Skips Along The Water heard it too and shifted their direction slightly.

"Come, this way," she whispered.

"Where are we going?" Cara asked.

"Shh. I will answer your questions when we are safely away. Now mount."

Skips Along The Water pushed Cara against the horse's flank, and Cara struggled to pull herself up.

"I can't. It's too high," she whispered in frustration.

Skips Along The Water moved her aside and leapt, pulling her body onto the mare's back.

"Jump high and pull yourself," she instructed softly. "You must do this, Cara. You cannot walk in the dark too far. It is not safe."

Cara bent at the knees and leapt as high as she could. She was not strong and the struggle to pull herself up was causing the horse to become nervous. It began sidestepping, despite Skips Along The Water's whispering assurances in its ear.

After several minutes, Cara lie across it's rump on her belly, and Skips Along The Water spurred the horse into a canter.

"Wait, I'm not on," Cara cried softly.

"You are on enough. We must move. When it becomes daylight, we will find a stump or a rock for you to climb upon."

"And how long before sun up?" Cara asked, her belly already beginning to ache against the constant jarring.

"Many hours. Now please, be silent. We must not draw attention to ourselves. I am sorry for your discomfort, but please be strong."

By Cara's estimation it was it was at least six hours before the hues in the sky began to change from black to gray to dark blue. As the morning slowly made its appearance, Cara was able to start making out the scrub grasses passing beneath her face. She lifted her head several times over the last several hours, because it would begin to pound as the blood flowed painfully to her head. Her extremities, on the other hand, had gone numb. She could not recall a time when she'd been so uncomfortable, so out of control of her body.

Oh, yes I can, she thought, generating a nervous tingling in her belly. *River Runner's assault in the woods had left her feeling completely incapacitated—mind and body.* She shook the thought free just as Skips Along The Water pulled the mare to a halt along a stream. With a massive tug, she pulled Cara from the horse's back and helped her to the ground.

"You will be unable to walk for a while," Skips Along The Water said sheepishly. "I am sorry for this, but it was necessary. I will go hunt for berries. When you feel your legs again, try to stand and walk. It will help."

Without awaiting a reply, Skips Along The Water moved away, scouring the nearby area for anything that they could eat. By the time she returned half-hour later, Cara was on her feet. She was unsteady, but at least she was standing.

"Sit," Skips Along The Water instructed. "We need to eat and then leave quickly. We have no time to stay. My brother will have wakened and will know you are gone."

Cara sat and began munching on the proffered berries. There were many questions swirling about in her head, but she would eat before asking them. Skips Along The Water's warning about River Runner struck her deep in her core and elicited an intense fear, so she would heed her words and eat before satiating her curiosity.

Once the berries were gone, Skips Along The Water latched hold of the horse's mane and led it along the river bank, apparently searching for something.

"Can I help you find something?" Cara offered.

"A stump or a rock that you can stand upon to mount," Skips Along The Water stated.

"Ah, right." Cara began scanning the area and within fifteen minutes had located a boulder near the riverbank. "There!"

Skips Along The Water nodded and tugged the horse in the direction Cara indicated. As soon as she stopped the horse, she took a step, leapt, and mounted.

"Now you climb," Skips Along The Water instructed, her tone urgent.

Cara climbed onto the boulder, bent at the knee, and pulled her body over the horse's rump. As soon as she was stable, she slid her leg around the bottom and pulled herself up to a sitting position.

"Hey, not bad," she congratulated herself. "First time I've ever sat a bareback horse."

Skips Along The Water kicked the horse into a gallop and Cara quickly latched onto her waist as the sudden jolt threatened to unseat her.

For most of the morning, they maintained that speed, until Cara became concerned over the horse's well being.

"Should we be pushing the horse so hard?" She called over the rush of wind blowing in her face.

Skips Along The Water called back over her shoulder, "It is what they are made to do—run with the wind."

"Yeah, but not carrying two people," Cara rejoined.

Skips Along The Water tugged on the mane and the mare began to slow its pace until it was at a walk. She then turned part way so she could face Cara, "It is unwise for us to move slowly. Do I need to tell you this too often?"

Cara shook her head, blushing at the reprimand.

Skips Along The Water sighed heavily, "I will run the horse and walk it too. Will that be okay?"

"Yes, thank you," Cara replied softly. "Can I ask you why you're doing this for me? You're risking your brother's wrath."

"Wrath?"

"Anger," Cara clarified.

"Yes, and my husband's."

"I didn't know you were married?"

"Only last night did I go to my new husband. He will be very angry when he sees that I have gone. He may think he was not a good lover."

Cara blushed again and Skips Along The Water huffed at her reaction, "River Runner will be equally angry. You have challenged him too many times, and he will not be forgiving. And I will pay for my help of you also."

"Why did you help, knowing that your husband and your chief will be beyond irate?" Cara asked again.

"Does this word mean angry too?"

Cara nodded.

"It is what needs to be. You saved my life, and I now owe you the same. You were right. You should not be made to stay where you do not wish to stay; and even though I know my brother to be a good man who would take much good care of you, it is wrong for him to make you stay with him. In that, it is not different from the man called Rankle. If your white man was dead, I would not help you."

Cara didn't know what to say, so she simply replied, "I'm sorry."

Skips Along The Water closed her eyes and shook her head, the irony of their circumstances, reversed, not lost on her at all. "I am sorry also," she whispered, then turned and spurred the horse into a gallop again.

"How long before we catch up to Casey and the others?" Cara yelled.

"We will not go to them," Skips Along The Water yelled back. "The warriors with him would beat me and take us back to the tribe."

"Then where are we going?"

"I am taking you to your people. You will be there to meet your Casey Scott when he comes back there."

"How do I know he'll make it safe and sound?" Cara asked, worry over his fate causing her body to tense.

"We do not know if he will live, but Crow Woman is a good medicine woman. She will make him well again."

Cara hoped so. Without Casey by her side, she wasn't certain how she would survive alone, a possible outcast among the whites.

CHAPTER 27

"Where are we?" Casey whispered hoarsely, the cottony feeling in the back of his throat making it difficult to swallow, let along talk.

Crow Woman immediately moved to his side, lifted Casey's head and made him drink. Casey gagged at the smell and tried to fight her insistence, but he was too weak. She poured the liquid down into his mouth and he choked, but she closed his mouth and would not allow him to spit it out. She spoke words, foreign to his ears, but they sounded as if they were encouraging. He looked into kind, but resolute eyes, crinkled around the sides with age. She nodded and smiled, then held the liquid up for him to drink some more. He didn't fight her this time and forced the liquid down his throat. She nodded, smiled again, then lowered his head before turning to speak to someone standing nearby.

Casey closed his eyes as a feeling of floating overwhelmed his body.

"You are feeling better?" A voice asked, intruding upon his feeling of euphoria.

Casey cracked open one eye and then forced the other to open also when he recognized the person speaking to him.

"You?"

"We are taking you back to your people," Crazy Beaver said. "Crow Woman has tended to you so that you return well."

Casey looked over to where Crow Woman sat, busily crushing herbs, "Tell her I said thank you."

"I will."

"How far are we from Martin's Landing?" Casey asked, forcing himself to remain awake.

Crazy Beaver looked confused.

"My home. When will we get back there?"

"Ah. We have one more day to travel," Crazy Beaver explained.

"Cara," Casey whispered and then the herbs the old woman gave to him worked their magic, and he drifted back into a dreamless sleep.

Crazy Beaver sighed. He did not know what would happen when they took the white man back and he discovered his woman was not among his people. He worried that he would not react well. One thing that Crazy Beaver discovered about this white man was that he was much like a warrior—he fought for the ones he loved and he did not give up easily.

"Let us go," he called to those traveling with him. "We are nearing the end of this journey, but it will take many days longer for us to return to our home, since the tribe will continue to move while we are away. I, for one, miss my woman."

CHAPTER 28

River Runner awoke to find Cara missing. At first he thought she'd wakened ahead of him and went to do her woman's business in the woods. He stretched languidly, a feeling of victory embracing him, because he knew he'd won and that Cara was his; that no man could take her away.

He stretched once more and stood, rolling up their blanket and returning it to the horse, which was munching contentedly on some nearby grass. River Runner patted it on the rump, "We will go soon, my friend."

He reached into his bag and pulled out some Pemmican. He munched on the stick, leaning against his horse, as his gaze moved about the camp. Many of his people were already awake and working to pack up for the next long leg toward their winter grounds. He smiled at the children playing chase, while their moms rolled up bedding. It was a life he was happy to share with Cara, if she would just accept him as she should.

The thought of her caused his gaze to shift toward the tree line near where they had bedded down. She still had not returned. His brow knitted and he walked toward where his sister and her new husband were bedding down.

As he neared their area, the knit in his brow deepened. Their camp had already been picked up, and neither Skips Along The Water nor Soaring Eagle were anywhere to be seen.

River Runner stopped a passing female, "Have you seen my sister and her husband?"

The woman shook her head and then moved along her way.

"River Runner!" Someone called, and he turned sharply. It was Soaring Eagle running his way.

"What is wrong?"

"Skips Along The Water is gone. I can find her nowhere. I have searched since daylight broke, and there is no sign of her," Soaring Eagle huffed, breathless from running around for over an hour.

River Runner's eyes widened and breathing became suddenly difficult as a weight of disbelief settled inside his chest, "No!" He cried, running toward the tree line. "No!"

Soaring Eagle ran along with him, realizing that there was something wrong, and River Runner knew what it was.

"Cara!" River Runner screamed over and over, but there was no reply. Much as Soaring Eagle had run, frantically, for over an hour, so did River Runner. Finally, he fell to his knees as the anguish of her disappearance overwhelmed him.

"You are sure your woman is missing also?" Soaring Eagle asked, flopping down on the ground next to his chief.

River Runner nodded.

"But how? Where would they have gone? I do not understand any of this. I thought Skips Along The Water was happy to be my wife."

"She is," River Runner replied softly, "but Cara was not happy to be mine, and your wife knew this to be true. She must have come in the night and taken Cara away from me."

"She would not stand against you in this way, my chief," Soaring Eagle replied, incredulous.

"There is much you do not know, Brother," River Runner stated, anger slowly replacing grief, "but when we find them, you will know what I speak is true and you will be the one to punish her for what she has done."

Soaring Eagle nodded, his face solemn. When he agreed to take the chief's sister as his wife, he did not know that she would be trouble to him. His anger began to burn, much as River Runner's was burning.

River Runner saw the anger on his brother's face, "We will return our women to us and they will never be allowed to leave us again. Bring the warriors to me, and select one to continue guiding the people to our winter home."

Soaring Eagle nodded.

"And hurry," River Runner called. "They have been gone many hours. We must get to them before they reach the white man's home."

CHAPTER 29

"We have much trouble now," Skips Along The Water said, smashing the ground with her fist. Just before dawn of the second day, their horse stepped in a hole and fell, toppling the girls from its back. Both suffered no more than bruises, but the horse broke its leg. It lie on the ground, its eyes rolled back in its head from the pain it was in.

"What are we to do now?" Cara asked, stroking the horse on its haunches. She knew she could not relieve its pain, but she felt she needed to do something.

"Come, we must continue on foot," Skips Along The Water stated emphatic.

"We can't leave this poor animal like this!" Cara cried. "Is there no way to put it out of its misery?"

Skips Along The Water sighed heavily, "Look around for a rock. We will bash it in the head."

"No! I can't do that," Cara replied aghast. "Surely there must be another way."

"We hit it on the head, or we leave it. Those are our choices. If you cannot hit it, we must go," Skips Along The Water stated callously.

"We'll go," Cara whispered sadly. She stroked the horse once more, "I'm so sorry," she whispered, then stood to follow along after Skips Along The Water.

"Without a horse, we'll never get to Martin's Landing before being overtaken, will we? Assuming you're right and your people will come for us."

"They will come for us," Skips Along The Water said emphatic. The certainty in her voice made chills race along Cara's arms and she turned instinctively to look back the way they'd come; just to see if there were warriors bearing down on them. She breathed a sigh of relief when she saw no one.

"So, what are we going to do?" Cara reiterated.

"We walk, and if we are lucky, we will find horses."

"From your mouth to God's ears," Cara said, "because if it was two days more on horseback, it will take ten times as long on foot."

"We do not have ten times as long, so let us hope we find horses."

"This is not going as smoothly as you thought it would, is it?" Cara asked out of the blue after they'd been walking for more than an hour.

"No," Skips Along The Water huffed.

"I can empathize."

"What does this word mean?"

"It means, saving you didn't go as smoothly as I thought it would either. I expected I'd stop Rankle, the doctor would heal you, and we'd return you to a grateful people. Instead..."

"I do not need to be reminded of what happened. I know what happened. I was there. And I will say again that I thought my brother did what he thought was right."

"Yeah, well, if you thought he was right, why are you helping me now?" Cara retorted, pulling her dress free after it became snagged on a pricker bush.

"I told you that too. If you continue to speak on this matter further, I will simply leave you here to walk home alone."

Cara huffed but dropped that particular subject. It was another hour before either spoke again.

"Oooh, I am so tired of walking I could scream."

"I would prefer you did not, since this could tell my people where we are, if they are near. There are berries here. Pick them and eat as we walk," Skips Along The Water instructed, pointing to a massive blackberry bush growing along the edge of the field through which they walked.

Again, Cara's instinct was to look over her shoulder, so certain was she, every time Skips Along The Water spoke, that River Runner was on their heels. When she'd assured herself, again, that they were not yet being followed, she began to pick and eat berries by the dozens.

"Oh, I'm so hungry, I could eat every berry on these bushes and still not satiate my hunger," Cara groaned, shoving another handful of berries into her mouth.

"As long as you do so as you walk...wait, stop!" Skips Along The Water said suddenly, ducking behind one of the bushes. She reached out and pulled Cara behind her.

"What? What is it?" Cara asked, unable to see what had caught Skips Along The Water's attention.

"I see horses," Skips Along The Water stated, her tone filled with glee.

"Wild horses?" Cara asked, wondering how they were supposed to capture wild horses, let alone ride them.

"I do not know," she replied, "but we will approach carefully. See if we can capture one."

Cara sighed, her thoughts of a moment earlier crashing back to the forefront. This time, however, she verbalized those concerns, "How are we supposed to capture a wild horse and ride it?"

"My people are horse people. Many times a year, we capture horses and ride without harm—well, almost without harm."

"Oh, that's comforting," Cara replied sardonically.

"We need rope," Skips Along The Water stated, searching the ground around her.

"Do you really expect to find rope in the grass?" Cara asked, her tone sarcastic.

"I expect to find that with which to make rope. Like this!" She exclaimed, holding up a thin switch. "Find many of these. We can bind them together to make something to catch the horse."

"Wow, I would never have thought of that," Cara admitted, admiration in her tone.

"That is because you are a white woman, and white women are useless," Skips Along The Water retorted, but Cara could not tell if she were teasing.

"Well, I may have been useless once, but I've learned a lot...." Cara stopped, suddenly realizing what she was about to say, but Skips

Along The Water had already determined her train of thought and completed it for her.

"Yes, you have learned much from being with the people. I think that, perhaps, you could even take care of yourself one day; but not now. You learned much, but not enough. Perhaps if you stayed...willingly?"

Cara shook her head and fell quiet, deciding it best to concentrate on locating thin switches.

It took yet another hour for Skips Along The Water to fashion a usable rope, but Cara was convinced it would do the job. The girl truly impressed her with her ingenuity and survival skills. Though reluctant to admit it, Cara really had learned a lot in the months among the people, but that didn't make her an Arapaho. She was still white and belonged with her own kind, despite River Runner's resolve that she remain with him.

Skips Along The Water glanced around the bushes again to be certain the horses were still there and sighed. They were, and they'd moved nearer still. "Now be quiet. It is important that we not startle them, or they will run and we will never capture one. Follow me, and stay low."

CHAPTER 30

"Everyone out! I will speak with Casey alone!" Governor Martini stormed into the doctor's office like a dust devil whipped up by a heavy wind, and all of Casey's friend's scattered as if the governor were just as injurious. "Well, doctor, where is he? Is he awake?"

"He will be if you keep shouting like that," the doctor retorted. "Now shut your trap and let the boy rest. He's been through quite an ordeal and is lucky to be alive."

"So I heard," the governor said, lowering his voice. "Is it true the Arapaho brought him in?"

"I assume so. I wasn't there," the doctor wisecracked.

"What of my daughter? Was there word of my daughter?"

"If there were, the men would have told you before telling me," the doctor replied. "Now, if you don't mind, Casey needs to sleep. I will send for you when he wakens."

"I'll wait here," the governor insisted.

"Suit yourself," the doctor snapped, "but it will be morning, most like, before he comes too, and I ain't got but the one bed—mine; and I can tell you now, I ain't sharing."

"Fine, send someone as soon as he wakens," the governor snapped, turning to leave.

"Oh, governor, would you mind having the diner send some food around. I can't leave with a patient in the back room and I haven't eaten since this morning. Can't have the doctor fainting dead away while tending to the sick, now can we?"

The governor huffed and left the office, leaving the doctor standing there shaking his head, "Men in important positions sure do like to demand their way, don't they?" He jested to no one, but Casey responded.

"They sure do, doctor," he whispered, his tone full of sarcasm.

"Yeah, but I really *am* important," the doctor quipped. "So, how're you feeling then? You've been knocking pretty hard on death's door. Thought maybe you were determined to walk on through to Hell."

"No, I'm satisfied with good old Martin's Landing," Casey remarked. "So, now that we've satisfied ourselves that I'm not dying, think maybe you could fetch me some food too? I haven't eaten a decent meal in months. And send the governor back around," he continued, his tone suddenly serious again, "it's urgent that I speak with him."

The doctor would have quipped about someone else feeling a mite bit self-important, had Casey's tone sounded anything but humorous.

He nodded, lifting his hat from the peg by the door, "I'll be back shortly, and I'll make certain the governor knows you're awake."

"Thank you, doctor, and thank you for saving my life."

"T'weren't none of my doing. The old Arapaho woman did that. All I did was put you to bed," the doctor replied, and then left Casey alone.

The mention of the medicine woman brought back to the forefront of his mind the last three days in the company of the Arapaho warriors, his mind drifting in and out of consciousness; and in and out of the realm of sanity. He wasn't certain he'd heard it correct when the warrior told him they'd sent Cara home when Rankle was discovered dead, but he felt certain that if that were the case, she'd have been at his bedside at lot faster than her father had been.

Had he heard correct; or had that been a figment of his fevered brain? Had the Arapaho released Cara to go home, or was she still among the tribe? If she'd been with the tribe the entire time, had they mistreated her? When he didn't get Rankle back to the tribe before they began the move, did they really kill her, as they claimed they would?

He slammed the door on that thought fast, before it could get a foot in and begin to fester. The last thing he needed right now were horrific thoughts swilling about his brain making a mess of things, when it needed to be clear for thinking straight.

All he was sure of right now was that Cara was missing, and the first words out of the governor's mouth, when he came storming in, confirmed that.

"Where's Cara?" He demanded. "Why isn't she with you? We haven't heard hide nor hair out of you for nigh onto a month now, and when you finally get back, you're near death and in the company of savages. Now I want to know what happened, and I want to know now! Why was my daughter put in that position in the first place? She said you two eloped and were planning to marry. Is that true? Did you go behind my back and take my daughter away from me?"

"Governor, enough!" Casey shouted with what little strength he could muster.

"I want answers, damn you, and I won't rest until..." The governor clasped his chest and sank to his knees. Casey tried to get up to assist and fell on his face.

"Dear God almighty, don't die on me!" Casey groaned, rolling onto his back.

"Casey, where's my daughter?" The governor gasped before collapsing on his side into unconsciousness.

"What in blue blazes?" The doctor yelled, dropping both plates of food onto the floor and racing to check on the governor.

"He collapsed," Casey breathed, fighting to stay conscious himself.

"Damnation!" The doctor exclaimed, rolling the governor onto his back. He bent down to check his breathing, "Well, he's alive, but his breathing's shallow." He looked at Casey when he didn't respond and started cursing up a blue streak. Casey had passed out on the floor beside the governor, and now the doctor had two men to tend to—one, he didn't know what do about and the other he done what he could already. He sat on his haunches and sighed, wondering whatever possessed him to go into medicine in the first place.

CHAPTER 31

River Runner refused to allow the men to stop come nightfall, so they had ridden hard for two days straight without food, water, or rest for themselves or their horses. When one of the warrior's horse tripped and threw him ten feet in the air, River Runner was forced to stop.

"Are you okay?" He asked, pulling his stallion alongside the winded warrior.

"I will live, but I think my horse..."

It was as far as he got before River Runner turned his mount and approached the wounded animal. He slid from his mount's back, pulled his knife from its scabbard and stabbed the horse in the neck. It was cathartic, for River Runner had been building up anger and tension for the two days since Cara had left and he was in a murderous rage.

Soaring Eagle rode up, hesitant to mention what was to be done now that one of their warriors was dismounted. Still, if anyone could speak to River Runner without being killed right now, it was he, "Brother, we are down a horse and we cannot ride hard with two men on the back of one horse. What should we do? We are but one day from the white man's home, and we have not yet found our women? It is likely they are already there, and if that is so..."

River Runner retrieved his knife with a flourish that silenced Soaring Eagle; he then stood abruptly, and walked back to where the warrior still lie, gasping for breath.

"I am sorry you are injured, my brother. Can you move?" River Runner queried, kneeling next to him and placing a reassuring hand on his shoulder.

"I cannot," the warrior whispered, shame in his tone.

River Runner nodded, then stood and approached another of his men, "Take him home," he commanded simply, then turned and remounted his stallion. Without another word, he spurred the horse into a gallop, his men following without hesitation or reservation.

CHAPTER 32

Skips Along The Water had managed to rope one of the wild horses, but it had taken the remainder of the day and well into the next day before they were able to mount it successfully to ride. The stallion bucked and kicked and whinnied in protest at being restrained until it was too tired to do anything but stand there and stare at them. Skips Along The Water walked up and stroked it on the cheek, whispering words of kindness and encouragement in her native tongue. All Cara could do was stand out of the way of the flailing hooves.

In the middle of day three, Skips Along The Water announced the horse ready to ride, "We have wasted much time, so we need to find a way to climb on its back, fast." She led the giant beast, which was at least two hands taller than their mare had been, to the first tree she located, then shimmied up a branch closest to the horse's height, and climbed aboard, holding tight to its mane in the event it decided against having her on its back. When it did no more than stand there, she released a loud sigh of relief.

"Climb up the tree and onto its back. I chose this tree because it looked easy to climb, and I knew you could not climb unless it was easy," Skips Along The Water said brusquely.

"You know," Cara grunted, tugging herself up onto the lowest branch, "you have been snappish at me since you rescued me from your people, and I'd appreciate it if you would stop now. I'm out here too, you know, and it's not like I'm eating or resting any better than you are..."

"Are you helping to capture and tame horses?" Skips Along The Water snapped in reply.

"No! But if I could, I certainly would be doing so!" Cara snapped back, maneuvering onto the horse's rump. "But if you hadn't ridden our mare into the ground, you wouldn't be having to wrangle horses either, so there!"

Skips Along The Water spurred the horse into a gallop, and Cara latched onto her waist tightly, "We have time to make up if we are to get to your people before my brother catches up to us," she yelled, "so if I have to run another horse into the ground, I will!"

Cara understood her reasoning, but her curt attitude was beginning to wear thin. She also understood why she was behaving poorly—because this rescue attempt was proving more difficult than she thought it would be. She knew that Skips Along The Water probably thought it would be a simple three-day ride back to Martin's Landing where she could dump Cara at the edge of town, bid her a quick farewell, and be back to her people within another three days. It just hadn't turned out that way, and now they were a day behind of when they thought they'd arrive. She'd bitten off more than she could chew and it made her angry; an anger she was taking out on Cara.

Cara was hanging onto her own mental patience by a thin thread also, so could readily empathize with how Skips Along The Water was feeling. It was why she so easily snapped her retorts when the maiden snarled at her or made a snippy comment. She sighed. In another day or two, they would be back in Martin's Landing, and this whole nightmare would be behind them. Unless, of course her own people rejected her; or Casey wasn't there waiting for her, or if Skips Along The Water's people caught up to them first. Cara shuddered. None of those thoughts would result in a pleasant outcome, so she did what she could to shove them from consideration. Instead she attempted to dwell on something pleasant, as her mother taught her to do when she was a young child: kittens and puppies. Her mother would repeat that to her when she awoke from a nightmare, or fell down and skinned her knee: kittens and puppies.

She smiled at the memory, a thought she hadn't had since she was very little. *It's amazing what the mind conjures under stress*, she thought and then closed her eyes and tried to picture kittens and puppies playing in her parlor back home. *Perhaps I'll find a kitten and a puppy when I return.*

A sound reached her ears from far away, and the pleasant thoughts scattered, as if in fear; and that raised her hackles. She dared to glance over her shoulder and cried out, "Dear, sweet Jesus, no!"

Though the riders were still far distant away, Cara knew that the dust cloud meant horses, and horses riding fast enough to kick up that amount of dust, meant it could be no one other than her companion's people.

"Ride faster!" She screamed, causing Skips Along The Water to duck away.

"Why do you scream at me?" Skips Along The Water called over her shoulder.

"I'm sorry," Cara said loudly, "but you must make this horse go faster."

"What is it? What has happened?"

"I see riders in the distance," Cara announced, expecting Skips Along The Water to interpret her meaning, dig her heels into the horse's haunches, and coax more speed from the already rapidly-moving animal. That's what she expected, but it isn't what happened.

Skips Along The Water pulled on the animal's mane until it came to a halt.

"What are you doing? They're going to catch up to us. Move, horse, move!" Cara screeched, kicking at the horse's bottom, but Skips Along The Water was in control, not her, and with a resigned sigh, the maiden turned the beast toward the direction of the riders. "You can't be serious!" Cara yelled. "They'll kill us now, or do you think that they are just going to welcome us with hugs and kisses."

Skips Along The Water lowered her head and shook it slowly, spurring the horse into a canter, "There will be a price to pay for what we have done. I will suffer for my part, for you would not have left had I not come to get you. I will suffer more; and I will tell my brother that it was my doing, so he will not punish you too harshly for running away."

Cara's jaw dropped in disbelief. She couldn't believe they'd come this far only to fail.

"Skips Along The Water, we're so close. If you'll just turn us around, I know we can reach the safety of Martin's Landing before they reach us, I just know we can. Please, just turn this horse around. Please, I beg of you."

But Skips Along The Water was already shaking her head. She'd made up her mind and she cared not that Cara would suffer also as a result of that decision, but Cara cared. She could not face River Runner again. It was hard enough when he was kind and pleasant to her, but she shuddered to think of what life would be like now that he was enraged with her. The thought actually made her fear for her life and she began scanning the distance between where she sat and the ground below. *We aren't moving too fast*, she reasoned. *Perhaps it would be possible to leap and land without injury to myself.*

She had just about talked herself into taking the chance, when Skips Along The Water kicked the horse's haunches, sending it into a faster gait. Cara looked at the riders, fast approaching. It was easy to distinguish them now, and she knew, beyond a shadow of a doubt, that it was the Arapaho.

"Please, Skips Along The Water, listen to me. I understand that you think you have no choice but to return to your people. I understand that, I do. But you can't possibly expect to make that decision for me. I am not of your people..."

"You are River Runner's wife," Skips Along The Water rejoined, "and I was wrong to take you away from him."

"No! Remember Rankle? You said that I was right about that. That my being held captive by your brother was no different than you being held captive by Rankle. Remember? You agreed it was the right thing to do, to help me get back home. Listen to me! Please!" Cara's pleas were becoming more and more desperate, but everything she said fell on deaf ears.

"I was wrong, and I will not make that mistake again," Skips Along The Water said, her tone without inflection.

Cara closed her eyes to pray, but either God wasn't listening, or he didn't care what became of her, for when she next opened her eyes, the warriors were upon them.

River Runner and Soaring Eagle slid from their horses, and Skips Along The Water did also, moving quickly to place herself between her brother and Cara, speaking rapidly in her native tongue in the hopes of calming him before he reacted badly.

The anger in his head, clouded his hearing, and he shoved his sister aside brusquely before approaching the horse and pulling Cara down to the ground. She stumbled and fell, but had no time to regain her footing, for River Runner began dragging her to where he'd left his horse.

"Let me go!" She screamed, but ceased her yelling when she heard Skips Along The Water cry out in pain. It was hard to turn her head and see what was happening, but when she did, she began to cry in fear, and for her companion.

Soaring Eagle had pulled her over his legs and was whipping her hard on her bare bottom. The whacks on her skin were so loud that Cara cringed at each assault.

"Please make him stop," Cara cried, the moment River Runner yanked her from the ground to face him. "He's hurting her. Please, make him stop."

"Why should I listen to a lowly white woman?" River Runner snarled.

Cara closed her eyes and fought against the fear welling in her belly. Gone was the man she'd known for the last few months, and in his place stood a savage. It frightened her to her core. Still, the assault continued and it tore at Cara's heart; and she realized that had Skips Along The Water not come to her aid, she would not be suffering so now.

"I will take her place, just please make him stop," Cara whispered softly. Her eyes remained closed, for she was too afraid to look at the rage blazing in River Runner's eyes. Still, she knew if she could stand up to a man like Rankle and stop an injustice from happening, she could stand up to River Runner.

But Rankle didn't frighten her. River Runner did.

River Runner said something loudly in his native tongue, and the sounds of flesh striking flesh stopped. Cara drew in a deep, unsteady breath of relief, "Thank you."

"You will receive the remainder of her punishment, so do not thank me," River Runner replied, his tone menacing. He abruptly shifted to one knee and yanked Cara down and across it. With the speed of a viper, he tugged aside all barriers to her bare flesh, exposing her bottom. Without pause, he began striking her with the palm of his hand, hard and swift.

The first strike sent a shock through Cara's system so powerful that it sucked the breath from her lungs and she was unable to cry out, but it didn't stop the tears welling. The strike after felt as if someone pressed a hot poker against her flesh. She screamed, and her head began to swim.

After the fifth strike, she fell silent again. Her flesh became numb, as did her mind, drifting not away to kittens and puppies; rather to the day she stood against Rankle. She knew then, without reservation, she'd done the right thing, for if the pain felt from the strike of a hand was excruciating, she could only imagine the intensity of pain caused from the strike of a whip. What Skips Along The Water suffered strapped to the post that day made her struggles since a mere twinge by comparison; yet she knew she'd do it all again if it meant stopping the maiden from suffering more than she'd already done. She also knew that, if she didn't accept her fate, others could suffer. Her mind drifted to Casey and her heart began to pound in pain. He'd nearly died in his quest to save her from her captivity, and could die if he were to come for her again. Skips Along The Water suggested she needed to put the past behind her and accept what her life was meant to be now.

"Please," she whispered loudly, "I'll not leave again. Just please stop."

River Runner's hand paused in midair, the shock of her words drifting through to the haze in his brain. His jaw clenched tightly, but he accepted her words as truth and shoved her from his lap. She landed in a heap on the ground and stayed there, too drained to move.

A few minutes later, Skips Along The Water scooted up next to her, "I am sorry, Sister," she whispered, her voice still tinged with the pain of her own thrashing.

Cara sat up and wrapped the girl in her embrace and they hugged each other tightly, allowing the tears to flow unfettered.

"Do you think they'll stop hating us soon?" Cara asked, swiping at her nose. "Quite frankly, your brother is very scary when he's angry."

Skips Along The Water sniffled loudly and swiped at her own tears, "I do not know, but it is my hope. I, too, never wish to suffer their anger again."

Soaring Eagle approached and spoke to Skips Along The Water in their language. She nodded and then turned back to Cara, "It is time for us to return." The pain on her face and the tears welling in her eyes at the admission stabbed at Cara's heart.

"Do not weep for me. I will be okay," she assured her, but she'd changed so much in the last couple of months, and she wondered whether she would ever be the same again.

CHAPTER 33

"Cara should be here," Murph said sadly. "Nobody should be buried without family in attendance."

Governor Martini had suffered a heart attack in the doctor's office several days prior, and had not survived it. Casey awakened after falling from his cot to find himself lying next to his future father-in-law on the floor, the doctor seated next to them, his head hung in depressed resignation.

"Will he be okay?" Casey whispered.

The doctor shook his head, "You will. He won't." With a heavy sigh, the doctor got up off the floor and bent over Casey, "Let's get you back on the cot, and then I need to go get the undertaker."

A few days later, Casey stood beside his business partner, Murphy, and other members from the community, laying to rest their governor; an esteemed member of their society.

"It just ain't right," Murph reiterated.

"Murphy," Casey said softly, as the men carefully lowered the casket into the hole, dug only this morning, "as soon as we conclude this business, we need to discuss what's to be done about Cara."

"You don't think she's still alive, do you?" Murph asked, trying not to sound callous. "If the Arapaho sent her back like you said the warrior told you, she'd have been back by now. So, either the man was lying or Cara and her escort were attacked and killed coming back here; or the Arapaho killed her when...well, you know. Either way, it isn't likely after all this time that she's ever coming back. Don't you think?"

The people began singing Amazing Grace, which cut their conversation short. Casey didn't sing with the others. His mind was too preoccupied with how to go about finding his Cara—whether she was dead or alive, he needed to find her. He wouldn't be at peace until he knew.

The service concluded and the people began milling about, conversing in respectable tones. Members of the town congregated near the gravesite, murmuring in hushed tones and then moved over to where Casey was speaking to Murphy.

"Mr. Scott," an elderly, bespectacled man said softly, "we wish a word, sir."

Casey nodded, "What can I do for you, gentlemen?"

"As a man of high regard in our community, we would like you to consider taking up the post of governor. We are in need of strong leadership and can think of no one more suited to the post than you."

"This isn't exactly the time nor the place, gentlemen..."

"We are aware of our lack of decorum, and extend our apologies; but with so much happening of late, our concerns are great, and we fear that we may not have a better time or place in which to broach the subject. If you accept our offer, we would like you, Mr. Abernathy, to consider the post of chief magistrate, since that post would be vacated..."

"Whoa," Murph interjected. "I think perhaps Casey is right, gentlemen. While we appreciate your faith in us, this is neither the time nor the place."

The elder gentleman sighed, "Very well. Still, the seed is planted, and we hope to hear word soon..."

"I should let you know, before you get too set on our acceptance, that we intend to be gone for several weeks," Casey stated.

The eyes of each council member widened, and their spokesman sputtered, "But, who would there be to protect the citizens of Martin's Landing, sir? I fear without the assurance of strong leadership, people will move away, fearful of the future of our small town."

Casey and Murphy looked at each other and realized the council's fears were not unfounded. Many a town had suffered hardship because of lack of a firm leader to guide their way. Still, Casey could not accept any posting until he'd satisfied himself he'd done all he could to locate his fiancé. He said as much and the councilmen shook their head. In understanding or distress, he didn't know.

"I'll stay and stand in as magistrate," Murph offered. "Think any important decisions or paperwork can hold until Casey gets back?"

"Very good, sir, and yes, yes, we can postpone any township decisions until Mr. Scott's return," the elder man agreed readily, pumping Murphy's hand with exaggerated enthusiasm.

Reassured, the councilmen walked away. Casey turned back to Murphy, a look of incredulity on his face.

"What?" Murph exclaimed.

"Are you aware that you just committed us to serve in office without consulting me at all?" Casey snapped.

"You could have spoken up," Murph shrugged. "Besides, they're right, there isn't a better man for the job; and I'd make a really good magistrate..."

"And what about our business? Are we just going to let it fold?" Casey asked, trying to maintain his patience.

"Oh, well, since this ruckus started, I kind of hired out men to run the business for us," Murph admitted, scratching at the back of his neck sheepishly. "I would have told you sooner, but...well, you weren't exactly well enough, were you? And besides, when you aren't running the town, you can always keep yourself busy supervising the business."

Casey sighed, "I was kind of hoping to have you by my side in my search for Cara."

Murph laid a reassuring hand on Casey's shoulder, "I know, and I'm sorry. Still, you'll have some good men riding with you; fair with a gun. Just promise me that if you haven't found her in two weeks, you'll come back and get on with your life."

"You don't think I'll find her, do you?" Casey asked, dread shrouding his heart.

Murph shook his head and lowered his gaze, "I'm sorry, Casey. I just think that...well, she's one tough lady, and I think if she was alive, she would have found a way to get back to you."

"I was thinking along the same lines," Casey admitted softly, "but you know I've got to try. I can't just assume she's dead. She may be injured, laid up at a farmhouse somewhere, or...I just have to try. You understand?"

Murph nodded, "Yeah, I understand. We best get back to town, the men will be waiting to head out with you. They've been preparing the supplies while we took care of what was needed here. The sooner you head out, the sooner you get back."

"You have my word, Murphy, that in two weeks, I'll ride back under that town sign down there and put the past behind me. Hopefully with Cara by my side, but if not...well, I'll move on. You have my word."

"I know, Casey..."

"But I'm not doing this without you. You'll come with me. We can put one of the other men in charge as magistrate until you come back. I can't do this without you by my side."

"Casey..."

"I need you by my side, Murphy!"

Murphy nodded with a heavy sigh, "Understood. Let's get going, then."

CHAPTER 34

The trek back to the people passed in silence. Neither River Runner nor Soaring Eagle spoke to their women, still fuming over having to race to retrieve them. For Cara and Skips Along The Water, the silence was simultaneously deafening and welcomed. If the men responded to their queries, it would have been less deafening, but they ignored all attempts to communicate. Primarily it was Skips Along The Water who attempted to communicate with them, for Cara chose to spend the time in quiet meditation and reflection. She had fought against her place as River Runner's wife, but now the fight was over and she needed to come to terms with what was to be. The idea still chaffed at her, and it was this she worked to change during the trip back.

She'd been so deep in thought, that she didn't realize when the people came into view. They'd reached their winter grounds and were busily setting up their teepees next to a rapidly flowing river, which fought against freezing despite the dropping temperatures that signaled the coming winter.

"I need to wash," Skips Along The Water admitted when she spied the river. "Want to come with me?"

Cara nodded. Skips Along The Water was her only ally presently among a people that treated her with courtesy, but never bothered to speak directly to her. Skips Along The Water had told her early on that many didn't speak her language, most were too old to try to learn a new language; so if she were going to become a member of their tribe, she was going to have to make the effort to speak the language of the people.

"We will need to hurry. The men will expect us to get the teepees ready and our food cooked. The men will have to hunt quickly for food; they would have already done so had we been here as we should have been," she continued her self-chastisement, grabbing a change of clothes from her pack; items they never thought to bring along with them when they'd run away; items Cara never thought she'd see again. She pulled out one of the outfits she'd sewn before fleeing and sighed loudly. This was a skill she'd have to perfect now, eyeing the crooked seams critically.

"You will get better," Skips Along The Water assured her as if reading her mind. "Come, we smell bad. We will collect some bear berries to clean our hair, and then maybe clean our skin with some maize husks. It will feel good to be clean."

Cara smiled at her enthusiasm, but it wasn't a happy smile, rather a smile of resigned acceptance. She followed her, now-accepted-sister, to where the stores for the people were kept and watched as she located the supplies for bathing. She would need to know this now so she could bathe without having to rely on someone to come with her. Skips Along The Water was instructing her, as she always was, on how to find the right thing, "You want your hair shiny," she concluded, "not falling out by using the wrong thing."

When she'd collected their bathing supplies, they both moved to the water.

"This is going to be very cold," Skips Along The Water said, and she wasn't wrong. Cara squealed when her foot stepped in the river.

"How are we supposed to bathe in that? We'll be a block of ice before we're done." It was the most she'd said in many days and Skips Along The Water didn't miss that it was because she had a complaint to lodge.

"You must learn to be accepting of what is..."

"I know. You don't need to remind me again," Cara sighed. "Okay then, how do you propose we get in that frigid water to bathe?"

"Jump in and move fast."

"Yeah, right," Cara muttered, but it appeared that she wasn't joking.

She dove into the water, sputtering when she surfaced, "Hand me the berries," she said, her teeth chattering.

Cara sucked in a deep breath of determination and dove in, quickly swimming over to hand Skips Along The Water some of the berries. They both washed as quickly as they could, shedding their dirty clothes and tossing them on the riverbank. Within a few minutes, their extremities were numb, but they were clean again.

They climbed out and dressed quickly, then headed back to toward their respective teepees.

"You can clean and cook your meal?" Skips Along The Water asked, concern lacing her tone.

Cara sighed and nodded.

"Remember, the wild onions..."

"I know," Cara interrupted. "You taught me well. I'm no longer a useless white woman."

Skips Along The Water gave her a tight hug, "Maybe if the food is good, River Runner will not be angry anymore."

"It's going to take more than a good meal for him to forgive what we did," Cara said, wondering what precisely it would take.

"Be strong, Sister. All will be well."

"You too. Will I see you again after we eat?" Cara asked, realizing she was clinging to the only person within a hundred miles with whom she was close—as close as she could be, considering their differences.

"No. I will see you tomorrow. Tonight, I must work hard to make my husband happy again," Skips Along The Water stated with a sheepish grin, which made Cara smile; her first genuine smile in days.

When Cara made it to their area, she was surprised to see the teepee erected and two rabbits laid out by their fire pit, skinned and gutted; ready to cook. Even the sticks had been placed and needed only to be lit. She looked around, but could not see River Runner anywhere. She took the flint stones that Skips Along The Water had given her the first week with the people and quickly lit the fire; then speared the rabbits and hung them to cook. The fire felt so warm and inviting, that she was hesitant to walk away, but she needed the herbs to rub into the rabbits and some maize to roast.

Once dinner was underway, she settled onto the ground, allowing the heat to penetrate her bones, still frigid from her earlier bath. The smell of the food made her belly grumble loudly and she found it difficult waiting patiently for the meal to finish cooking. She was so hungry, she could eat it all raw.

"The food smells good."

The intrusion caused her to jump. She looked up to see River Runner watching her intently from the other side of the fire. He settled to the ground and sniffed at the food.

"You did good."

Cara swallowed and her breathing intensified. He was being nice again. Did that mean that he was no longer angry? She didn't know him well enough to know for certain. *Still, if he's making an effort, I guess I should too*, she thought, trying to force words to form.

"Thank you for getting things ready. Your sister and I really needed a bath..." she trailed off lamely, not knowing what to say to this man—her husband. Communicating with him was new and did not come as easily to her as it did with Casey. She lowered her gaze so he wouldn't see the sadness that suddenly enveloped her at the thought of her former fiancé.

"Yes, you both smelled like skunk," he replied and when Cara looked up quickly, prepared to verbally retaliate, she was taken aback again at how handsome he was when he smiled, as he was doing now.

"I suppose you think you're funny," she snapped lightly, standing to check their food. "Never mind, don't bother answering. I can tell you do. It's time to eat now," she said quickly, hoping to head off any more need to converse. It was too unnerving for her to pretend an affinity for him.

He stood quickly and handed her two wooden plates. She didn't know what to make of his desire to assist. It was as if he felt guilty over mistreating her and was trying to make amends; but did the native male truly ever feel guilty over his actions? She knew nothing about them beyond what she'd learned during her stay with them.

What she did know about River Runner was that he was fiercely protective of his people—both against perceived enemies and within the people themselves. She recalled his coming to the aid of the pregnant woman and her two children. He could have turned a blind eye and allowed the abuse to continue; in fact, she knew many white men who abused their families that were never interfered with. What did that say about the differences between her people and these?

She also knew that River Runner would go to the ends of the earth to retain possession of that which he thought to be his—namely her. Would Casey do the same? Was he out searching for her now, even as she sat dining with someone new? She looked across the fire and her breath caught in her throat. River Runner had finished his meal and was watching her with that stare of intensity that he reserved when he wanted to bed her.

"Finish your food, wife," he said simply and then fell silent. Cara did eat then, but slowly, the food getting repeatedly stuck on the lump in her throat. The moment the last of the food cleared her plate, River Runner stood and took it from her.

"I will wash these. You go prepare for bed."

He walked away, leaving her sitting there panicking; her brain conjuring all possible ideas of what took place in "bed". She'd felt his body next to hers many times; been on the receiving end of the strength of his passion. But they had yet to consummate in the way that a husband and wife were meant to. The thought terrified her. Of course, the thought of mating with any male terrified her, including Casey; but with Casey she wanted to experience it, terror and all; wanted to know if it felt as good as his caress and his kiss.

River Runner, on the other hand, was all-consuming in his desires and it left her breathless, uncertain what to feel. Would his mating with her be as forceful and extreme as his introduction to lovemaking had been in the woods? As with conversation, she didn't know him well enough to engage fully, and that was most terrifying of all. What did he expect from her?

Her brain jarred at the word "expect", for she knew that he expected her to be in his bed upon his return from the river and here she still sat, stewing in fear and apprehension. She stood abruptly and headed inside the teepee, but stopped short of shedding her clothing. It was expected she sleep unclothed, but tonight was different; tonight the expectation of what was to come was too great for her to bear, and she stood rooted, staring down at their sleeping mat.

She jumped when she felt his hands on her shoulders and she closed her eyes, working hard to maintain level breathing.

"Do not fear me," he whispered next to her ear, then bent and nipped her neck. "I will never hurt you again. My honor." He slid his tongue along the flesh of her neck and then nipped her gently on the shoulder, causing the sparks to fire in her brain. Whatever this man was to her, he was adept at lovemaking, and Cara was helpless to fight against the feelings he ignited.

He continued to kiss and nip her exposed flesh, while his hands slid around her waist and up to cup her breasts; kneading them firmly, pinching gently at the nipples until they awoke beneath his ministrations. Cara moaned loudly and her head fell backwards, landing against his chest.

He continued his assault, sliding his hands beneath her dress to stroke her abdomen, his fingers like butterfly wings against her flesh. She shivered and her knees weakened. His hands moved upward, pulling her dress up and over her head; and he met little resistance when he pressed his chest into her back, moving her gently toward the mat.

With firm pressure against her belly, he bent her at the waist, holding tight as she collapsed face first onto the bedding. He quickly shed his clothing and slid atop her, moving with snake-like ease from her legs, across her bottom, his flesh caressing her flesh. When his face reached hers, he lie his weight atop her and heard her breath whoosh from her body.

She groaned loudly when his teeth nipped at her ear, and then at her neck, sliding further down to run his tongue along her spine. He heard her gasp and smiled. As his tongue worked its way along her bottom, he slowly maneuvered himself to a kneeling position, then clasped her hips firmly, pulling her to her knees, slowly lowering her hips until she settled pliantly atop his member.

His hands slid from her waist and around to her thighs, tugging lightly until they parted, allowing him to slide inside of her fully. He took his time, slipping into her moist warmth with little hurry, until he could press no further; then he went still. His eyes closed against the throbbing pain and he wanted nothing more than to withdraw and slam into her over and over until he reached his release; but he wanted her to remember her first time with him; with any man. He wanted her so full of need that instinct kicked in and she started to move with him.

It didn't take long.

She groaned at his going motionless and instinctually rocked backward, causing her to gasp at the pressure filling her. Still, he didn't move, but her action did cause him to release a groan of his own.

"Please," she whispered. She didn't know what it was she was seeking, but she knew she hadn't found it yet. She pushed her hips back again and the lights fired in her brain.

"Oh ..." she murmured and pushed into him again. This time she heard the moan he emitted and it registered somewhere within the fog that what she did must feel good to him too.

He allowed her to rock against him a few more times and then he clasped hold of her hips, held her firmly in place, and withdrew, returning inside with a firmness that caused lights to flash in her eyes; caused her to cry out. This is what he'd done with her in the woods, with his fingers. He'd driven her to the brink of madness. But his fingers did not fill her as he was filling her now; they did not reach as deeply into her womanhood as now, when he retreated and slammed into her again. He stole her breath away as he penetrated deeper and deeper with each thrust, until she felt him stiffen; then she felt an unfamiliar moisture enter her womb. Just as she moved toward unconsciousness, he released his grip and she slipped back down onto the mat, her body completely incapable of movement. She was only barely aware that he slid down to lie beside her, and then she was floating away in the arms of slumber.

CHAPTER 35

It had been a week of tracking every possible route from the Arapaho summer grounds to Martin's Landing; every conceivable way in which they could have traversed when returning Cara—if they'd been truthful about having set her free; having sent her home. If something happened to her along the way, wouldn't the warriors have been capable of defending her? If she'd died, wouldn't they have sent word so that he'd know and stop searching? Would there not be a trace of her remains anywhere if she had met an untimely demise?

The other option was the threat that was made were he to fail and not return within the given time frame. He'd been told that she would die. Had they killed her then, and lied to prevent being attacked? They certainly seemed to go out of their way to ensure the people in Martin's Landing were informed of how cooperative they'd been in the search for Rankle, so that there would be no chance of retaliation. Still, if they didn't want retaliatory action, why threaten to kill her at all? Could it have been a ruse to ensure his compliance; to ensure that Rankle was found and killed? If that were true, then it was highly feasible that the warrior was telling the truth and she'd been set free to return home.

"So then why didn't she make it?"

"What'd you say, Casey?" Carl asked.

Casey shook his head, "I'm just trying to reason out why Cara never made it back to Martin's Landing. There's just no reason why she shouldn't have, especially if she had an escort to guide and protect her."

It was nearing late November now and there was a dusting of snow on the ground, which was making it more difficult to track any activity that would have taken place in October. Carl said as much and then added, "I'm not certain we'd be able to find any sign of her anyway, Casey. I mean, realistically, we can follow predetermined pathways, but that doesn't mean the warriors did. There are hundreds of square miles between Martin's Landing and the tribe..."

"I get your meaning, Carl. I do. I just couldn't bear the thought of giving up without knowing for sure."

"I'd do the same, if it were my woman," Carl sighed, "but we have to face the reality that she may still be with the tribe. They may never have released her. Cara is a beautiful woman; and forgive me for saying, but she'd be mighty hard to resist."

Casey drew in a deep breath and let it out slowly. He'd thought the same, but dismissed it because he couldn't come close to dwelling on the notion that his Cara was still a captive of the Arapaho. Carl was right though, she is beautiful, and it may have been difficult for the male members of the tribe to overlook that beauty.

"Damnation!" Casey exclaimed loudly, shaking his head. "I can't believe...I just can't..."

"I have a thought, if you're willing to hear me out," Murphy offered.

Casey nodded, rubbing his hand wearily across his chin.

"Me and the men continue riding north..."

"It's going to be snowing heavy soon. You'd never make it back to Martin's Landing before..."

"We ride hard. Can't be more than a week out and back," Murphy continued. "We confirm whether Cara is with the Arapaho."

"I don't understand," Casey replied in exaggeration. "What good will confirmation do, if you can't take her out of there and get her home. In two weeks, the plains could very well be impassable; you'd be lucky to get back with news, whether good or bad. And let's say it's good, and she's there. It'll be spring before we could mount a rescue operation..."

"I ain't saying a winter rescue would be easy. Ah, Hell, Casey, I don't even know whether we'd be able to snatch her from under the noses of the Arapaho. I'm just saying that, if you want us to try to get your woman back, we're willing to try. Who knows, God may just grant us a reprieve from the snows until we return, yeah?"

"If you're going, I'm going with you," Casey asserted.

"No," Murphy said, shaking his head emphatically.

"Why in Hell not?"

"Because they know you. If they get sight of you heading toward their camp, they're going to know what you're after. They see us, and all we are to them are passersby; ranchers or settlers. They won't have no cause to think otherwise. You know I'm right."

"Y'all had dealings with them too, remember? When Cara was taken? You think they aren't going to recognize any of y'all?"

"We weren't with them that long to make an impression. Likely they won't remember us anymore than we'll recognize them. You go on back to Martin's Landing and keep busy. If she's there, we'll know for a fact, soon enough, whether we'll be able to take her out safely; and if possible, we'll head for the nearest town to fire off a telegram to you. Hell, if the plains become impassible, we may have to hunker down in the nearest town until spring. Which means...we're going to need coin."

Casey laughed humorlessly and dug out his wallet, "For an off-the-cuff plan, you sure sound as if you've been giving this a lot of thought."

Murphy chuckled, "Nah, I just know what I'd do if it was me going after mine. I'd cross through Hell itself."

"You go up against Arapaho warriors and you may just find yourself there."

"There's plenty of daylight left, so we're going hit the trail. You head back. I'll let you know something within the next week or so. If you haven't heard anything by Christmas, you'll know to bury a few empty coffins along with an empty one for Cara."

"Don't say that, Murphy," Casey protested.

"I'm serious, because the only way you won't hear from me by then, is if I'm lying dead somewhere. Same goes for the rest of the men. And if we're lying dead somewhere, that means we crossed on the wrong end of some arrows."

"God go with you, Murphy," Casey said, clasping the man's hand firmly. "I won't ever be able to repay you for this kindness. I'll owe you a debt for the rest of my life."

Murphy nodded solemnly, "Let's just cross that bridge when we come to it. Find a fat turkey for Christmas. God willing, we'll all be joining you at the dinner table for some raucous celebrating." Murphy nodded, smiled, then turned his horse toward the north, whistling to the others to follow suit.

Casey turned the nose of his stallion to the south and said a prayer that his men would find Cara, and when they did, they'd get her out and get her home.

"Please, God. Let her be safe."

CHAPTER 36

Three days in, the snows started, a light flurry disconcerting to the men who'd prayed hard for clear skies and fair weather. Murphy started grumbling beneath his breath as the winds gusted and subsided repeatedly. When gusting, it felt as if God were slapping at his face with frosty gloves, challenging his manhood; his ability to withstand the assault. He pulled his hat down low on his brow and his collar higher up on his neck; then shifted the bandana from around his neck to cover his nose and mouth. It was the best he could accomplish short of finding cover somewhere; time he wouldn't waste as long as he was able to see far enough ahead to stay on track.

He glanced over his shoulder at the men. All had followed suit and had hunkered down as much as was possible on the back of a steed. As the day turned into night and the fourth day of their trek began, the sun peered over a clear horizon, promising a brighter day.

It was early afternoon when they reached a stream and Murphy called the procession to a halt, "We need to afford the horses a rest. Dismount!"

The men, used to riding for shorter stints, groaned with stiffness as they slid from their saddles. They led their horses over to the stream to eat and drink, pulling their own meal from their saddle bags. They wanted to settle down to rest, but the ground was soggy with partially melted snow, and wet trousers made for an uncomfortable sit in the saddle.

"We should find the tribe in the next day or two," Murphy said, moving over to eat with the men, "so we need to formulate a plan on what to do if we spot Cara."

"If it were me, I'd just ride in and ride out with her," Carter quipped and everyone shook his head and sighed simultaneously.

"Okay, now for serious suggestions, please," Murphy said. "I gave Casey some mighty high hopes that we'd do what we could to get Cara back..."

"If she's even there," George said softly. "I mean, we're risking frostbite and death by Arapaho on a "maybe"".

"Yeah, and before we set off, Casey told each and every one of us that we didn't have to come, so stop your jawing," Luke snapped. "Now, Murphy is right, we need to know how to proceed once we run into the tribe. We have to seem like we're just passing through. They've been known to host white travelers, so maybe we can appeal to them to let us stay for a meal. Maybe we can poke around a bit..."

"Okay, so that'll be our first course of action," Murphy interjected. "We'll see about getting into the main tribal area to see if Cara is even there. If she is, we'll need to know how to proceed. We need to get back to moving, so if anyone comes up with a rescue plan, ride up and let me know. Let's ride."

The ride had been incident free through the next night and by midday on day five, the group topped a small rise to see the activity of a tribe in the distance. They pulled up beside each other, looking over at Murphy for guidance; everyone nervous at the prospect of riding into an Arapaho camp; knowing they didn't have much in the way of a choice.

"Okay," Murphy sighed, drawing a deep, nerve-balancing breath, "it's important we don't give away our fear or our intent. They sense something off, and we'll likely be served to their dogs for dinner. Got that, everybody? We're just passing through."

"How do we know that this is even the right tribe?" George asked.

"We don't, but it's likely, since this is the direction the Arapaho traveled to their winter grounds. It isn't like we'd run into a dozen tribes in the area. They tend to give each other a wide berth. Now, we can sit here devising ways to postpone heading down there, or we can just get it over and done with." Murphy clicked his tongue and headed down the small hill toward what he hoped wasn't his imminent demise. He didn't look behind, knowing that the other men would have followed. If not, he'd borrow a bow and shoot them himself.

"Warriors headed this way," Carter called from behind him, confirming he wasn't alone. He'd seen the warriors headed toward his position and his skin crawled thinking the men would desert him. He sighed loudly, thankful they weren't cowardly.

The men drew closer together, a mere foot in distance between each horse.

"Remember what I said," Murphy said, just as the warriors halted in front of them. He smiled at the Arapaho and hoped he didn't look like a complete fool, "Hi, um. We're glad to see some folks out this way. We got a bit turned around...um, do any of you speak English?"

One of the warriors nodded stiffly.

"Excellent!" Murphy exclaimed. "Glad to hear it. Which tribe are y'all?" He tried to make the question as innocuous as possible, but they needed to know that he'd been right about his assumptions that this was the tribe they were seeking.

"We are the Arapaho," the English speaker announced proudly.

Murphy nodded, keeping his facial expressions blank, "Nice to make your acquaintance. Anyway, as I was saying, we got ourselves turned around a bit, and haven't seen hide nor hair of anyone in days. We're a bit trail weary, if you must know. Do you think your chief would object to hosting a meal for some weary travelers? We'd be happy to conduct some trade in exchange for a hot meal."

"Stay. We will speak with our chief." The English speaker spoke a few words to the other warriors and then turned and headed back to the camp.

"Um, do any other of y'all speak English?" Murphy asked, but his question was anything but benign. He needed to know if he would be free to speak to his men without revealing anything to the warriors. They all just sat staring at them, gazes blank. Not a one registered recognition at his words, so he felt safe assuming they couldn't understand him. Still he needed to be cautious, "So, what do we have to trade?" He asked. "That offer was shot from the hip, and I admit to not thinking it through."

"I think we can scrape together a few things. I have a shaving mirror," Carter offered.

"Yeah, me too," George said.

"I have an extra pistol," Luke stated and everyone gave him a look as if he was insane.

"I'm not certain it's a good idea to arm one of them," Murphy replied.

"It's something they will receive well," Luke persisted, "and it ain't as if they aren't already armed. One pistol won't make a difference."

"Okay, well, we'll hold it in reserve if they look for more than the shaving mirrors," Murphy said, nodding thoughtfully.

After half-hour, nerves getting twitchier, Murphy began to think that they weren't going to be welcomed, but then the warrior returned and bade them follow.

"Okay," Murphy said softly, "play it cool everybody, and keep your eyes open."

"I'm thinking that if they have white women, they aren't going to parade them in front of us," George whispered. "So, eyes open or not, how are we going to confirm if she's here? We aren't exactly going to be able to go teepee to teepee..."

"We'll cross that bridge when we get to it," Murphy interjected. He'd had the same concern from the moment that he offered to go on this ridiculously perilous mission; but he'd been sincere when he'd told Casey that he'd do everything possible, as if it were his own in harm's way. He didn't know how he was going to find Cara if the Arapaho kept her hidden, but if it meant asking for a moment to relieve himself every few minutes to go snoop around, then that's precisely what he'd do. That still didn't solve the problem of what to do if they found her, but as far as he was concerned, this was a think-by-the-seat-of-your-pants undertaking to begin with, so he really meant it when he said he'd cross that bridge when it came up.

The children, unused to seeing too many white people, ran up to the horses, laughing. As far as they were concerned, any person invited in by their elders meant it was safe to approach them; and approach they did. As soon as the men dismounted, they looked at each with wide eyes, as if expecting to be given something.

Murphy shrugged, "Got anything suitable for a kid?" He whispered, and each started patting pockets. Before it became an embarrassment of nothing to give, River Runner approached and shooed the children away.

He nodded to each, his eyes seeking their leader. Murphy recognized the look and stepped forward, "I'm Murphy," he said, extending his hand. River Runner just looked at it.

"I am River Runner, chief of the Arapaho. Welcome to our village. Come. The women are working on preparing food. You will dine with us."

"Much appreciated," Murphy said, thrilled to hear they wouldn't be hiding the women. That didn't mean that they wouldn't be hiding any white women though.

River Runner led them through the camp and waved to sit around an open community fire near the center. The women—all native—bustled around them, preparing meat and maize.

"What has brought you here with winter fast approaching?" River Runner asked, and Murphy didn't miss the tone of suspicion.

"We're family. We buried our parents not long ago," Murphy weaved his off-the-cuff story, knowing that any mention of family would put these people at ease. At least he'd heard that family was important to native people. "My brothers and I decided to head out this way to seek new opportunities and...well, being unfamiliar, we got turned around a bit. Do you happen to know which direction the nearest town is? How long a ride?"

River Runner nodded, "There is a town in that direction," he said, pointing slightly northwest, "about two days ride. It is small, but you will not make it further before the winter snows close the way."

"That's good to know, and I certainly appreciate you pointing us toward a place we can hole up for a while. We were hoping to make it to a place called Martin's Landing. Do you know of it?" Murphy kept working to keep his tone as bland as possible, but he needed to gauge the man's reaction and had to prevent a smile forming when River Runner's gaze widened.

The chief nodded slightly and pointed southerly, "It is four or fives days ride, depending on how fast you are on horseback. It will not be safe to ride so far with winter coming. The plains will be horse deep in snow soon. Did you not come from that direction?"

Murphy shook his head, "We came from that way," he said, pointing east. "If we'd veered more southerly, we may have run across Martin's Landing, but apparently we veered more northerly."

River Runner nodded solemnly, "There is not much snow now," he said. "You may be able to get to this place if you ride fast, but your horses may not if they have come so far already. They will be tired."

Murphy nodded, "We have been riding a fair bit for many days. Perhaps we can bunk down here tonight and leave at first light? Give the horses time to rest? That will make it easier to push and make it to Martin's Landing before the plains become impassable."

River Runner pursed his lips, "I will think on this. For now, we will eat. If you will excuse me, I must take food to my wife. She is not well and cannot join us. I will return in a moment. The maidens will serve you."

He collected a plate from his sister, stood, and walked toward his teepee. Five maidens held out plates with food. Murphy politely acknowledged, but his gaze glanced sideways, watching where River Runner went, careful to denote the location. A shiver had crawled along his spine at the mention of River Runner's wife, and his stomach sank. Something in his gut told him that River Runner's "wife" was Cara. As chief he would have first choice of any white woman to enter their village. At least he figured he would. But his gut wasn't fact and he needed to be sure before placing his men at risk.

"Think that the chief's woman is Cara?" Carter asked quietly, biting into his deer meat.

Murphy nodded, "I was thinking along those lines, yes. The problem is, how to go about finding out for certain."

"I think one of us should excuse himself to go for a piss. Maybe duck behind the chief's teepee for privacy?" Luke suggested. "Then we can call through the teepee. If it's Cara, she can let us know..."

"And if it isn't, the maiden may raise an alarm," Carter concluded.

"Well, if that happens, then the person who decides to go can just say he was talking to himself during...well, you know," George interposed. "The only thing we got to decide on is who's going."

"And what to do if she is in there," Carter added. "This plan has more holes than Swiss cheese. It's like we've been flying by the seat of our pants since we started..."

"And I told you, you cawing over it ain't exactly helpful," Murphy interrupted, "so why not set your brain to helping and turn off the complaining. Between the five of us, we should be able to come up with some type of plan. We've gotten this far, haven't we?" The men nodded in unison. "Right, so I think maybe I should be the one to go," Murphy said, then fell silent when he saw River Runner returning. The look on his face showed signs of displeasure and he wondered whether Cara was giving him grief over being made to hide away while the white men were there. The Cara he knew would be raising a ruckus for certain. She didn't like anyone ordering her about. He couldn't stop the smile forming at the thought.

River Runner settled nearby and accepted a proffered plate, digging into his food in silence; obviously deep in thought.

"Your wife feeling okay? You look a mite concerned," Murphy asked, again attempting to feign a cross between indifference and sincerity.

River Runner nodded briefly and returned his attention to his plate. In fact, his wife had given him grief at not being permitted to dine outside of the teepee simply because of the presence of white men.

"Why should they care about the color of my skin?" Cara snapped, taking the plate of food and setting it next to the mat.

"I will not have them telling others that you are here!" River Runner said sharply. *"I will not lose you!"*

"You think that it would be possible for anyone to take me away?" Cara replied, equally sharp. *In the back of her mind she was eager to make an appearance in the hopes these men would notify the army and they would come for her, yet at the same time, she knew that any attempt to remove her from River Runner could result in all-out war. Still, it gnawed at her that she was being forced to stay hidden and she was never one to be forced into anything...until now, she thought, and her shoulders drooped.*

River Runner took her into his embrace and kissed her hair lightly, *"Stay here, wife. I will return soon."*

The meal ended in silence. The women collected the plates and moved to the river to wash up.

River Runner stood, "We will keep the fire going and you may bed down here for tonight. The women will locate skins for you to cover yourselves with. It will be very cold tonight."

"Much obliged, but um, I was wondering if I could speak with you for a few minutes before you retire for the night?" Murphy asked quickly, realizing that he'd not excused himself at dinner; not that he'd had much chance, since the entire dinner was abbreviated.

"What is it you wish to speak on?" River Runner asked, impatience in his tone. Still, as chief, he was required to be at the disposal of his guests, even if he didn't want to be.

George caught the diversionary tactic and spoke up, "I need to excuse myself," he said, working hard to look sheepish.

River Runner shook his head and sighed, but waved him away before turning back to Murphy. The other men moved toward their horses, but Murphy stalled them, "If the women are going to the trouble to find us blankets, then we should respect that and not pull out our own bedding." It was code for "we may have to ride out fast, so don't unpack anything". The men received the message loud and clear and settled back down by the fire. Murphy turned back to River Runner.

"You have been very kind, and I want to extend our gratitude," Murphy started. "But could you be a mite bit more specific as to how to reach Martin's Landing?"

"It is not hard to find," River Runner stated, walking towards the edge of the camp. Murphy fell into step beside him. "If you point your horses straight toward this direction," he said, again pointing south by southwest. "If you keep the sun to your left in the morning and to your right toward nightfall, you will come across the town you seek within five sunsets."

"Excellent, um, I know this might be a sensitive question, but better to be safe than sorry, so, um...well...do you know if we might encounter other tribes that might not prove as friendly..."

River Runner had already begun shaking his head, "We are the only tribe near to the town you seek and many of the people there we count as friends."

"Well, that's wonderful to hear. I certainly hope that we can be counted as friends too," Murphy said enthusiastically.

River Runner nodded, "I will count you among those with whom we may trade in future. For now, I must return to my wife."

"I understand, and thank you for speaking with me."

When they turned to head back to the camp, he saw George seated by the fire with the other men. His back was tense, which meant something had happened.

"We'll be leaving before sunup," Murphy said impulsively, "so I will wish you farewell now. It was a pleasure making your acquaintance."

River Runner nodded, "Safe journeys."

The two parted ways and Murphy settled near to his men, each accepting a buffalo hide from one of the women. They spread them out close to each other before settling back down. When everyone had headed to his or her teepee for the night, Murphy quickly turned to George.

"What did you find out?"

"Cara's here," George whispered hoarsely. "I didn't really think we'd find her," he admitted.

"Now what do we do? Go notify the army?" Luke asked.

"I told their chief we'd be leaving before sunup," Murphy sighed. "I wanted to give us a chance to be well away before anyone woke; preferably with Cara in tow."

"Yeah well, she may have gotten the impression we're here to rescue her," George said, uncertainty lacing his tone. "I just couldn't reveal our appearance and then leave her hanging, wondering whether we would take her home."

"Yeah, but since we're completely unaware of precisely how we're going to accomplish that, and Murphy told the chief we're leaving before sunup," Luke snapped nervously, "how are we going to accomplish a rescue?"

All the men fell silent, each trying desperately to formulate a workable escape plan, but with Cara sleeping beneath their chief's nose, it wasn't like they could just stroll in and snatch her away.

"Anybody got any brilliant ideas?" Murphy asked, desperately.

Everybody shook their heads.

Murphy sighed, "Maybe y'all should try to get some sleep. It's a long ways to us leaving and we're going to need some rest. Maybe with a couple of hours sleep under our belt, an idea will come to us."

"I can't sleep," Carter admitted, "not knowing that Cara is less than a hundred feet away and in the clutches of a savage."

"I can't either," George admitted. "My head's too messed up right now to think straight too."

"Okay, well, sleep if you can. I'll try to keep thinking of something," Murphy said, and then everyone fell silent again.

CHAPTER 37

Cara was still pacing when River Runner ducked into their teepee.

"Why are you still clothed, wife? It is time for us to sleep." River Runner walked up and pulled Cara into his embrace, holding her tight against him.

"I'm too tense, River Runner. I am not ready to be abed yet; and I'm too chilly to remove my clothing tonight."

"Hmm, you are disagreeable this night. Is it because of the white men?"

"I'd rather not talk about that," Cara said, attempting to pull from River Runner's embrace, but he held fast. "I am not going to release you so stop fighting me."

His words held double meaning for Cara and she stopped squirming, sighing loudly.

"Better," River Runner praised, lowering his head to kiss her on her neck. "And since you are not sleepy," he continued, his tongue moving from her neck to her ear, "I will find a way to make you drowsy." His teeth nipped at her ear, but Cara was too tightly wound to succumb to his seductions.

"Please, don't. I do not wish your attention tonight."

"You may not wish it, but you will not deny me," River Runner said sharply and pushed her down onto her knees, kneeling behind her. Having the white men in his camp, so close to his teepee made him tense and he knew of no better way to relieve that tension; and her rejection only made him more frustrated and more determined that neither would allow the white men to keep her from him.

He reached around and cupped her breasts, kneading hard and pinching her nipples even harder. Before she could cry out, one of his hands reached up and clamped over her mouth, so that all that escaped was a muffled yelp. He held firm to her mouth as she squirmed against his assault on her breasts.

"I will cease when you submit," River Runner said in a whisper next to her ear and she immediately went still. River Runner grinned humorlessly, and then bent her at the waist, quickly moving aside their clothing so that he could access her with ease.

He positioned himself behind her and then bent over her, placing his hands on either side of her head, "You will not yell out," he commanded and Cara felt tears prick. She didn't know what he intended to do, but his tone was ominous and it worried her. Prior to now, he'd made love to her, building her ecstasy along with his until they both reached release. His demeanor tonight was different; it was if he wanted to punish her for the white man's presence. She pressed her face into the furs, muting her shrieks of discomfort as he slammed into her over and over. She felt his release enter her womb and sighed with relief. The battering had been short lived.

Without further acknowledgement of her presence, he rolled over onto his side, facing away from her, and was asleep within minutes. She remained where she was for over an hour, listening to his resonant snore. It hadn't escaped her notice that he'd been too angry to pull her into his embrace; a feeling she'd come to realize was more an imprisonment to ensure she didn't sneak off into the night.

For another hour, she sat mulling over what that meant. Was he so certain he'd hear her if she moved; so arrogant that she'd never attempt to escape again that he felt there was no longer a need to trap her within his arms at night? Was he so certain that she'd come to accept her place as his wife that she would not even consider leaving again? But she was considering it, especially since there were men outside who were there to take her home.

Home.

Casey.

That had her sitting for a while longer, worrying over whether Casey would have her now that she'd been defiled by another. The stories of rejection slammed through her mind repeatedly causing as much pain as River Runner's lovemaking had been.

She drew in a slow breath, worried that the slightest sound would waken River Runner. With as much stealth as she could manage, she slid to her knees and then slowly to her feet; pausing repeatedly to listen for his snoring. She tiptoed from the tent, her heart thudding loudly in her ears.

If he hears me, I'll simply tell him I had woman's business to tend to, she thought, moving as slowly and silently toward the campfire, now dwindling, as she could manage. The men saw her approach and stood quickly, and just as quickly she placed a finger on her lips to prevent them speaking. If the talking, even quietly, didn't wake River Runner, it may very well wake someone closer by. She kept walking past them and straight for where their horses were resting.

In continued silence, she lifted the reins of one of the horses, indicating that they were to walk with them. Murphy nodded, knowing that the sound of horses galloping away could very well alert the entire tribe to their intent. Murphy took the reins from her and nodded, then started walking, praying all the while that none of the horses would let loose a whinny. They needed complete silence.

Half-hour later, they reached the knoll that they'd sat on earlier when they'd located the tribe. As soon as they topped that gentle rise, Murphy spoke up quietly.

"We need to know which way to head. I'm of mind the head due west."

"What?" George asked, incredulous. "What's due west?"

"I don't know, but I do know that the chief of this people will send men to look for us both northwest and en route to Martin's Landing. Those are where known civilization is to these people and it's where he'll assume we'll head. When we reach a town, we'll hunker down and wait for word from Casey that the coast is clear. If we can get somewhere before the winter's snow hits, we may just be in the clear. The natives won't be able to track us in the snow and are likely to give up the chase if we aren't where they expect us to be, or if they can't find us before the plains get snowed under."

"How will Casey know where to find us?" Carter asked.

"Because you're going to ride Hell bent for Martin's Landing and tell him, that's why, but I don't want you taking the direct route," Murphy said firmly, his meaning clear. If he rode straight back, he may easily be overtaken by the Arapaho, if they send men to look for Cara. "Now go. And remember, tell Casey we're headed due west and the first town we come to is where we'll be holed up. If there's a telegraph office there, I'll wire as soon we get settled."

Carter mounted and spurred his horse into a gallop, his nerves firing nervously. He knew that Murphy was right about taking a different route, but he was alone and scared that he'd get lost.

"I'll just ride fast and hard and won't rest until I get there. The Arapaho won't be able to catch me," he said to himself and then bent over his horse's neck, encouraging him into great speed.

Murphy watched Carter ride off and then pulled out his watch, "Okay, it's about six hours to sunrise. We're going to have to put considerable distance between here and anywhere pretty fast. Cara, you're with me. Let's get out of here."

"Cara, I need to lift you up, okay?" Murphy said as a way of apology for having to put his hands on her.

Cara nodded and fought back tears at his gentlemanly conduct, something she'd not been the recipient of for quite some time.

When she was settled, Murphy jumped up and settled in the saddle, "You're going to have to hold tight, Cara. We're going to be riding pretty fast and I don't want you slipping off."

"I understand," she murmured, wrapping her arms around his waist. "Murph?"

"Yeah?"

"Why didn't Casey come for me?"

"Because these people know his face and he didn't want to risk your life."

"Ah, okay."

"Ready to go now?"

"Yes, please."

Victim of Love Barbara Woster

Murphy held back his natural instinct to yell out his command, instead silently spurring his horse into a gallop with his boots and reins. Cara held on tight, but refused to release her built-up tension, because she knew, no matter which way they rode, it was possible for River Runner to track her.

As the snow began to fall, the tension slowly left her body. Not even River Runner's best warriors would be able to find them if the snow covered their tracks. She released a long, heavy sigh and laid her head on Murphy's back, tears of joy and relief slipping down her cheeks.

She was going home, at last.

CHAPTER 38

For only the second time, River Runner woke and discovered his woman not asleep by his side. The first time, his sister had done the unthinkable and stolen her away; determined that she should be returned to the white man. They both had suffered greatly when River Runner and his warriors caught up to them. Suffered so that River Runner doubted their either would ever attempt to leave again.

That thought brought him a modicum of peace. *She wouldn't dare attempt to flee again*, he thought smugly. He stretched and then flung the skins aside, a shiver racing through his body as the frigid morning air assailed his flesh. He pulled on his leggings and moccasins, then wrapped a lighter skin around his shoulders. When he stepped outside there was several inches of snow on the ground.

As he trudged toward the community fire, he stopped suddenly, turning to gape at the trail of footprints in his wake. His were the first to lead away from his teepee.

He turned back rapidly, his gaze frantically searching the faces among those already gathered for the morning meal. None of the white men were present, nor did he see Cara. His breathing intensified and a sense of panic pressed firmly on his chest.

Wait! The white man said they would be leaving before the sunrise, so Cara must be gathering food or water or perhaps she's visiting Skips Along The Water. Just then his sister rounded the corner, her arms laden with food she planned to cook for her and her new husband. He hadn't spoken to her in weeks; not since she absconded with his woman, but now he needed answers.

"Sister, have you seen my wife?"

"Oh, so now I'm your sister again, Brother?" She snapped scornfully.

"I do not have time for your foolishness. Have you seen Cara?"

"No," she answered tersely and then moved to pass him.

She really hadn't seen Cara, and her curiosity was great as to where she could be, but she wouldn't seek to assuage that curiosity with her brother. He'd behaved badly and she would only converse with him when he spoke to her. In her eyes, he had behaved no better than the man named Rankle. Cara had been right: her brother was holding her against her will, forcing her to be what she did not wish to be. He had once been a good man in her eyes; a man of honor, but he'd changed when he brought the white woman among the people. He was no longer the brother she once knew.

River Runner dismissed his sister's petulance and began to search everywhere, but no one had seen Cara since before the white man's arrival. River Runner closed his eyes as the truth assaulted his senses— she'd gone with the white man. She'd run away again.

"Well, I warned her that what belongs to me will never be taken from me," he growled, then went to find Crazy Beaver and Runs With Deer.

"We must go," he said as soon as he found them. "The white man has deceived us and have stolen my wife. We will go find them. This time, we will show no mercy."

The two warriors looked at each other concernedly, then Crazy Beaver spoke up, "Perhaps it's best that she's gone. If they were unafraid and came among the people to steal her away, then it would be dangerous for us to go after them. Unless they went back to her home, we will not be able to track them; or did you not see the snow that now covers the ground?"

"I saw it, but we don't need to track anyone. We know they will return to her home, but there is only one place other that is nearby that they may try to hide. The white man was asking about it last night. Runs With Deer will take a warrior and go northwest to the small town. They have allowed us to enter there before, so they should allow us to enter again. Look around quickly and return. If they are not there, then there is only one other place they would go—Martin's Landing."

"The winter snows are upon us. We will never be able to ride safely. The horses will move slowly as the snows deepen. We have never ridden far when the snows come; yet now you ask us to risk our lives for a woman? If your woman is gone, perhaps the Great Spirit willed it to be.

You have not been yourself since you brought her here. Now that she is gone, maybe you will see your people again."

That comment stopped River Runner in his tracks, but even if what Runs With Deer said was true, he could not allow the white man to steal what was his and said as much.

Crazy Beaver nodded, "I agree that it is not good for the white man to steal from our people. Already they stole our maiden, and the white woman returned her to us. Perhaps because she returned her, she is happy to be a part of the people..."

"She *is* a part of the people. She is my wife," River Runner persisted. "And she is happy to be my wife. The white man did not see this, and stole her from me. We must not allow them to keep taking what is ours. If they take what is ours, then they will keep doing so, and then maybe, one day, they will come and take our lives. We must stop them now!" River Runner felt things begin to swing in his favor. It was not hard to incite his warriors against the white man, and he would do what it took to take back what was his. "I will go after her..."

"You are our chief," Crazy Beaver interjected. "You need to be here."

River Runner shook his head, "I will seek the council and remove myself as chief. You are right, Runs With Deer, I wish my focus to be on my wife, and I do not do my people good if I cannot think on her and them. I would like for the people to choose my sister's husband as chief. He is a good man, with a good heart, and a smart head."

Crazy Beaver nodded, "I will accept this, and will ride with you to return your woman."

"Thank you, my friend."

"I will accept this," Runs With Deer said less enthusiastically. "I will speak to the warriors. We will take many with us and fight for your woman. You know that, if we do this thing, we could make war with the white man? It is something we have not done before."

"There will be no cause," River Runner said softly. "Once my wife is returned, I will take her north to Canada. We will make a new home far away from the white man, so there will be no war."

This response seemed to please Runs With Deer and he acquiesced, "I will be by your side gladly then, my friend."

"I know the snows are heavy, Brother," River Runner said to Runs With Deer, "but it is still light on the ground. Would you ride north to the small town there to see if my woman is there? It will take no more than two sunsets to go and return."

"I will leave now," Runs With Deer agreed, "Crazy Beaver can talk to the other warriors on your behalf." Without another word, he turned and strode to his stallion, mounted swiftly, and rode off toward the north. River Runner watched him go and breathed a sigh of relief.

"You know if he finds her, he will bring her back, even if it means killing the white men," Crazy Beaver observed.

"It is why I sent him," River Runner admitted. "He is the one who should be called Crazy. Why did your mother name you that when you are less crazy than your brother?"

"Because when I was born, she thought she would go crazy raising another son," Crazy Beaver laughed. "Come, let us go tell Soaring Eagle, he will now be chief and then start to prepare for the long trip to Martin's Landing; and hope it does not snow again until we come back."

CHAPTER 39

It took two days longer than Carter intended before he rode down the main street of Martin's Landing. The snows began to fall heavily the day before and it became more and more difficult for his horse to high step through the ever-deepening, frigid slush. By the time he pulled up outside of the stables, his horse was in such bad shape, he feared he'd end up having to put it down. He prayed it wouldn't come to that, since they'd been together for five years now, and he didn't fancy losing a friend and retraining another.

He slid off the saddle and walked around, patting his horse appreciatively on the cheek before walking up to the stable manager's door. He banged loudly to ensure he heard, in case he was asleep, since night had fallen hours prior. When the stable master opened the door in his dressing gown and nightcap, Carter apologized for the disturbance, quickly explained his need, and then turned the horse over the stable master's care, with extra coin for extra attention.

When he was assured his horse would be well tended to, he trudged calf-deep across to the closest boardwalk and straight to the only place still open at that hour—the saloon. The raucous laughter from inside indicated that many of the menfolk were still up and enjoying some local flavor before heading home to a dark, quiet homestead.

He pushed through the door and went straight up to the bar. After ordering a whiskey, he turned to scan the men, hoping to see Casey in attendance. It would mean not having to fight his way to the man's house.

At first he missed him, sitting in a shadowy corner, his head bent over an untouched glass of Bourbon. He grabbed his whiskey and walked on rubbery legs across the small room. It wasn't until he scraped out a chair, loudly, that Casey looked up.

"Dear God, Carter! Y'all made it back?" He asked, scanning the room.

"Just me," Carter said, and then waved his hand to stop the flurry of questions he could see swirling in Casey's eyes. "Just let me down this, and I'll get to explaining. My word." He closed his eyes in exhaustion, then lifted his glass to his lips, tipped his head back, and downed the contents in one gulp, gasping and coughing as it burned its way down his esophagus. It landed in his empty belly and immediately sent a wave of warmth through his appendages. He sighed.

"Okay," he murmured. "We found the Arapaho. They did have Cara. The chief claimed she was his wife." He shook his head, still reeling over what they'd accomplished beneath the noses of the Indians. "Um, whew," he started again, wiping his hand across his forehead. "So, we found her, like I said. We just didn't think we'd be able to get to her because the chief had her stashed away in his teepee. So imagine our shock and surprise when that girl managed to sneak out in the dead of night, on her own accord."

"That's my girl!" Casey exclaimed softly.

"Yeah, she's something! Anyway, she snuck right up to us and led us straight out from beneath the Arapaho's noses. I rode back here and Murphy and the others..."

"Where are they?" Casey interrupted, his nerves a jumbled mess.

Carter waved, "Calm down, Casey. That's why I'm here. We couldn't risk the Arapaho leaving this alone. In fact, after meeting their chief, I don't think he's going to let this go. He's a fairly fierce man, if you must know my opinion. Still, we figured they might not let it lie, so Murphy took off dead west, a direction we were quite certain the Arapaho wouldn't think to go."

"What's due west?" Casey asked, furrowing his brow.

"See, now that's what I asked," Carter said, waving at the bartender to bring him another glass. "And what Murphy said was that they was going to ride due west until they came to the first town. Don't know what town that would be, but...well, that's the fact of the matter. Figured they'd be safe there until the plains were passable again. Oh, and, uh..." he paused when the bartender placed another glass of whiskey on the table. "Excuse me a minute," he said, then tipped the glass back, coughing and sputtering as it followed the path to his stomach.

"You might want to take it easy on that, Carter. You haven't got any food in your stomach, do you?"

Carter blinked rapidly, the effects of the whiskey rapidly replacing coherence in his head, "Nope, can't say as I do, have food that is," he murmured.

"Well, if you have anything else to tell me, now might be the best time. Before you pass out. Like, maybe, how I'm supposed to find Cara?"

"Oh oh oh, yeah, that, yeah."

"Come on, Carter, hang on a little longer, will ya?'

"Yeah, okay, um. Murph, he's uh, yeah, um, something, um. Oh oh, yeah, um, telegraph, yeah. If he can." That was all she wrote. Carter laid his head down on the table and was asleep within minutes.

"Dang, talk about a light weight," Casey muttered, but was grateful he'd imparted the remainder of the news. When Murphy reached the safety of the nearest town, he'd wire him and let him know where they were. He picked up his hat and stepped outside, then turned around and walked back in, "Carl, do you have a room I could use? Snow's coming down real hard out there, and I'm not of a mind to walk home in it."

"Two bits," Carl said, pulling a key from the board behind him.

Casey tossed the coin on the counter, took the key, and headed upstairs. He barely made it to the bed before his mind shut down. Relief flooded through him so hard, and the stress at wondering over Cara's safety fled so quickly, that he could not remain awake if he wanted. The noise from the bar could get louder and he'd be able to sleep right through it. The nagging worry over the snows tried to filter through, but it was stamped out by slumber. He fell face first on the bed, snoring before his head hit the pillow.

CHAPTER 40

Murphy was getting a mite bit worried. The snows had started, coming down hard, which meant more work for the horses. Still, he encouraged them to keep pushing, sending up prayers hourly that a town would come into sight before nightfall. If they were forced to continue into another day, in heavy snows, they may not survive the trek.

"How're you holding up?" Murphy called over his shoulder, his concern for Cara great. She was dressed in Indian garb, which was ill-suited for the weather. She'd told him, when the snows started, that the Indians relied on heavy skins to cover them during the cold. Since she didn't have that...

"I'm cold," she said, and he believed her, since her teeth were chattering rapidly. Along with the fear he had of not coming across a town soon enough was the worry over whether she'd survive much longer if he didn't get her safe and warm.

"Try to hold on, Cara. I'll get us safe. I give you my word."

She didn't reply, but he felt a slight nod against his back.

A few hours later, as the sun was lowering on the horizon, one of the men called out to him, "Lights to the East!"

Murphy turned and looked, "Hallelujah!" He shouted, turning his horse toward the lights. It took a few hours more, but eventually they made their way beneath the sign of the smallest settlement he'd ever seen: Jacks, Oklahoma. The lights were coming from one of only three houses in sight, which meant no hotel, and not likely would there be a telegraph office.

"Damn," Murphy muttered, pointing his horse toward the porch of the biggest house. "Sure hope they're friendly," he murmured. "Cara, I've gotta get off the horse. You need to let loose."

He felt her hands fall away and he slid carefully off the mount. She nearly toppled off with him.

"George, get over here and help her," he called, holding on to her unconscious form.

"She okay?" George asked, pulling her into his arms.

"Can't say. Let's hope we're done riding for now. I don't think any of us can make it further," he said in an exhausted tone, then hauled himself up onto the porch. He knocked, praying the whole while that the people who lived there would be considerate and compassionate folk; not crazies who would turn them away because of Cara's state of dress.

A young man answered, eyeing the group warily, "Help you, mister?"

"We've been traveling for nigh onto five days now; got caught in the snows. We'd be mighty appreciative of some food and a warm place to bed down for a while; and, well, if there's a woman in the home, maybe she can spare some clothes for our lady friend? Truth be told, we snatched her back out of the clutches of the Arapaho, and...well, she's in serious need of kindness. We all are."

The man looked them over once more and then nodded for them to enter. They all plodded into a small foyer, dragging feet tiredly. A woman rushed forward, and gasped when she saw Cara.

"It's all right, Miss, she not Indian," Murphy said quickly. "She's just..."

"Bring her this way," the woman interjected, turning toward one of only three rooms off-shot from the entryway. "I'll tend to her, Mr. Caleb. Have Miss Nancy make some food for the men, and send along apologizes for the delayed departure."

"Yes, Miss Genevieve," Caleb said, nodding in deference, which had Murphy and the men giving each other puzzled glances. Still, the offer of food outweighed the need to assuage their curiosity and they followed like sheep after Caleb, entering another room off-shot from the foyer. It was a small dining area with a corridor leading to a cook shed. Caleb walked over to the entryway to the cook shed and yelled for Nancy. A black girl came rushing in and quickly nodded respectfully to the men in attendance.

"Miss Nancy, Miss Genevieve requests that you put together some food for these men before heading off to your sleep. She sends her apologies for delaying your departure."

"No need for worries, Mr. Caleb, I jes throw somethin' t'gether real quick like."

"Thank you, Miss Nancy," Caleb responded and then waited for Nancy to depart before returning his attention to the men, "So, may I inquire as to what has transpired, sir?" He asked Murphy, but Murphy was too taken aback by the mode of address between the individuals within the home to respond. Instead, he waved toward where Nancy was working on food and shook his head, struggling to formulate words, but Caleb quickly picked up on his confusion and grinned.

"We are all outcasts from society, sir," Caleb explained. "Each having been forced from our homes for reasons which we'd rather retain privately. Miss Genevieve, being the kind soul she is, took us beneath her wings and gave us a purpose again. It didn't matter to her what our occupation, skin color, or proclivities. During our time with her, we're each required to work and assist in obtaining provisions..."

"But I've never heard a slave addressed in the formal," Murphy said, unable to hide his incredulity.

"She is not a slave here, rather the better of the cook among us; therefore, she has been given that role in our little community. Others, men more strong, are tasked with building. Still others hunt or garden. Those fleeing persecution or those simply seeking a better home, are welcome to come live among us. Until we build enough shelters, we are required to share quarters, of course. Some people merely use it as a wayside en route to Independence..."

"How many residents live here?" George asked, also awe-struck over the living circumstances of this tiny communal township.

"Currently, we have seven individuals who have made their home here. Others, such as yourself, merely stop for assistance; and we offer what we can, when we can. So, may I inquire as to the circumstances which have brought you here?"

"Our dear friend's fiancé was abducted by the Arapaho. We managed to free her, but because of the lateness of the year and the risk of being tracked, we decided to veer off our route to seek shelter in a place not likely to be found by the Arapaho; to wait out the snows. We were hoping to find a place with a telegraph office..."

"We haven't any amenities of that kind here," Caleb interrupted.

"Yes, we discerned that much upon our arrival," Murphy sighed.

"Independence is but a day's ride west of here...well, in fair weather, it is. They have a telegraph office there."

"That's great news," Murphy said again, feeling less trapped and more capable. "We'll head out tomorrow and make our way there, that is, of course, if Cara is well enough to travel."

"She'll be well enough," Genevieve said, coming into the dining room. "She's just exhausted and underfed. I'm fair certain with some nourishment and a good night's rest, she'll pull through just fine."

"I'm very glad to hear it," Murphy said, nodding. "We owe you a debt, but...well, all I can offer right now is to pay for our food and lodging for the night," he continued, pulling out his wallet.

"It will be welcomed," she smiled. She collected the bills from Murphy and tucked them into her bodice.

Just then, Nancy returned with a tray laden with flatbread, deer meat, and cheeses, "It don' be much..."

"It's perfect," Murphy interjected. "Thank you for making it."

Nancy nodded, smiled, and curtsied, "If there be nothing else, Miss G'nvieve."

"I think this will serve. Goodnight, Miss Nancy, and thank you for your kindness. I'll see you on the morrow."

Nancy curtsied again and then left. Genevieve turned back to face the men, devouring the food hungrily, "Gentlemen, I hate to interrupt the feast...." She paused and grinned when the men stopped eating and looked up. Their full cheeks reminded her of chipmunks gathering acorns for winter hibernation. "Oh my," she murmured, trying hard not to laugh. She waited for them to swallow and then continued, "Before y'all consume all of the food, I would like to put a small plate together for Miss Cara."

The men exchanged sheepish glances and stepped back from the platter.

"Well, it's a good thing I spoke up when I did," Genevieve laughed, looking at the nearly depleted food. She served a plate for Cara, then waved the men back to their eating before heading from the room and back to Cara's room.

"I certainly didn't expect to see you awake," she exclaimed, as she pushed through the curtain hanging over the entryway. "How are you feeling, Miss Cara?"

"Where am I?" Cara responded sleepily.

"You're nowhere important, dear. What is important is that you eat and sleep so that you can regain your strength." Genevieve placed the tray on the ground, "Here, let me help you sit up to eat."

Cara gasped as the woolen blanket slid down her chest, nearly revealing her breasts to the stranger. She quickly tugged it back up to her chin, her eyes wide and questioning.

"My apologies. I forgot that I removed the clothing you were brought in. It was my intent to give you one of my day dresses once you awoke. I suppose now would be that time. Let's get you clothed, and then we'll see to getting you fed."

Genevieve turned and reached inside of a sizable trunk to pull out a floral-patterned emerald green day dress. It had been so long since Cara had worn any civilized attire that she felt tears sting her eyes.

"Now, now, child. There's no cause for tears. You're safe now, and among friends. Now, lift your arms and let's slide this down. Hopefully, we're close enough in size that this will fit. Otherwise, we may have a problem, since I'm the only woman close enough to your size that would have anything for you to wear." Genevieve slid it down over her head with ease, "There now, it's a might bit giving in the bosom area," she said, her cheeks tinting at how much more ample her bosom was compared to Cara's. "Still, at least it fits. You'll need to stand to slip it all of the way down..."

"I'll wait, thank you," Cara replied softly. "I don't know how to thank you enough for sharing your clothes and your food...oh...my friends...have you seen..."

"The men are in the other room, wolfing down the remainder of the food. They kindly explained everything. Now, let's worry over speaking later, and eat your own food. Your men folk plan to ride out tomorrow, in the hopes of reaching Independence—a more sizable town with a telegraph office. They won't be able to accomplish that, unless you eat and rest."

"I *am* hungry," Cara admitted, accepting the food and consuming it ravenously.

"I'll go fetch you some cider. I'd offer something else, but I'm afraid we haven't anything other. I'll return momentarily."

Cara nodded, and quickly put away the remainder of food on the plate. She'd just swallowed the final bite, when Genevieve returned with her cider. Just as ravenously, she drank the contents, drawing in a deep breath when done.

"Ah, that was refreshing," she sighed.

Genevieve collected the dishes, "I'll let you get some sleep now, dear. I'll be bedding down in here a bit later also, so don't be alarmed if you hear someone coming in. It won't be no one other than me."

"Thank you again for tending to our needs so graciously," Cara said softly, stifling a yawn.

"T'weren't nothing. It's why I came out here—to help those in need."

"I should call you Sister Genevieve," Cara said, smiling. "It would suit you to be a nun."

"I *was* Sister Genevieve once, but no longer," she said, then turned and left to see to the men's accommodations.

Victim of Love Barbara Woster

"I wonder whether her attempts to help some person in need caused her trouble as it did me," Cara wondered aloud, and then allowed her mind to close down for sleep.

CHAPTER 41

"What have you discovered?" River Runner asked as soon as Runs With Deer returned a week later from his reconnaissance of the town to the north.

"She is not there," Runs With Deer said, exhaustion in his tone and lining every inch of his face. "The white man must be very brave indeed if he took her to her home with the snows coming down. We will never be able to take her away now, if she is back with her people."

"We have warriors ready to take back what belongs to the people. We are all in agreement that no man will take what is ours any longer," Crazy Beaver inserted. "River Runner has agreed to take the white woman away from the people to protect us from the white man's guns, when she is returned. She is his wife..."

"She is a white woman who preferred to leave than to remain..."

"She came to stay with the people willingly. The white man stole her away," River Runner said with quiet hostility.

"River Runner is right," Crazy Beaver asserted, "if we allow the white man to keep taking away what belongs to us..."

"We will wait until the snows are gone from the ground, then?" Runs With Deer interrupted, uncertain he liked where this was headed.

"We will not wait," River Runner said. "We have waited only for your return. We will leave with the new sun. Go be with your wife now. She has missed you. I must go prepare to leave."

When River Runner walked away, Runs With Deer turned to his brother, "His mind is gone. He is crazy for the woman. Should we not be concerned?"

"He is no longer chief of our people. He has removed himself and given it over to his sister's husband, but with the request that he be allowed to take the warriors to the white man's home to take back his woman. The council agreed since he has been good to the people."

"I do not like this, Brother. We are putting our warriors in much danger for a white woman."

"No, we are standing side-by-side with River Runner against the white men who stole from the people, as we should. Now, go to your wife. I see her standing in front of your teepee. She knows you are home. Make her very happy tonight, for tomorrow we go take back River Runner's wife."

Runs With Deer left his brother and headed for his teepee, but his mind was in turmoil over leaving for the white man's home. It was a mistake, but he could not persuade River Runner nor Crazy Beaver of that mistake. *Still*, he thought, *if River Runner did not make it to the white man's home, there would be no need to make war with the white man.*

CHAPTER 42

"Thank you again for everything you did for us. We will never forget it," Cara said, wrapping the supplied blanket around her shoulders as she stepped onto the front porch. She was about to head toward where the men were, readying the horses, when Genevieve stalled her departure.

"Miss Cara," she said softly. "I do not know what you have been through, but I do know what you may face when you return to your home."

"You think that my family will shun me," Cara stated, raising her chin a notch to show that she was confident it would not happen. Genevieve noticed her attempted confidence, but still felt compelled to offer a warning.

"Many women stolen by the natives of this land often find they have no place among their own kind any more, once they are freed. It is possible your fiancé may turn his back..."

"My fiancé sent these men to rescue me. He won't turn away from me."

Genevieve's countenance grew more somber and she felt tears sting her eyes, "My dear, I was taken by the Comanche and my own sisterhood turned their backs on me—women sworn to honor God's law. Your fiancé may simply have sent these men to remove you from the clutches of those perceived savage. It does not mean he will willingly have you...
"

"Enough!" Cara snapped, closing her eyes to block out a reality she was unwilling to face. "My fiancé loves me, and will not reject me."

"He will be a good and honorable man then. I offer you blessings upon your life; but if anything should go different from what you hope, please know you may always come here to live with us."

"People shunned by society," Cara said softly.

Genevieve nodded, then turned and returned inside.

Cara headed across the yard, still calf-deep in snow, her mind sending up prayers that Casey hadn't just sent Murphy to free her only because he couldn't bear the thought of her in the clutches of savages.

What would she do if he decided he didn't want her? Where would she go? Here, to live among the shunned and rejected?

By the time she reached Murphy's horse, her feet were numb with cold, but her heart began to burn with incensed thoughts of being rejected simply because she'd come to the aid of a squaw. She'd done a kindness, but had suffered greatly since doing so. Her thoughts turned to Genevieve, rejected by those who were supposed to put all others above themselves. If nuns could show no mercy, how could she expect a simple white man to?

"Murphy?"

"You ready, Cara?" He asked, reaching for her waist so he could lift her onto his stallion's back.

"Wait, um, can I ask you a question first?"

Murphy's brow knitted, but he nodded, "Make it quick or our toes are going to get frost bit for certain."

"Was it Casey's intent for me to return to him, once you rescued me?" Cara's question came out in a strangled whisper, uncertain she wanted to hear the answer.

"Cara, that man loves you so much, that he wanted to ride into the Arapaho camp himself and kill every one of those lying, conniving red skins for keeping hold of you when they promised to release you. I had to talk him out of coming with me for fear he'd do something stupid. Does that sound like a man with bad intent towards you?"

Cara shook her head, tears of relief streaming down her cheeks.

Murphy latched hold of her waist and hoisted her up onto the saddle, "Now, I have a promise of a Christmas turkey, so if you don't mind, I'd like to get to Independence, fire off that telegram, and see about getting us home in time for Christmas dinner."

"Thank you, Murphy," Cara whispered. "You risked your life for me and have been a dearer friend than I've ever known. Whomever you decide marry will be a fortunate woman indeed."

"Ah, ain't no woman wanting an old, haggard buzzard like myself," Murphy replied, embarrassed. He clucked his tongue and the beleaguered group headed west toward Independence.

"I don't believe that for a moment. If you didn't notice it, I did," Cara said conspiratorially.

"What are you talking on?"

"Miss Genevieve was looking at you in a more than passing manner; and she's fair to look upon," Cara intimated with a wide grin.

"Ah c'mon, Cara, you aren't joshing this old man, are you?"

"No joshing."

"Well, um," Murphy started, clearing his throat loudly, "that's interesting news to be sure."

"I do hope that your assistance to me will not prohibit your returning to Jacks and..."

"Now, Cara," Murphy interrupted, "this is hardly an appropriate topic of discussion; however, I'll keep Jacks in mind."

"Don't you mean you'll keep Genevieve in mind?" Cara laughed.

"Now enough of that kind of talk," Murphy chastised lightly. "What would your fiancé think..."

"He'd tell me I'm always into mischief..." Cara interjected, then suddenly stopped speaking, reminded of recent mischief that landed her in the clutches of River Runner.

"You okay, Cara? I wasn't really upset with you, you know?" Murphy said over his shoulder when Cara stopped talking.

"I'm fine, I just realized that you need to focus on the horse's footing," she fibbed, but the horse chose that moment to stumble lightly, lending credence to her little white lie.

"Yeah, I might ought to do that," Murphy said, pulling lightly on the reins. "We've a long way to go and some mighty treacherous territory to cover. Next time we decide to return a squaw to her people, we might ought to consider doing so at a better time of year."

"Oh, there won't be a next time," Cara said softly, her tone full of indignation. "I'm done assisting others."

"What did you say?" Murphy asked. "Hard to hear when the wind gusts up like this." He pulled his hat lower on his face and tugged on the lapels of his coat.

"I didn't say anything," Cara replied loudly, burrowing in behind Murphy's back, pulling the blanket tighter around her shoulders. Once she was nestled against the cold gusts of wind, her mind drifted back to what she'd said to Murphy. She'd meant it. She'd spent most of her life coming to the aid of others, but this last disaster showed that kindness wasn't always rewarded. She shuddered at what her life may have become had Casey not given up searching for her; had he not sent Murphy and the men into a nest of vipers to rescue her. She'd cried so much in the last three months, and the tears weren't done, starting again when her mind shifted to what she'd done with River Runner; what he'd forced her to do, because he'd lied and manipulated her into his bed. Would Casey be able to forgive her that particular indiscretion? Would he still be willing to marry her knowing she'd lain with another man?

That thought jarred another to the surface and she suddenly felt physically ill, "Please stop!" She yelled.

Murphy pulled his stallion to a halt and Cara slid off the back, bending over just in time to empty the contents of her stomach onto the unblemished snow.

"Dear sweet Jesus!" Murphy exclaimed, climbing down from the horse. "Are you okay, Cara?"

She scraped some snow, untouched by her stomach contents, and used it to wipe the residue from her lips, then scooped another bit into her mouth, swishing the intensely frigid frozen water around until she felt cleansed. Only then did she stand erect again, turning to see Murphy and the other men standing in a semi-circle around her, concern etched on all of their faces.

"Are you all right, Miss Cara?" George asked.

Cara sighed heavily, suddenly feeling drained—and embarrassed, "I'm fine. Just a little sick of being on horseback, I suppose."

"Um, well, we kind of have to be on horseback for a long while yet. Are you sure you're going to be up to it?" Murphy asked, concerned etching his features.

"I'm sure I'll be just fine, Murphy, but thank you for the concern. I'll be okay because I have to be in order to get home to Casey. Help me remount?"

"Sure thing, Cara, but if you feel sick again, don't hesitate to speak up, okay?"

"Oh, I don't think that will be a problem."

In fact, it was only a problem once more prior to reaching Independence. The following morning, just after the sun rose, Cara's stomach began to heave again, but this time she had nothing to throw up. Still, the men waited patiently while she knelt beside a mound of snow, heaving and retching pitifully.

"You know, if you was a married woman, I'd say you was having morning sickness," Luke said off the cuff, not realizing that his words had a bigger impact than anyone realized they could.

Murphy and George exchanged glances of concern, and Cara kept her gaze averted, her face reddening. All suddenly coming to the realization that she could very well be carrying a red man's baby.

"Um, do you think you're up to continuing now, Cara," Murphy asked delicately, deliberately avoiding the disturbing subject now hanging over all of their heads.

She nodded in silence. Murphy helped her mount and they continued on their way, no one speaking. The following morning, the small town of Independence came into view.

"Climb down, Cara," Murphy said, pulling his horse to a halt on the hilltop overlooking the town.

"Why?"

"You'll ride in with Luke," he said, and then yelled, "Luke, come here!"

"Yes, sir?"

"You're going to pretend you're Miss Cara's husband. We don't want no trouble with the town folks; and trouble we'll have in spades if a single woman rides into town with three men."

"Can't we just say I'm your sister? You three could pass for brothers. I don't mean any insult, Luke. I'm sure you'll make a fine husband..."

"I understand," Luke interjected, "and she's got a fine idea..."

"No!" Murphy insisted. "Then we'll have trouble with single men fawning all over her, making things more interesting than they need to be. We don't know how long we'll be hole up here. You'll play her husband. No more talking about it. Now help Cara mount behind you. She can't ride into town with me if she's married to you. Slide off my mount, Cara." Murphy's tone brooked no argument, so Cara slid down and then mounted behind Luke. She hadn't felt this discomfited since being in River Runner's company. Murphy she didn't mind because he was right— he was a haggard old buzzard; but Luke, like River Runner, was young, fit, and all male. It was too close a similarity which made it impossible to relax on the way down the hill.

"We'll find a place to settle in and then I'll find the telegraph office. Let Casey know where we are now. After that, we'll go down and get some food..."

"Murphy," Cara said softly, "if Luke and I are married, we'll be expected to share a room and..."

"Don't concern yourself, Cara. I thought of that. We'll check you in as a couple, but then Luke will bunk down with me. If anybody notices, we'll just tell 'em y'all are having a fight; and since married folk fight all the time...well, it'll be believed, is all."

Cara sighed loudly and then thought of another thing, "I sure could do with a bath."

"I'll have one ordered up for you before I go to the telegraph office," Murphy offered. "I'll get one ordered up for us too. Time we men stopped smelling like skunk spray."

Victim of Love Barbara Woster

They dismounted in front of the building in town that said HOTEL, each sighing heavily as they pulled their weary bodies up the steps to the front door.

"I hope we're going to be here for more than a night," Cara muttered, every bone and muscle in her body aching from so much time in a saddle.

"Just a few. We'll have to saddle up and head to Martin's Landing at week's end if we're going to get there before the snows get so bad..."

"Not bad enough right now?" Cara asked, glancing over her shoulder at the ankle-deep snow on the ground here. Far less than what they'd come through, to be sure, but still work for the horses to trudge through.

"Less snow further south, but it's not winter yet," Murphy said. "We really need to be in Martin's Landing before Christmas or we may not be as fortunate in finding a place to hole up as we were this time."

Cara sighed heavily, but she realized the wisdom of getting home sooner rather than later. Still, the thought of facing Casey, now that she knew what she knew made her less certain of not being shunned; made her fearful, wanting to turn and flee back to Jacks to hide away from society forever.

CHAPTER 43

River Runner and the other warriors fought through calf-deep snow for the three of the six days it took to reach Martin's Landing. By the time they topped the ridge overlooking the town, none had spoken in days, their tempers at an all-time high at making such a treacherous trek. It didn't help that the first part of the journey was made with Runs With Deer whispering malcontent in their ears over River Runner's obsessions with a white woman; how River Runner's obsessions were going to cause a war with the white man.

But instead of causing the desired rift, all it did was to create more hostility toward the white man. Had the white man not stolen River Runner's woman, they grumbled in reply to Runs With Deer's whispered ravings, they would not be on horseback in deep snows, going to snatch back what was taken.

The warriors may be angry, but Runs With Deer was livid—and not at the white man; rather his rage was directed at River Runner. Their former chief had caused nothing but trouble for the people from the day he took the white woman; and that trouble had been escalating ever since.

"How are we to find her?" Runs With Deer asked, unable to keep the snide tone from his voice. "There are too many people; too many white women wearing hats upon their heads. We cannot simply ride in..."

"Yes, we can," River Runner said confidently.

"You will kill us all if we..."

"When night falls," River Runner continued, ignoring Runs With Deer's fuming interruptions, "we will move about unseen as the warriors we are. We will find where she is being kept and take her away."

Runs With Deer drew in a deep, calming breath through his nostrils. River Runner was correct. Under the cover of darkness the warriors could accomplish anything. They had done so many times before; and this made his anger toward River Runner greater than ever. It angered him that River Runner could think logically when he obviously had no brain to think with because of the white woman. River Runner must have finally sensed Runs With Deer's malcontent, for he sidled up next to him.

"The reason you make a good warrior," River Runner said, "is because you are not afraid to kill for what belongs to the people; nor are you afraid to die for the people."

"I do not think that what we are doing is right," Runs With Deer snapped.

River Runner nodded, "I know. Your angry words have been spoken clear and loud for all to hear; but answer me this—if it were you woman..."

"I would never cause trouble for a white woman."

"If it were your woman..."

"I would kill anyone who stole her from me," Runs With Deer admitted. "But not if she was white," he added huffily.

"But I would, because she is my wife. She has lain with me on my mat, and perhaps carries my son inside of her."

Runs With Deer's eyes widened.

"All I ask, my friend, is that you help me take her back. Then I will take her far away, so that the white man does not make war with my people," River Runner concluded. He knew that, if he didn't calm Runs With Deer soon, he could very well end up with a knife in his back.

Runs With Deer nodded.

"Thank you."

The warriors slid from their horses and led them away from view of the townspeople, then nestled down to chew on their Pemmican while they awaited nightfall.

When the sun finally sunk below the horizon, the warriors crept over the rise, moving rapidly to the edge of the town before the area around them became completely dark. Once blackness settled over the area, all they would have to maneuver by would be the lights from the houses. They needed to check the houses quickly before everyone settled to bed and the lights were extinguished.

"Be careful when looking inside that the people there do not see you. Check every place where light is. Whoever finds her is to signal so the other warriors can join him."

The warriors bent low and took off running towards the houses lining the street behind the main town. River Runner reached the first home and peered inside. His hope rose when he saw a woman with hair the color of the winter grasses standing over a stove, preparing food. Then she turned and his hope shattered. Not her.

He moved on to the next house and his heart sank further. She was not there either. A few minutes later, he heard the hoot of an owl, and he smiled. Someone had found her.

He quickly ran toward the sound, and spotted Crazy Beaver. The other warriors soon joined them.

"You have found her?" River Runner asked expectantly.

Crazy Beaver shook his head, "No, but I have found the man named Casey Scott."

River Runner quickly peered into the window. Casey was lying on a bed, atop a colorful blanket, but he was not asleep. He lie with his arms behind his head, staring at the ceiling. Cara was nowhere to be found.

"Why is this important?" River Runner snapped softly. "It is obvious that Cara is not with him."

"No, but if she was here in this place would she *not* be with him?"

That stopped River Runner in his tracks and his brow knitted in concern. Still he couldn't quit looking.

"We do not know the white man's way. He may not want her now so she could be in a different home. We must search them all."

The warriors looked at each other, but then Crazy Beaver shrugged, "We are here, so we will look."

Without another word, the warriors bent at the knee and took off toward the other homes again, but River Runner stayed with Crazy Beaver, asking the one thing that was on his mind—besides Cara.

"Why?"

"Because you are a good man, River Runner, and were a good chief. I think that Runs With Deer is right though—your mind is not right over this woman, and she may cause you more trouble, but that is not for me to say. I am here because we cannot let a white man take away our women anymore, even if that woman is white."

"Thank you."

"Let us keep looking. The lights will go out soon and darkness will make it hard to see."

The two were about to continue their search when a pounding sounded from inside the house. They peered inside and saw Casey leap from the bed, moving toward the front door.

River Runner looked at Crazy Beaver, nodding toward the side of the house. They ran swift and silent, looking around the side of the house, just as Casey pulled open the front door.

"Mr. Scott, I've received word from Murphy. The men and Cara are hole up in Independence. They're just waiting on word from you..."

"Tell them to stay put for a few more days. If the Arapaho show up here, I don't want them finding her."

"Yes, sir, um, but Murphy is also concerned about the snows that far north; and I think he's right. They wait too much longer, they may be stuck there until spring."

Casey closed his eyes and drew in a deep breath, "I know, Albert, but right now, the Arapaho have no idea where Cara is..."

"What if they just let it go? I mean, isn't everyone making a huge assumption that they'll want her back?" Albert asked. Ever since he'd been told what to expect and the circumstances surrounding that expectation, his curiosity soared. Mainly over what Miss Cara would be like now that she'd been a captive of savages; and why Casey was going to so much trouble to get back an unclean female.

"He'll want her back," Casey said, and the confidence in that one statement put the matter to rest. "Now go back and tell Murphy to stay put for three more days. If the snows aren't too heavy then, it should be safe enough to head out. Oh, and tell him I'm on my way."

"Sir?"

"Include in your telegraph that I'll meet up with them, either in Independence or on their way back. Do you have something to say, Albert?"

"It's just that...well, Independence is a good four day's ride, to the north. With the snows up yonder, a ride could easily stretch to double that time. If Murphy heads back before you get there, y'all could easily bypass each other..."

"I get your point. Tell Murphy to stay put. I'll be there within the week."

Albert shook his head, but turned to go deliver the message.

"I don't see what all the fuss is about," he muttered as he sat down in front of the telegraph machine and started tapping on the button, "I certainly wouldn't be going to all this trouble over spoilt goods."

Casey, on the other hand, knew precisely what the fuss was about—he wasn't about to fail; to allow his woman to fall into the hands of savages and then wash his hands of her. He'd sworn to her, just before this disaster befell them, that there'd be sunshine in Hell the day he wasn't able to tend to his woman's needs. That had been in response to her jab about having seven men with them to protect her when returning the Indian maiden to her people. Well, they'd all failed. Not a one of his men had been able to defend Cara; had prevented her from being snatched from right beneath their noses.

He'd been proud of his men when they'd managed to snatch Cara back from beneath the noses of the Arapaho warriors; but something Carl said, just before the men went to rescue Cara, bothered him -- *Cara is a beautiful woman; and forgive me for saying, but she'd be mighty hard to resist.*

That statement ate at Casey's soul, night and day, and he knew it was unlikely, in the nearly three months she'd been held captive, that she was still pure, untouched. He closed his eyes as the rage welled. He stopped packing his bags, closed his eyes, and drew in several deep, calming breaths.

"What am I going to do about that?" He whispered, then knelt down and laid his face on the bed, praying for peace and understanding.

River Runner and Crazy Beaver watched Casey for only a moment more, then knelt and ran across to where the warriors had agreed to meet once all of the houses had been searched.

"We found nothing!" Runs With Deer started as soon as Crazy Beaver and River Runner joined them, but the smiles on the two men's faces stopped the remainder of his tirade. "You have found her?"

River Runner nodded, "Come, we must get back to our horses and ride, before the white man leaves."

Runs With Deer's brow knitted in confusion, but he had no time to query further before everyone took off at a dead run for the hilltop. He'd hoped to ask where they were off to as soon as they reached the horses, but River Runner leapt onto his stallion in one smooth motion, spurring the horse into a gallop the minute his butt contacted the horse's back.

The other warriors quickly leapt onto their horses and took off after River Runner, who was soaring across the ground as a cheetah after prey. Runs With Deer kicked at his stallion's side, spurring him to greater speeds, until he was riding side-by-side with River Runner.

"What have you found out?" He yelled.

"Where Cara is," River Runner called back.

"Where?"

"She is with Casey's men in Independence," River Runner yelled.

"Independence is a bigger town with more men than Martin's Landing. How are we going to take her away with even more people around her?"

River Runner looked over at Runs With Deer in frustration. This warrior, his friend, had been questioning everything since his woman came to be taken from him; had been fighting against his finding Cara, "You have something to say, but I will not slow to hear you say it," River Runner shouted.

Victim of Love Barbara Woster

"I have said it," Runs With Deer shouted back. "Your mind is not working right. You are going to start a war with the white man over a white woman."

"Enough! I will hear no more," River Runner yelled. "I will not start a war with the white man. I have *not* started a war with the white man. These thoughts in your mind are what is not right. I will think straight and take my woman away and no man will even know I was there; and then I will take her to Canada to find a new home for us, so that they will not come for her or blame my people. If you cannot see this, and will not help me, then go! Return to the people!"

Without waiting for a reply, River Runner leaned over the neck of his stallion and kicked at its side. The horse responded, increasing its already rapid stride. River Runner shot over the prairie at speeds the others had difficulty maintaining. It wasn't until they encountered the deeper snows that River Runner was forced to slow.

CHAPTER 44

Casey reached Independence seven days later. Riding beneath the sign, he sighed in relief at knowing that he'd won. He had outwitted the chief of the Arapaho and had taken back that which did not belong to the Indians. As he rode down the snow-covered main street toward the hotel, he wondered, again, how things would be between him and Cara. Would she be the same spirited woman he loved, or had time with the Arapaho broken that spirit? His greatest concern though was whether she was still untouched.

He dismounted and entered the hotel, Carl's words still resonating in his brain, refusing to allow his mind peace: *Cara is a beautiful woman; and forgive me for saying, but she'd be mighty hard to resist.*

"Casey," he heard someone call out, and turned to see Murphy, Luke, and George headed his direction. He smiled and headed over.

"It's mighty good to see you all," he greeted, shaking each man's hand. "I owe you each a debt, getting Cara out the way y'all did. That took courage above and beyond anything I've ever encountered in my lifetime. Makes me proud to call each of you my friend."

The men grinned ear-to-ear at the profusion of compliments, "T'weren't nothing," George muttered.

"T'weren't nothing!" Murphy exclaimed. "Were you with us during the whole time, George!?"

Luke laughed, "What Murphy meant is, it was damned near the hardest and scariest thing we've ever done."

"How *did* you do it?" Casey asked.

"Let's get a drink and we'll tell you all about it. Might add a few gray hairs to your head though," Murphy said, heading toward a table in a corner. He waved at the bartender as he sat down.

"Where's Cara?" Casey asked as he settled onto a chair. "Is she...well, how is she faring?"

"She's okay," Murphy said, then turned to the bartender, "four whiskeys." Once the bartender walked away, Murphy turned back to Casey, "She's been through quite an ordeal; not that she's told us anything. It's just how weary and tired she looks."

"Of course," George interjected, "that could simply be from all of the riding we've done of late. She's spent the last few days hole up in her room sleeping. We've had food sent up so she can have some privacy...oh, and we best let you know that people here have been...well, we didn't want folks thinking poorly..."

"She's married to me," Luke blurted out, and then quickly amended his statement when Casey shot him a look meant to kill, "That is, folks here *think* she's married to me."

"What Luke-smooth-talker is trying to say is that, I decided it was best if folks here thought Cara was married, so that her reputation wouldn't suffer from being in the company of three men when we arrived. Luke was the best candidate, since he is closest in age to Cara," Murphy explained, shooting Luke a "watch how you put things" glare. "Anyway, getting here was easy compared to getting into and out of the Arapaho camp. We're still scratching our heads over how *that* went so easy."

"How *did* you manage it?" Casey asked, sipping on his whiskey. While he truly was interested in how his men had pulled off a successful rescue operation, he was also stalling. As long as his men had information to impart, he wasn't going to have to climb those stairs to see Cara. He wanted to see her, and he didn't. Right now, just knowing she was safe was good enough for him. Until he came to terms with her life among the Arapaho, it would have to suffice as good enough.

"We gambled that the Arapaho wouldn't see us as a threat if we just told them we were brothers passing through the region," George supplied.

"Surprisingly, it worked," Luke stated, shaking his head in remembrance.

"They invited us to dine with them," Murphy added.

"And we kept trying to decide on how to locate Cara while we ate, *if* she was even there, which, of course, she turned out to *be* there," Luke inputted.

"Admittedly, we was running out of ideas as the night wore on," George continued.

"But then Cara just strolled out of River Runner's teepee, pretty as you please," Murphy picked up.

"River Runner?" Casey asked.

"Yeah, the chief of the Arapaho," Murphy clarified. "He'd called Cara his wife, and, I have to say that, he was mighty fierce about that claim."

That comment had Casey's mind reeling, confirming what he'd feared—that his Cara had been claimed by another man and that the Arapaho were likely to come after her. It did relieve his mind knowing that they wouldn't think to look here, in Independence. He forced the negative thoughts aside, "You said Cara strolled out of ..."

"Yeah," Murphy interrupted. "Without a word to any of us, she walked straight to the horses and led us out of camp on foot."

Knowing Cara left willingly with his men lifted Casey's spirits a bit. Perhaps she hadn't been taken by the chief yet; perhaps the chief was merely laying claim ahead of consummation. He shook that thought aside quickly and changed his focus, "Carl said it was your idea, Murphy, to head due west. Did you get the impression that the Arapaho would come for Cara?"

Murphy nodded, "I don't know about all of the warriors, but River Runner seemed obsessed with making sure we knew she was his wife. To me, it sounded almost like he was in love with her. I'm sorry, Casey, I know you don't want to hear that..."

Casey shook his head, "It's okay, Murphy. Something in my own head was telling me that they'd come for her. You're just confirming my suspicions and the reasons why they would. You made a good call."

"Did the Arapaho show up in Martin's Landing?" Luke asked.

"If they did, we didn't see them, but that doesn't mean they weren't around."

"So, what are we going to do then? We need to get back to Martin's Landing before Christmas, but if the Arapaho are determined to get her back, then they'll likely go there to find her."

"I was thinking on that very thing on the ride out here," Casey said, "and I think I have a solution."

"You going to share that idea?" Murphy asked.

"We head back to Martin's Landing via an indirect route," Casey replied.

"And what route would that be?" George asked.

CHAPTER 45

"I'm not going, and you can't make me!" Cara shouted, moving away from Casey's embrace. He'd come upstairs a few minutes earlier and she'd never been happier to see him, until he sprung his intentions on her.

"Cara, you must see reason," he said softly, watching her warily as she paced the room near the window. She was still as beautiful, but she'd grown far too thin; the dress she'd borrowed from the woman in Jacks hung like a sack on her, concealing fully what figure she had. "If we take you back to Martin's Landing, there is a risk that River Runner will find you."

The mention of River Runner caused Cara to tense. She wrapped her arms about herself protectively and stopped pacing, turning to stare out the window. Casey saw the transformation from angry animation to sullen silence and moved up behind her. He placed his hands on her shoulders and was astonished at how she jumped, turning quickly.

When it registered that it was Casey, she relaxed her guard, "I'm so sorry, Casey. I didn't mean..."

"It's okay, sweetheart," he said, folding her into his embrace. "You've been through quite an ordeal, which is why we need to keep you safe until we know for certain the Arapaho will give up the search."

"But a convent? Really, Casey, you'd lock me away in a convent?"

"Not lock away, Cara. Just pay them to board you until spring," Casey replied, trying his best to sound convincingly certain that his way was the only viable way. "That's only a few months away."

"But I want to come home," Cara cried against his chest and it was Casey's turned to tense slightly. Would Cara even be able to come back to Martin's Landing? Would the people there welcome her back, knowing that she'd been a captive of savages? The white man was not the most forgiving of people, and his standing in the community and his new position as Governor may not be enough to wipe away the taint that now hung over Cara. The thought of his being governor brought to mind a new thought—Cara's father had passed away a couple of months after she'd been abducted, and he hadn't yet told her the news. *Nor am I going to,* he thought to himself. *She's been through too much already, and she has much more to contend with before this is all said and done. I don't need to be adding to her woes with such depressing news.*

"I'll return for you in the spring, when I'm certain the threat has passed," Casey whispered, kissing her lightly on the head. "Being in Martin's Landing is going to cause far more stress than staying somewhere away, where you'll be safe. Please, Cara, you need to trust me that this is the right thing to do." Casey felt the smallest of nods against his chest and sighed loudly, "Thank you, darling. Now why don't we head down and join the men for supper. Luke—um, your husband—is waiting outside to escort you down."

Cara looked up, her cheeks tinted red, "That was..."

"...Murphy's idea," Casey concluded with a grin. "Yes, I know. The old goat was just doing what he thought was right, but that doesn't make it any easier on me, knowing I can't fawn over you in public right now," he joked, trying to lighten her spirits.

"I've missed you so, Casey," Cara whispered, lowering her gaze shyly.

Casey lifted her face and placed a light kiss on her lips, "I've missed you too, darling," he said softly. He could see the anticipation on her face, knowing she wanted him to deepen the kiss as he'd done in the past, but now his uncertainties prevented his doing so. "Let's go down to supper," he said, drawing her from the room.

Cara didn't miss his reticence and felt close to tears again. Something had changed in Casey, just as it had in her, and it was creating a chasm between them. She could feel it widening as if she were standing beside the creation of a new canyon.

CHAPTER 46

"What do we do now?" Crazy Beaver asked, as they lie on the snow-covered grass across from the hotel, out of sight from the passersby. He and River Runner snuck into town on foot at twilight, when a majority of the people were home. They'd seen Casey ride into town and tie his mount to the hitching post out front of the hotel, so they knew *he* was there, but they needed to confirm Cara was there.

"We wait for sight of her," River Runner said and then pointed at an upstairs window. "There she is," he exclaimed quietly, his gaze softening at the sight of her standing next to the window. His gaze quickly hardened and his anger intensified, when he saw Casey lay his hands on her. Her reaction, however, gave him hope that she no longer wanted Casey as her man. She'd jerked away from him, as she'd done to him when he first went to claim her as his own. "See, my friend, she is not happy to be back among the white man," he declared, using the action as confirmation that his warriors were doing the right thing in taking her back.

"Do we wait until darkness and then take her?" Crazy Beaver asked, knowing that it would not be an easy thing to climb the building and climb back down with the woman; but he was willing to do so if it meant getting this done and returning to his own woman.

"No," River Runner sighed. "Runs With Deer is right. It would be too dangerous to risk taking her from here. There are too many white men with guns."

"Then what are we going to do?" Crazy Beaver asked, he too preferring a solution that did not require going to war with the white man.

"Come, let us return to the others. I have an idea," River Runner said, then slid backwards until he felt it was safe enough to stand and run.

CHAPTER 47

"It's been years since you've been that far south, Casey," Murphy commented as they mounted their horses the next morning. "Are you even sure there's a convent around Verbeck anymore? We sure are going a long way around for an unknown, so it ain't likely we'll be home in time for that promised turkey Christmas dinner."

"You aren't coming with us, old friend. You, Luke, and George have done enough. I'll be taking Cara on my own. It's time for me to take responsibility of her, and that's what I intend to do."

"Casey, it may not be safe for you to make that trek alone. You'll need men..."

"I had seven men with me when the Arapaho abducted her the first time, remember?" Casey snapped and then sighed. "I'm sorry, Murph. I just don't think that four men against Arapaho warriors is going to make a difference if they try to take her away again. Also, if you three are back in Martin's Landing when the Arapaho show up, it will lend credence to your story that you were just passing through, that you don't know Cara or anything about her."

"Less likely they'll attack the town. That what you thinking?" Murphy said softly.

Casey nodded.

"If it didn't make sense and if I wasn't ready to get home, I'd argue with you further," Murphy admitted sheepishly. "Instead, I'll bid you Godspeed. When do you think you'll get in touch to let us know of your progress? I certainly am not fond of waiting to hear something until you get back to Martin's Landing next spring."

"I'll wire when we pass through a town with a telegraph office. My word." He glanced up to see Luke and George escorting Cara from the hotel. He quickly reached inside his coat pocket and pulled out a letter, "I wrote this up quick like last night. It's to inform the town council that you will step in as interim governor..."

"Wait, I thought I was to be the new magistrate," Murphy said, confusion knitting his brow.

"Yeah, well, I'm placing Luke in that position and George and Carter in charge of the business," Casey said, grinning at his friend's facial expression. "We'll right it all when I get back."

"And if you don't?" Murphy blurted, instantly regretting where his thoughts went.

"Then you four will take good care of Martin's Landing," Casey replied sincerely. "You're a good man and the townsfolk will be honored to have you in charge of things. Still, it's my intention to return soon and then return next spring—or sooner, weather permitting—to retrieve Cara from the convent."

"Sooner might not happen. It's going to take you months just to get to the convent," Murphy said, unable to hide the worry in his tone over his friend.

Casey just nodded, reaching for Cara's hand when she approached, "You ready?"

She nodded, but didn't smile. She understood the wisdom of Casey's plan, but was far from pleased at the idea of sitting on a horse for many more weeks, running from the Arapaho; especially since she knew, almost with a certainty, that she was carrying River Runner's child.

"Murphy?" She said softly, "thank you again for everything you did for me; and don't forget Jacks."

Murphy blushed and she did smile then.

"Maybe I'll head out there in the spring," he whispered, giving her a hug.

She wished the best for the older man and hoped he would remember Genevieve and make his way to Jacks in the spring or summer when or if she and Casey returned to Martin's Landing.

She then turned to George and Luke, "Thank you for risking your lives to bring me home. I will never forget your kindness nor your sacrifice."

Both men bowed their heads in embarrassed gratitude.

"T'weren't nothing, Miss Cara," Luke said softly, and Murphy laughed, wanting to repeat that it was most definitely not nothing, but he held his peace.

"Y'all go safely," he said instead.

"Go with God, my friends," Casey said, then helped Cara mount. If he didn't get on the trail soon, the daylight was going to fade. Still, it wasn't easy saying goodbye to his friends. Murphy was right, the trail to the convent was going to be as treacherous as any they'd traversed thus far and he could very well not make it back to Martin's Landing after dropping Cara off at the convent. Anything could happen. That made saying goodbye harder than at any other time in his life. Without looking back, he turned his stallion to the west and spurred the animal into a gallop. What made it even harder was his indecision about whether or not to return for Cara come spring. He told her and everyone else, he intended to, but his heart was having trouble facing the realization that she was no longer his. He had some hard thinking to do between the time he left her and the following spring.

Murphy, Luke, and George stood outside the front of the hotel until they rode over the hillside.

"Well, I think it's time we head..." he started, and then stopped speaking suddenly, dread and fear slamming into his gut with a vengeance. "No! It's not possible!" He cried.

"What is it, Murph? What's wrong?" George asked, scanning the area that Murphy was watching intently.

"I thought...I thought I saw Indians," Murphy replied, suddenly uncertain what he'd seen.

"Indians! Where?" Luke cried out, scanning the horizon carefully.

"I'm not sure," Murphy admitted. "I saw what looked like black hair."

"Sure it weren't just ravens? They're so big and black that they could be mistaken for a man's head," George offered, "and there's no way the Arapaho knows we're here."

Murphy shook his head to clear the concern and just sat for a while longer, watching the area carefully. After more than ten minutes, he sighed heavily, "I guess I was mistaken. Must have been ravens."

"Yeah, ravens," Luke said, relief in his tone. He'd had his fill of Indians and rescuing. He was seriously ready to get back to his dull life in Martin's Landing. "Are we heading home now?"

"Yeah, we're headed home," Murphy said, mounting his stallion. The three men pointed their horses to the southeast, not knowing they were leaving Casey and Cara to face the Arapaho alone.

CHAPTER 48

"They are leaving," River Runner said, gleefully, "and they are on their own."

"This will be easy to do after all," Runs With Deer said, relief in his tone. "But you know we will have to kill the white man, or he will just keep coming for her."

River Runner nodded, "He must die, yes."

"If he dies," Crazy Beaver inputted, "then there will be no need for you to leave the people, my friend. No man will know how he died, since he will be alone. His body will be food for the wolves. He will never be found."

"And if he is found, no one will know he was with a woman," another warrior added eagerly. "He is not with people who know him."

Each man readily, and thoughtlessly, contradicted earlier concerns over killing a man considered important to the white people. Each warrior was so ready to return to the people that they no longer worried over whether Casey would be found; whether the white people would send their army to attack.

"He is going a way that no man would think to look for him..." Another interjected.

"I do not need convincing, my friends," River Runner said, moving toward his horse. "Casey Scott must die."

"They will be out of sight of the town very soon," Runs With Deer said. "We will kill them quietly, without our cries of victory. We must not alert the white men that we are here." Although he was happy that the white woman was protected only by a weak white man, he still had a feeling of dread creeping along his spine that made him want to use caution.

"We do not need to worry about being quiet, my friend, because we will follow them," River Runner interjected, "until we are far away from the white man's town. Then no one will find his body. Let us go, and stay low. Stay in a line behind each other. That will make us more unseen."

The warriors leaned over their horses' heads, ensuring as much inconspicuousness as possible when they rode alongside the hill leading away from town. When they were well away, they sat upright, but did what they could not to alert Casey and Cara of their presence; making certain to stay in a line behind one another's horses.

The tactic worked, for Cara didn't notice the trail of Arapaho until many hours later, near sundown, when she just happened to glimpse over her shoulder at a flock of pheasant that had fluttered up nearby, startling her.

Her heart jumped into her throat when she peered back and saw River Runner leading six warriors well behind. Though they were still well away from her, and she couldn't make out their features, she knew how River Runner sat a horse; knew his body, and remembered the last time she'd fled and saw him riding toward her. There was no mistaking that determined sit on his horse.

She didn't know if they knew she'd spotted them, but the last thing Casey needed to do was to try to outrun them. She knew the futility of that act. Though Casey was a good rider and had a strong stallion; there was no way that two on a single horse could outride six single riders. Why they hadn't overtaken them yet, she couldn't begin to fathom, for they were as helpless as newborn babes left out in a winter storm—as good as dead.

Still, if she let Casey know of the impending danger, there was a possibility that they could outwit them, even if they couldn't outride them.

"Casey?" She said near his ear. She hadn't spoken all day, so wasn't surprised when he jumped. She couldn't help but smile at his reaction, but the smile was short-lived. They were in danger.

"Yes, sweetheart?" Casey called over his shoulder.

"I need you to listen to me, but I want you not to turn around," Cara said, and instinctively, Casey moved to turn around. Cara leaned into his line of sight and scowled at him. "I'm serious, Casey," she snapped loudly.

"What's going on, Cara?" Casey replied, his brow knitting.

"River Runner and his warriors are following us," she said, trying to keep the fear from her tone—to no avail. "I don't know how they found us, but they did. I need you to believe me when I say we can't outride them, so I don't want you to do what you're thinking and spur this horse into a gallop."

Casey drew in a deep breath, pulling back on the instinct to do just that. Still, he knew Cara was right—there was no way a horse carrying two, could outride a single rider, especially one practically born on the back of a Pinto.

"If you're so certain it's them, why haven't they attacked yet?" Casey snapped, fear slamming into his heart.

"Perhaps they know we can't escape and are playing with us," Cara said, fear causing her body to quake.

"They're cats and we're mice," Casey muttered, anger replacing the fear.

"They are a fair distance away. Do you think we could pick up the pace, just to a canter? Not fast enough to put them on alert, but maybe just fast enough to reach the woods in the distance before they realize we're moving faster than we are?"

"Attempt to hide in the trees? Sounds like you've done this before," Casey said, giving the horse the command to trot.

"I have," Cara admitted, cringing in remembrance. When she fell silent, Casey pressed her for the details, which she reluctantly revealed, "River Runner's sister tried to help me escape."

"Was that the girl whose life you saved?" Casey asked. He couldn't imagine anyone else caring enough about a white woman to come to her aid.

"Yes. She felt that River Runner had become obsessed with keeping me and that it made him no different than Rankle. We were very close to reaching Martin's Landing, and I thought I was going home, but we lost one of the horses and had to ride double. That's when we spotted the warriors in the distance, riding fast and hard to catch up to us. When they captured us, they beat us for running away," Cara whispered and then trailed off. She didn't need to say anything further. She'd made her point—you can't outrun a determined Indian, and they were in for a world of hurt if they were captured. The punishment for her alone was going to be severe. She shuddered again.

"The tree line is too far, Cara. I'm not certain we're going to reach it...how far are they? Have they noticed we've picked up speed?"

Cara tried to look over her shoulder casually, as if she were simply admiring the surrounding plains. She quickly turned back, "They too are trotting. They are getting closer, I think. Casey, I'm so frightened."

"We need to get to the trees. Are they far enough away that I can at least make it that far in a gallop?"

"Yes, we can make it to the trees before they catch us, but unless. . ." Cara got no further before Casey shouted to his horse and they went flying across the snow-covered ground toward the fast-approaching tree line. The sound of Indian cries reached her ears and she felt tears prick. The game was up. The war for her had begun—again.

A few minutes later, Casey tugged on the reins, drawing the horse to a walk, "Stay low behind me," he commanded, and then ducked into the trees, giving the horse its own lead to find a way through the thick underbrush. The branches slapped at his arms, but he protected his face, by pulling his hat low on his brow and lowering his head. The horse neighed and whinnied at being made to traverse such a precarious passageway, but kept moving forward, as if it sensed the lives of its riders were in danger.

"Casey, we're only stalling the inevitable," Cara exclaimed, reminiscent of the flight with Skips Along The Water, when the maiden turned their horse around in defeated resignation. "We can only go so far before the woods end, snatching away the only thing keeping us safe. They're trackers. Do you think we can hide forever from them?"

"What do you want me to do, Cara? Surrender?" Casey called back. "Well, I'm not prepared to do that, and if we're going to have even the slightest chance of surviving this, you're going to have to trust me, and we're both going to have to be quieter."

Cara fell silent, glancing periodically over her shoulder to see if she could catch a glimpse of anyone following, but the light piercing through the canopy was so sporadic that it made seeing anything beyond the nose on her face iffy at best.

"I hear water," Casey hissed loudly over his shoulder, and then leaned over his horse's neck, "Find the water, boy."

The horse bobbed its head as if in understanding and took the first available pathway to the right, its head bent low as it pushed through the ever-thickening branches. The way they were headed was not a well-used thoroughfare and the struggle was obvious. By the time they broke through into a tiny clearing, each had scratches and welts covering every exposed area of flesh.

"It's a river!" Cara exclaimed.

"Indeed, and it may just be what we need to throw the Arapaho off our scent," Casey declared, carefully leading his stallion into the icy water.

CHAPTER 49

"We waited too long to overtake them, and now they have escaped into the woods," Runs With Deer snapped angrily.

"Crazy Beaver, will you explain to your brother that the Arapaho are good trackers?" River Runner retorted and then pushed through into the woods.

The other warriors followed, but Crazy Beaver waited with his brother, "You will need to stop your anger, Brother. You know we are almost upon them and will take back the white woman soon. You should be rejoicing..."

"River Runner will get us killed over this white woman! I feel it!"

Crazy Beaver knew his brother was fast to anger and knew he was not likely to change, but he'd never heard him doubt the warriors' abilities to fight, "You do not think we can kill Casey Scott?"

"I do not think we will kill Casey Scott and someone not come kill us," Runs With Deer replied, finally expressing his fears.

"Go!" Crazy Beaver snapped. "Return to the people."

Runs With Deer's brow knitted, "I will not!"

"You cannot stay and doubt your brothers. It is not good for a warrior to doubt," Crazy Beaver said softly. "I am going now. If you follow, you will stop your anger and your doubts. If you cannot, do not follow."

Crazy Beaver turned his horse and worked his way through the woods, his eyes keenly searching the surrounding area for signs of which way the others had gone. Since the path taken was not well traveled, it was easy to see the broken branches and the hoof prints in the moist ground. He knew that River Runner would also be following the path and he would catch up to him soon.

He heard his brother behind and smiled grimly. He hoped that he would not do something stupid against River Runner or the people would banish him—or worse.

A few minutes later, he broke into the small clearing and saw the warriors riding down the river bank toward a stallion in the river, which was struggling to make it to the other side. He and Runs With Deer kicked their horses into a gallop, let out a war cry, and raced after them.

CHAPTER 50

"Shoot the horse," River Runner instructed as soon as they broke through into the clearing and spotted Casey and Cara in the river. "Shoot only the horse," he repeated, pulling his bow from his back. He kicked his horse into a canter, pulling an arrow from its sheath. The other warriors were doing likewise, each lining up their shot to knock their prey off their only means of flight.

With a whoosh of wind, the arrows soared through the air, three of which struck the horse's hindquarters. Its back legs immediately collapsed beneath the pain, but it valiantly struggled to right itself. Cara was holding on to Casey tight, trying not to slip off into the frigid water.

"Dear sweet Jesus," she exclaimed, staring down at an arrow that was only inches from her leg. "Dear sweet Jesus," she said again, looking over her shoulder at the warriors who were only a few feet from them now, with two others riding toward them fast. "Casey."

"I know," he replied, his voice strained. "Listen to me, Cara," he said harshly, trying to turn the stallion's nose toward the other bank, "our options are not many at this point. Either way, we're going to have to get to the other bank and back into the woods, before the Arapaho decide the game is over and come after us. Right now, I think they're enjoying the chase, which, believe it or not, gives us an edge."

The tears were streaming down Cara's cheeks as fast as the river water ahead of them, so she couldn't respond to Casey's plans, but she nodded her acquiescence. It was either follow him, or die, and she preferred not to die.

"I can't keep my horse on its feet much longer. When I release the reins, he's going to know it's okay to fall. I want you to slide off the back and move as fast as you can toward the bank. Stay low and use the horse as cover. Get to the tree line. Don't look back and don't stop moving. I'll be right behind you."

Cara nodded again and closed her eyes as the horse collapsed its hide legs again, followed by its forelegs. It sat in chest-deep water, its eyes reflecting the pain from the arrows piercing its hide and the frigid water spearing its sides. Cara immediately slid off the side of the horse and nearly froze in shock as the water assaulted her body from the waist down.

"Move!" Casey said harshly, pushing her toward the bank. "Move, Cara!"

Cara heard his voice penetrate the freezing fog threatening to overwhelm her brain, and sloshed toward the edge of the bank. She climbed up the other side and moved sluggishly toward the tree line, sending up prayers of thanks that it was closer than it seemed. She pushed through the thick branches, brushing each aside with more force than she realized she had. She kept her word to Casey, driving forward and not looking back—even after she heard the first gunshot resonate through the air.

CHAPTER 51

"Let her go, River Runner!" Casey yelled, remaining as hidden as was possible beside his horse. He knew the effort was futile, but he had to give Cara the opportunity to flee; so the moment he'd seen her push through into the woods, he'd pulled his weapon, taken cover behind his horse, and fired a shot toward one of the warriors. It was a warning shot, and he'd missed—deliberately—but it gave the Indians pause, just as he'd hoped it would.

He didn't know which of the warriors were River Runner, but he needed to find out. He didn't have enough bullets to take every one of them down, even shooting as good as he knew himself to be. He needed to ferret out the man for whom those bullets were intended. *Cut the head off the snake*, he reminded himself.

"She is mine. I will not let her go!" River Runner replied, and Casey had found his target. Yet something inside him needed answers.

"Why? Why do you insist on trying to steal my woman?" Casey yelled and saw the Indian stiffen.

"She is not your woman. She belongs to me, and she will return to me."

"If she was yours, she would not have run away from you—twice now!" Casey incited.

"She *is* mine. She has lain with me—willingly—and carries my child!" River Runner yelled back the taunt, knowing his declaration was pure speculation. He only guessed that his seed were strong and fertile and that after lying with a woman, he'd easily impregnate her. He'd never done so before, but he felt confident he had impregnated Cara.

Casey's blood froze and his mind ceased functioning with any logic. He'd wondered at whether Cara had remained untouched, and now he had his answer. Of course, he had no way of knowing whether this man was telling him a falsehood; but if he were...no, Casey believed him. No man would pursue a woman with such vengeance without a purpose; and an unborn child was the greatest purpose there was.

Still, if he were about to die, he wasn't going to allow River Runner an untainted victory, "She does *not* carry your child! I have lain with her for many days now," he yelled, lying his ass off, "and there are no signs that a child grows within her. If she carries anyone's child...."

An arrow whizzed by his head, and he ducked. He heard a shrill cry and River Runner's horse leapt into the water, headed straight for him. Casey took careful aim, and fired.

****

Cara heard the second shot, much further sounding than the first shot had been, but she kept moving. The instinct to protect herself and her unborn child, strong, driving her feet forward. She'd learned much in the months spent with the natives, and she was confident that she had the skills needed to survive until she found a haven of rest.

The sound of repeated gun fire sounded, and she finally stumbled. She fell to her knees as the echo of the last shot faded, tears soaking the ground beneath her lowered head. She settled back on her haunches and let out of a cry of agony.

****

Casey's first shot was off from his intended mark, but it hit River Runner hard just below his shoulder, knocking him sideways and straight off his stallion's back. Casey wasted no time, knowing that he wouldn't get another chance now to finish River Runner off, before the other warriors riddled his own body with arrows.

He quickly leapt to his feet and trudged through the ankle-deep water to where River Runner lay, mildly stunned from the impact of the fall. He took aim and fired again, this time striking him center chest, and again, and a third time. His final bullet went through the warrior's forehead, just as the other warriors let loose a maelstrom of arrows, each striking him with simultaneous and lethal might.

CHAPTER 52

For over a month, Cara made her way slowly to the northwest, subsisting off of berries, plants, and whatever animal she could stone and eat uncooked. She no longer feared that the Arapaho would find her, for had they even headed her way, they could have easily overtaken her. The only explanation for their sudden disinterest was that River Runner had been killed by one of the bullets fired by Casey; and that Casey, in turn, had been slain by the remaining warriors. Two men had pulled and tugged her in different directions, both determined she would be their woman; neither living to see it happen.

If they feared she would send the army after them, she thought it was feasible they would have continued to hunt her and killed her to ensure her silence, but they knew that it was likely the wilderness would claim her life; but they had underestimated her will to live.

As she made her way further north, the snow deepened, and she took shelter in a cave, sleeping many of the days and nights away, as a bear in hibernation; moving only when she found the determination to fight her way through hip-deep snow.

During one of those times of determination, her mind began to argue with the sanity of her continued efforts, willing her to lie down and give up. To release her body from the agonizing torture it had been subjected to far too long.

"I can't give up on my baby," she whispered, but the words issued weakly, unconvincingly. "Besides, someone's coming for us," she said, smiling wistfully. "Can't you see the rider in the distance? They'll help us."

Somewhere deep inside, she knew what she saw was an hallucination, but she clung to it for as long as her mind allowed, fighting for survival with her last ounce of will.

* * * * * * * * *

"Will she survive?" Caleb asked a few days later. He'd seen a woman in the distance a few days prior and rode out to save her. At the time, he had no idea that the woman was Cara, until he reached down and pulled her free from the snow, laying her across his horse's back. It was the dress she'd left in the first time she'd come that had given him a sense of her identity.

He carried her inside and immediately called for Genevieve, who'd yelled for Nancy to brew some broth.

Genevieve sat, slowly pouring broth down Cara's throat, "She's feverish, and I'm not sure she won't lose her legs to frostbite, but she's swallowing the broth, and that's a good sign. If I can get her strength regained, she might have a fighting chance."

"Think the doc will make it out here?" Caleb asked next.

"If anyone can get through to Independence, it'll be Mr. Jacob. He's tough and a good rider. He'll get the doc back, if it's possible to do so. Don't doubt him, Mr. Caleb. Doubt will kill Miss Cara, as quick as a bullet. Now go see how Miss Nancy is doing with the herbal remedy for the fever. We need to get some more into her soon."

Caleb left. Only then did Genevieve fall back on her old habits and bow her head in prayer, "My dear sweet Lord. There's a child here in need of your kindness and mercy. Put your hands of healing upon her body. Give her a chance to live and grow old."

The doctor arrived a week later to find a feverish and thrashing Cara, fighting for survival.

"What have you been giving her?" He asked.

"We've plenty of snow, so we've been washing her down with melted snow, to cool her body."

"Too cold can make her worse..." the doctor started but Genevieve interrupted.

"Yes, we melt the snow and it warms up a bit while we wait to use it."

"Okay, good. What else have you done?"

"I've been making a basil and ginger tea, drizzling it down her throat as much as possible, to bring down her fever; and some herbal broth for sustenance. As much as she's thrashing about, I'm not certain it's working very well."

"You seem to know your craft, woman," the doctor said, his tone a bit exasperated, "and I can tell you that it is likely working. What I can't fathom, since you seem to know how to tend to the sick, is why you had me pulled from my bed and hauled over knee-deep snow for a week in order to pat your back over a job well done."

Genevieve was used to the tempers of the Mother Superior and the nuns at her convent, so wasn't surprised or offended by the doctor's outburst. Instead, she merely stepped up to the bed and yanked the covers from over Cara's legs, then stepped back and waited for the exclamation that she knew would follow. She wasn't disappointed.

"Dear sweet Mother Mary of Jesus!" The doctor exclaimed, viewing the blackened dead flesh where pink, plump skin used to be.

"Frostbite," Genevieve said unnecessarily.

The doctor merely nodded, unable to form words for what this girl had been subjected to for such a severe case of frostbite to occur. He shook his head and sat down in a nearby chair.

"This is why I needed you here, Doctor," Genevieve said softly. "I fear there's no hope for saving her legs."

"There's not the slightest hope," the doctor replied quietly. "Not if she's going to recover at all."

"I had one of our men folk preparing our strongest saw; sharpening it and washing it down to clean it up. It's all we have, so I hope it will suffice," Genevieve said, trying not to dwell upon the words she was speaking, for if she did, she knew she'd be emptying her stomach contents on the floor. She'd tended to many injuries while at the convent—passersby with bullet wounds and snake bites—but never had she dealt with a case of frostbite larger than that of a few fingers or toes. Never had she seen someone's legs completely rotted from the knees down.

"I, um, won't be needing it. I, um, have a bone saw. I'll need some cloth to tie her down; keep her from moving about while I work."

Genevieve immediately called for Nancy, "Please find our oldest blanket, and have a couple of the men tear it into strips; and make haste."

"And have someone bring a lantern...do you have a lantern here?" The doctor added quickly.

"Yes, we do. Miss Nancy," she called, stopping the black girl in her tracks, "the doctor also needs a lantern brought in and...anything else, doctor? Before I send her on?" The doctor nodded, and Genevieve shooed Nancy to get the needed supplies.

"I'll need you to help me administer the morphine," the doctor said, moving over to examine the rest of Cara. "Are there any other injuries that I'm unaware of; of which you may be unaware?"

"I don't know. I've just been trying to get her fever down and keep food in her system," Genevieve admitted.

"Well, it's likely the legs are causing the fever's lingering. Once we've tended to that, she'll likely recover in a few weeks. Still, while we wait, let's make a cursory check for any surprises...oh my!" The doctor paused, his fingers fluttering over her abdomen again to confirm his findings. "Did you know she was with child?"

"Dear sweet Jesus, no!" Genevieve said, suddenly thankful that she'd only given her herbs for healing.

"Well, there'll be no morphine for the surgery or for the subsequent pain she'll endure; not unless we want her to lose this child. Of course, we may lose them both before the night is over, if this doesn't go well."

"God is on our side," Genevieve said softly.

"Then you best be praying that he keep my hands steady and my mind clear, because I'll be the one performing the surgery," the doctor said sharply.

Nancy returned with the requested items, but the doctor quickly amended his needs when he realized that he wouldn't be able to use morphine, "Go fetch me two of the strongest men, girl." Nancy dashed from the room and ran to get Jacob and Bill.

"Hold her down and hold her still," the doctor commanded the minute they walked in, "and if you're prone to being sick, curb it. We can't save this girl's life if you two turn into giant milksops. Am I understood?" The two nodded. "Good, let's get to work."

CHAPTER 53

Eight months later

"You're going to have to push, sweetie. It'll be a lot easier for the men to carry you about if you have twenty less pounds weighing you down," Genevieve teased, but Cara was having none of the humor.

"She won't be carried nowhere much no more," Nancy said, bringing some hot water and clean towels into the room.

"What are you blathering on about, girl?" Cara screeched and then yelled as another contraction tore through her abdomen.

"The doctor be here from Indepe'nce. He done brought you a chair with wheels on it."[2]

"If he hasn't brought a shotgun to put me out of my misery," Cara screamed, "I want nothing...arrgghhh."

"Tell the doctor the baby will be here shortly, and he'll be able to examine the baby and the mother...." Another screech stopped her in midsentence, "Ah, he'll be examining them real soon. I see the crown. The baby's coming. Now, Miss Cara, when you get the urge to push..."

She no sooner got the words out when Cara lifted her head and bore down with a loud yell, falling back against the bed when the contraction passed. Within a minute, another contraction swelled, and she felt the urge to push again.

"Oh, real quick like, Miss Gen'vieve, there be a man here; says he know ya."

"Miss Nancy, I don't think now is hardly the time."

"I don't...oh, dear...sweet...Lord ..." Cara huffed when she fell back again.

"Yes, Miss Gen'vieve," Nancy curtsied and then ducked out of the room. She quickly moved to where the man stood inside the front door, his hat twisting nervously in his hands.

"Sounds like a mighty ruckus going on in there," he commented.

---

[2] The first known image of a wheelchair was carved into a stone in the 6th century. Different forms of wheeled chairs have been in use since the 18th century (mobilityscooters.co.nz)

"Yessir," Miss Nancy confirmed. "It be Miss Cara. Her baby done on its way."

Murphy's eyes went wide as saucers and his breath caught in his throat. He'd spent the entire spring and most of the summer searching for Casey and Cara, but there wasn't a sign of them anywhere. When he hadn't heard from Casey, as promised, he resigned his post as governor, promoted Luke to the position, and then took off—back tracking the route Casey was supposed to have taken. When he reached the convent, the sisters said that no one matching his description had ever arrived. It was then he realized that he *had* seen Arapaho warriors and not ravens the day he rode out of Independence, and his heart sank in his chest. He continued on to Jacks, not knowing what he was searching for, but feeling as if he had nowhere else to go. He never imagined he'd hear that Cara was there, which meant..."When did Miss Cara get here? Was someone with her?"

"Miss Nancy!" Genevieve yelled.

"I sorry, but I's got to get," Miss Nancy said with a curtsy and then ran back into the room.

* * * * * * * * *

"Just one more, darling girl, and this baby will slide right out of you. I promise. Just one more push."

Cara lifted her head and with a mighty scream, pushed with all of her might. She felt the baby slide from inside her and immediately passed out.

"Let her sleep," Genevieve said when Nancy looked as if she was going to try to wake her. "You clean her up, while I clean up the baby for the doctor to inspect. Once you've got her cleaned, get those clean cloths put inside of her to staunch the flow of blood, then cover her and go make her some food and get some fresh milk from the cow the doctor brought. She's going to need to drink plenty if she's going to feed this baby proper like."

"Does it be a girl or a boy?" Nancy queried, washing the blood away from Cara's body.

"Well, I certainly am not going to inform you before I inform the mother, now am I?" Genevieve snapped lightly.

"I s'pose not," Nancy huffed, stuffing clean cloths into Cara's vagina before covering her and heading out to make Cara a meal. "Ain't as if she would be knowing if you told me though," she muttered, shuffling from the room.

Genevieve laughed and then turned her attention back to the baby, "Welcome to the world, little one."

* * * * * * * * * *

A few days later, Murphy shuffled into the room, and Cara's eyes lit up, "My dear, dear friend," she exclaimed, trying to shift herself to a sitting position.

"Here, let me take the little tyke, while you prop yourself up," Murphy offered.

"Thank you."

She pulled her body upright and then reached for the baby, not missing the shock that registered on her friend's face, "Lost them in the snow," she said simply.

"Dear sweet Jesus," Murphy whispered. "How? When?"

"The day we left Independence, the Arapaho found us. I don't know what happened precisely," she said, her eyes clouding over in recall, "because Casey had me run away; but I heard gunfire, and I never saw River Runner or Casey again. How did you find me? Did my father send you?"

Murphy's face turned a blotched red at the mention of Cara's father, "Cara, I found you because I set out to search for y'all when I hadn't heard from Casey. Casey didn't tell you about your dad?"

Cara's brow knitted.

"Oh Cara, I'm so sorry, but your dad passed a few months after your abduction. The doctor said his heart just stopped. Probably from the stress of...well, probably from stress," he concluded lamely.

Cara closed her eyes, but she didn't cry. She'd cried her last tears the morning after her surgery when she'd realized her legs were gone. She'd cried so many tears over so many months, that she simply had none left. She nodded solemnly, "So, I take it you came back for Miss Genevieve?"

Murphy nodded, "So, um, I take it that that's, um, River Runner's son?"

Cara shook her head, "No, this is *my* son," she whispered fiercely, folding him closer to her chest protectively, "and I'll not allow him to be a victim of a man's twisted love. We may be members now of the shunned and rejected community, but this little darling will only know true love; pure love. You have my word of honor," she concluded, placing a kiss on her newborn's forehead.

"What's his name?"

"What do you think I would name him?"

Murphy nodded and smiled, "Want me to carry you outside? Get some sunshine?"

Cara smiled, "No, he's squirming so I'll need to feed him now."

"Okay, let me know if you need anything. I'm not going anywhere." Murphy turned to leave, but Cara stopped him.

"Murphy?"

"Yeah, Cara."

Cara was about to say how much she missed Casey, but decided that it was time to put the past in the past, "I'm glad you're here."

"Me too," Murphy smiled and left the room, just as the baby started whimpering.

"Okay, my darling Casey, let's get you fed."

ABOUT THE AUTHOR

Barbara Woster is an educator and a business owner. She has been in love with the written word most of her life, which is what spurred her to become an author. Because her taste in books is eclectic, she writes in genres as she is inspired—generally by ideas or conversations with her husband or children. She is a mother to four wonderful daughters, and currently resides with her husband in Oregon.

Printed in Great Britain
by Amazon

22192046R00161